THE
GRANITE MOTH

A Novel

ERICA WRIGHT

PEGASUS CRIME

NEW YORK LONDON

THE GRANITE MOTH

Pegasus Crime is an Imprint of
Pegasus Books LLC
80 Broad Street, 5th Floor
New York, NY 10004

Copyright © 2015 Erica Wright

First Pegasus Books edition November 2015

Interior design by Maria Fernandez

All *The Iliad* excerpts are from the Robert Fagles translation.

Library of Congress Cataloging-in-Publication Data is available.

ISBN: 978-1-60598-893-1

10 9 8 7 6 5 4 3 2 1

Printed in the United States of America
Distributed by W. W. Norton & Company

8487

For my parents

"Sometimes you don't know who you are until you put on a mask."

—ALEXANDER CHEE, "GIRL"

CHAPTER ONE

Skeletons rattled their way up Sixth Avenue, spreading their green glow over the crowd. Puppeteers on roller skates navigated larger-than-human dummies to the delight of families and college kids alike. The next float seemed to be a pirate ship, if pirate ships came in pink and ghosts came in iridescent thongs. The annual Halloween parade was one of the few times when I felt at home, disguised among countless others disguised. That night I had donned a cheap but bedazzled mask with jeans, and I was feeling underdressed but unexposed. I was wedged between a Batman father taking turns hoisting twin girls onto his shoulders and a twenty-something woman dressed like a sexy raccoon. All had their arms outstretched as a man in an eyepatch and little else tossed bubblegum into the air. A few pieces landed at my sneakers, and I kicked them away.

The mass of people made the New York Police Department nervous, but they weren't my responsibility anymore. It had been three years since I'd turned in my badge to the surprise of exactly no one. If I glanced behind me, I was sure to see two or three mounted cops, hands patting their horses' necks to soothe them. I kept my eyes forward, trusting my source to find me under the 10th Street sign because it was my only choice. Optionless has never been my favorite date, but sometimes you have to make do. I had arrived two hours before the start of the event to make sure I could snag this prime viewing location, and part of me felt guilty about keeping a real enthusiast from seeing the elaborate homemade creations that kicked off the party night on a gleeful note.

An authentic-looking Marilyn Monroe blew kisses from the top of a birthday cake, complete with forty-five candles. I went onto my tiptoes to see if the Pink Parrot's contribution was visible, yet. Dolly had said that he and his fellow stars would mosey by around 7:30. And by "mosey," I assumed he meant sit gracefully as fireworks boomed above his head. The Pink Parrot was the premier drag club in the city, and the owner, Lacy "Big Mamma" Burstyn, wouldn't let Dolly's size 12 platform heels touch the pavement, of that much, I was sure.

The sun had long since dipped below the brownstones, and I was glad to be wearing a sweater instead of the bustiers and leotards popular amongst the adult attendants. I'd never lasted this long at the parade, getting tired before the final hurrah, but I was determined to stay until my informant found me. It had taken a few years and a busted face to convince me that I couldn't be a spectator anymore, but color me convinced. Kingpin Salvatore Magrelli may not have been involved with my last case as a private investigator, but that didn't make him any less of a threat. I knew for certain that he had killed a teenage boy for knowing too much about a shipment, and I had a pretty good idea that he'd pulled the trigger plenty of other times. To be honest, I'm not sure how I'd dodged a Magrelli-sized bullet as long as I had.

A cheer managed to carry over the steady din, and I scanned the avenue to see the Pink Parrot extravaganza making its way toward me. It was even grander than I expected: a mini castle complete with turrets, drawbridge, kings, and (of course) queens. The club name was lit in gold, and Dolly was dancing to Cyndi Lauper. He was a good thirty feet away, but I could still see why his performance sold out every night that he headlined. The black gown was more subdued than his co-stars' fuchsia and lime getups, but he downright emanated charm as he waved sparklers and grinned as big as the spotlight. Instead of his favorite blonde bob, he had donned a long brunette wig curled into ringlets. I knew who was responsible for the perfect hairdo and hoped I didn't need to visit Vondya Vasiliev anytime soon. I wasn't her favorite client; even so, I would fight anyone who said she wasn't the best wigmaker on the Atlantic seaboard.

As the Pink Parrot entourage drew closer, I glanced around to make sure I hadn't missed my contact. No one looked promising, and I turned my attention back, startled when I found Dolly's eyes locked on mine. He winked at me, and I shuddered. Not that I wasn't happy to see him, but being recognized still scared me. During my years undercover, I had dreaded the possibility that someone would know me on the streets and reveal my affiliation with the police. In that scenario, a quick death was a pipe dream. After I got out, I was afraid that someone from my past life would hunt me down. I made myself smile at Dolly, but didn't wave. I watched him turn toward the other side of the street and light another sparkler.

"Friend of yours?" a voice whispered at my ear.

I jumped and my hands flew to my mask, but it only took me a second to recognize the deep rumble of my former classmate, now decorated detective Ellis Decker. Despite his well-deserved reputation for dependability, part of me was amazed that he had actually turned up. He disapproved of my desire to go after Magrelli on my own, but a desire to protect his city must have won out. He knew the NYPD didn't have the time or resources to pursue every cartel with its hooks in the boroughs. If I were feeling sorry for myself, I would say that I had blown one of our chances. There weren't recruits lining up for full-time undercover assignments. I had been an anomaly to say the least. The younger Magrelli brother had gotten my criminal charges against him dropped, and I was hellbent on making up for my failure. I'd collect enough evidence for five judges and juries, never mind what puppetmaster was holding their strings.

Vigilantism aside, I wasn't sure if Ellis would be happy to see me in any capacity. We could work together, but a great yawn of time and experiences stretched between now and when we had been close. I wiggled around until I faced him, his tortoiseshell frames a few inches from my face. The bright streetlights made his eyes look white behind the glasses—the eyes of a prophet, I always thought. I wondered if he knew my eyes were gray, or if he mistook them for brown and green and blue as most everyone else did. My unmemorable appearance made me a decent private investigator—able to trail people without being spotted—but probably wasn't a quality envied by most. A glance at the attention-seeking revelers confirmed my theory. Why wear a tiara or fishnets if not to be noticed? Disappearing was my superpower, like it or not. There's no sending that sort of thing back to the manufacturer.

"A friend?" Ellis repeated.

"Almost," I replied, which was an accurate description of my relationship with Dolly. It was difficult to make friends when you spent your time pretending to be different people, but somehow Dolly had managed to squeeze his way into my life. "Did you find anything I can use?"

The crowd jostled me toward Ellis, and he caught my elbow. He didn't let go right away, and I could tell that he was holding back on another lecture about the risks involved. That would be falling into old patterns, back to when I was cowed by the authoritative tone he had developed by age nineteen. We had been undergraduates together at the best criminology school in the city, and he had been the best of our class, valedictorian, an honor even his blueblood parents acknowledged. By that time, my own parents had died, and I was looking for an escape from reality. Undercover work had seemed ideal, selfish even. And perhaps my current motives were selfish, as well. I didn't want to worry anymore about hitmen crawling up my fire escape. I held out my free hand, and Ellis looked behind him. The celebration was a perfect screen; no one would notice or hear us. He reached into his jacket and pulled out a thick stack of photocopies.

"Not anything to build a case on, but I thought you might be interested in the restaurant."

I squinted at the top page, which showed grainy photos of a swanky place called The Skyview. Tables for two looked out over Central Park, and I guessed the height to be about twenty stories up. Couples in cocktail attire sipped champagne and gazed longingly into each other's eyes.

"When are our reservations?" I asked.

Ellis snorted. "It's members only, so even if I wanted to, darling, I couldn't take you."

I doubted that Ellis Decker would be denied entry anywhere, but didn't say so. I was already brainstorming how I could snag an I.D. card and an appropriate ensemble. Would my knockoff Jimmy Choos trigger some sort of commoner alarm?

"It could be legit, Kathleen, so don't get your hopes up."

I started at the use of my real name. I may have been christened Kathleen Stone, but I was more likely to go by Kat, Kathy,

Kay, Kitty, or even Keith. I made myself nod to acknowledge his warning, but the Magrellis didn't do legit. If the place wasn't laundering their drug cash flow, it was raking in illegal dollars some other creative way.

Another cheer erupted, and I turned to see that the Pink Parrot float had stopped for a brief show. Even better, Dolly had picked up a microphone. I was expecting Lady Gaga or Madonna to thud over the PA system, but instead, Dolly said a warm hello in his real voice, a honeyed timbre that drew catcalls. And when he started to sing "Rocket Man," the onlookers surged forward as if drawn like mice to their piper. It was an unusual choice, not as fast-paced as the occasion seemed to dictate. There was also the real singing voice after a dozen or so lip-synchers. No wonder Mamma Burstyn treated him like royalty. He was giving Sir Elton John a run for his considerable money.

When I turned back around to thank Ellis for the information, he had vanished, and I felt my spirits sink in disappointment. Maybe it was unrealistic, but I was hoping to grab a beer like in the old days. "Onward," I mumbled before standing on my tiptoes to see over the head of a Playboy Bunny who had scooted in front of me while I was distracted. Between her satin ears, I could make out the retreating Pink Parrot float, its red taillights casting an eerie sheen over the jugglers behind. They were dressed like macabre court jesters, their faces painted in green and purple scales. One tossed flaming batons into the air, snagging them a split second before they hit the ground. When he added a fourth pin, the audience added whistles to their applause. He caught it the first time effortlessly, then seemed to trip over something in the street. At first everyone assumed that it was part of the act, but the cheers turned to shrieks when the pin careened forward, way out of his reach, bouncing onto the Pink Parrot's makeshift stage.

"Dolly," I screamed, but the woman in front of me couldn't hear, much less the person I wanted to warn. Dolly had started to sing about Mars when he noticed the fire spreading quickly through the streamers and papier-mâché dragons. To his credit, he didn't panic. Most of the other entertainers ran for the sides, climbing over the railings even before the truck stopped. Dolly grabbed bottled waters and emptied them onto the burning surfaces, but it was hopeless. People started to stampede east, knocking over anyone moving too slowly. I wrapped my body around the 10th Street sign, determined to help if I could survive the exodus.

Roman candles began careening in all directions, and their high-pitched whine had never sounded less festive. A man fell nearby, his right foot engulfed until someone threw a jacket on top, slapping out the flames. I took a step toward them, then stopped, my eyes on the blue sparks emanating from what looked like audio equipment on the Pink Parrot stage. Then the float exploded, a deadly combination of sheet metal, scaffolding, and performers thrown into the night.

⊷

The blast threw me to the sidewalk, but I managed to absorb most of the fall with my arms. Blinking up into the smoke and confetti, I instinctively scanned the street for Dolly. I couldn't make anything out beyond vague shapes. I quickly checked myself for cuts, relieved not to find anything serious. Then I pushed myself up and sprinted toward the chaos. More people flew by me, coughing and crying, but I couldn't let myself slide into terror, yet.

"Dolly," I screamed again, but the sound was completely lost. I ran toward where I had seen him last, despite a sinking feeling that he would have been flung far from there. I nearly tripped over another victim before I stopped to check on him. I crouched down to see the man's face, but he was waving me away.

"I'm okay, I'm okay. Help the others," he said. I squeezed the stranger's hand before heading closer to the fire. It was hot, but the smoke bothered me more than the heat. I could feel my throat constrict, wanting to gag, but I pushed forward.

"Dolly," I tried again. Police officers were already on the scene, asking anyone like me who had run into the danger to stay back. I ignored them and kept calling.

"Ma'am," someone said, pulling my arm. I twisted out of his grasp and ducked closer to what remained of the float.

"Over here, kitty cat," said a strangled voice nearby.

Relief flooded my system as I dropped to the ground and crawled toward Dolly. He was sprawled on the pavement, his dress ripped and bloody. I scanned his body as best I could in the smoke, my eyes and throat searing. I didn't see any major injuries, but plenty of scrapes and burns. I maneuvered him until I had both arms wrapped around his torso, then scooted away from the inferno, pushing as hard as I could with my boots. I could hear sirens close by and tried to tell Dolly not to worry before being overcome by coughs. He had his eyes squeezed shut, but he was breathing. We were too close to the float for anyone to notice us right away, but after five feet or so, an officer came over to help. He dragged Dolly to safety then went back toward the blaze.

I rolled onto my knees and dry heaved, spitting black globs onto the pavement. It took a few minutes before I could do anything else. When I checked Dolly's pulse, it was strong, and I felt some of my nausea subside. I loosened his wig and took off his necklace, trying to cool him down. His pretty face had been licked by flames, and there was a angry pink mark across his forehead. When he finally opened his eyes, he smiled.

"I thought angels would have halos, not masks," he said before coughs racked his petite frame.

I laughed—a dry, aching sound—and rocked back on my heels, ripping the cheap Mardi Gras decoration from my face. I'd forgotten about the disguise altogether.

"Better," he said, reaching to brush my cheek. His hands were burned, too, but not as badly as his face. I stood up to look for an EMT. Ellis's frame was illuminated by the lights of a parked squad car. I waved to get his attention, and he turned toward me, mouthing something I couldn't make out. I knelt down quickly and told Dolly that I would be back with help then jogged toward the car.

"He's hurt. I don't know how bad," I said, reaching Ellis.

He gestured for a distraught parade attendee to stand back then yelled "Kurt" toward one of the two ambulances. "We have another 10-54 by the 10th Street sign, east side."

I looked back toward Dolly to see that I had been dragging him back to my viewing spot. When two EMTs rushed past me, I asked Ellis what else I could do.

"You'll be safer at home," he said.

Ignoring him, I went back to Dolly's side, as Ellis must have known that I would. The EMTs had applied an oxygen mask and were checking the burns for any that looked serious.

"Do you think he hit his head?" one of the workers asked me.

"He was standing on the float when it blew."

He nodded and strapped Dolly onto a stretcher. "Roosevelt Hospital," he said to my unasked question.

I kissed Dolly's temple before they wheeled him away, then noticed that he had my sequined mask tucked to his chest. I wanted to change my earlier answer to Ellis: Yes, Dolly was most certainly a friend.

CHAPTER TWO

Emergency rooms the world over must look particularly gruesome on Halloween, a combination of real and fake gore highlighted by glitter and fluorescent lights. The Roosevelt waiting area was packed. A few of the Pink Parrot performers were milling around, waiting to have their minor wounds examined. They told me that three of their coworkers, including Dolly, had been rushed back. I sunk onto the floor next to a child in a kitten costume. The girl's whiskers had been cried off, but she was remarkably calm considering the gash on her shoulder.

"I fell," she offered when she caught me staring, then adjusted her cat ears and leaned back into her mother.

"Me, too," I said, showing her the small cuts on my palms. She was more curious than horrified. Her mom smiled wearily at me and stroked her daughter's hair.

My own parents had been killed in a fire. Not an explosion of the sort I had just witnessed, but a run-of-the-mill kitchen fire, deadly despite its banality. You'd think by now I would be immune to tragedy, but staring at the distraught faces around me, I definitely wasn't. The sight of Big Mamma rocking herself in the corner disconcerted me. She had dressed up for the parade even though she hadn't been on the float, and her gold pantsuit looked gaudy in the hospital glare. One of her employees rubbed her back absentmindedly, but was equally upset. He had removed his wig, revealing a crew cut above his made-up face. I turned away when he caught me watching him, but his eyes were glassy, as if he didn't register me or anyone else. When the news came that two of the three performers had bled out during surgery, he was the first to leave, refusing to be treated for smoke inhalation. I had a feeling Big Mamma wanted to run away, too, but her sheep gathered around her, seeking comfort from her imposing frame and no-nonsense attitude.

When I learned that Dolly was not one of the two casualties, my vision dimmed, and I had to put my head between my knees to keep from passing out. My whole body was tingling, but I could make out a light patting on my shoulder, my kitten companion providing what little comfort she could. Of course, she didn't need to provide comfort because I was feeling giddy with relief—guilty for feeling relieved perhaps, but giddy nonetheless. When I sat up, Big Mamma was staring at me from across the room as if she knew I wasn't mourning the loved ones she'd lost. She was trying to say something to me, but I didn't understand. She raised her voice, and I shivered.

"We need to talk," she said, then turned toward the exit without waiting to see if I would follow. Of course I would.

⸺⸺

Paramedics took long pulls from their cigarettes as they watched us walk toward an unlit corner of the parking lot. I'm sure we were a sight, my face dirty from the smoke, hers tense from holding back emotions. Big Mamma had helped me on a previous case, providing key information about a fellow Manhattan bar owner, a rival that she was glad to see fall. I had been in awe of her at the time. Ms. Burstyn is something of a living legend—it says so right on her Wikipedia page. She was one of the first people to refuse to pay mob protection fees for her club, and she was also one of the first African American women to own a business south of Harlem. It was hard not to feel inferior to this pioneer, and I wanted to turn back. She seemed to sense that and clamped a hand around my arm as we continued. I winced, but let her lead me. When she stopped, so did I.

She didn't speak at first, and we both focused on the chain-link fence. There were drooping, plastic flowers entwined in the metal and a few burnt-out Saint Michael candles on the ground—forgotten remnants of a September 11th shrine from the month before. I didn't like looking at them, but didn't know how to hurry this impromptu meeting along. One of the sergeants at my old precinct used to say that all conversations are about power, who has it and who doesn't. At the time, I assumed he meant when talking to suspects, but over the years, I'd come to apply this principle to most interactions. What I'm saying is that Mamma Burstyn was in control. I shifted my weight from foot to foot in order to warm up, waiting for her to begin.

"Two men leave a SoHo club together, get harassed then attacked by an angry mob," she said. I watched her breathe out a few visible puffs before she continued. "Six to two are bullshit odds. Bullshit, right?"

I nodded, and she continued. "Bruises, gashes, broken ribs. Stitches and CT scans. Not to mention a lifetime of looking over their shoulders, not sure if it's okay to be seen together. Does this sound familiar, Miss Stone?"

I thought the question was rhetorical and didn't say anything. The story had been aired on the local news stations several nights in a row. All six men had been arrested and charged, but the sensationalist nature of the crime meant it was still talk show fodder. An array of civil rights experts weighed in while anchors murmured along gravely. When the pause stretched too long, I spoke as softly as I could. "Yes, ma'am, I remember. Did you know them?"

"Does it matter?"

I swallowed hard, the spit making my throat burn all over again, and shook my head.

"I try to keep my boys safe," she continued. "Cameras covering every square inch of The Pink Parrot. State-of-the-art alarm system. Professional security guards, not bouncers off of Craigslist. Cars home after midnight. I even set up a self-defense class. Only Bobbie—" She stopped talking, and I looked away as she composed herself. I guessed that he was one of the men to have died in the ER. "Only Bobbie took me up on it. Smart kid, that one. From Kansas."

She paused again, and I wondered who would tell his parents. That was probably her responsibility, too.

"Ms. Burstyn, are you saying that you don't think this was an accident?"

In response, she opened the lapel of her jacket, and I jumped, scared that she was about to pull a gun on me. My paranoia didn't go unnoticed, but Big Mamma didn't comment. Instead she handed me what looked liked a wedding invitation, and I expected an announcement of Bobbie's nuptials, feeling sick at the thought of his fiancé learning that he was a widow. On closer inspection, however, it was an invitation of a wholly different variety:

We regret to inform you of the passing of Darío Rodriguez, Roberto Giabella, Herman White, Ravi Sethi, Aaron Kline, Carlton Casborough, and Juniper

Summer. Services will be held at St. Mark's Church, date and time TBA.

I rubbed my fingers over the seven names, noting that they were raised on the silver letterpress paper. They were printed in an intricate crimson font, and at the bottom was a small, black noose. It was the fanciest death threat that I'd ever seen. A few of the seven names were familiar, but I knew most of the Pink Parrot stars by their stage names.

"Were they all on the float tonight?" I asked.

"Do I look stupid? I haven't even let them be in the same room together all at once. These are my headliners. Tonight, Dolly and Bobbie were up there. The other performers were understudies or busboys."

With Roberto "Bobbie" Giabella, one down and six to go, I thought before I started shaking.

"Nuh-uh," Big Mamma said. "You stop that right now. We need you."

"No way, this needs professional attention."

"You are a professional."

I couldn't think of a reasonable response and mumbled something about the NYPD.

"You mean the fine officers I met last month? They didn't even make a copy."

I knew the type. I could even imagine their faces, blowing off this woman's concerns because of apathy or fatigue. Two gay men getting beat up—followed by a media frenzy—warranted a quick response. But a threat? Bottom rung of the priority ladder.

"But they'll investigate now." Explosions tended to get official attention.

"I don't give a flying fig about now. Now, they can do whatever they want. Me? I want somebody's undivided attention."

She had it, and she knew it. Dolly's name was on that list, Darío Rodriguez, and he was one of about three people who might miss me if I was gone.

"Don't tell me you trust New York's Finest as far as you can throw them," she continued. "After what they did to you. Most people jump when a car backfires. You? You jump when someone reaches into her jacket."

She has the power, I thought again, not in the least surprised that she knew about my past life. If anyone had hidden eyes and ears in this city, it was Lacy Burstyn. Her connections must have made her more rather than less frightened, aware of the chinks in her finely tailored armor. While I sympathized, I wasn't sure that I was the right person to help and said something about the NYPD doing their best with limited resources. Plus, I had volunteered for my undercover assignment, however much havoc it had wreaked on my life.

"How old were you? 21? 22 maybe? One of my waiters came to my office last week and offered to turn tricks in the private bathroom. You know what I said to him? I said if I caught him so much as staring at a stranger, I'd kick his pretty white tush out the door. If someone wants to grab a tiger by the tail, you don't get out the first aid kit. You tell them to leave the tiger alone!"

She yelled the last words, and a door slammed behind us, the paramedics retreating inside. Not everyone wants to be a witness.

"I'll need access to all your employees," I said. "It won't be easy," I added, knowing she would understand I meant questioning them would be emotionally charged to say the least. Memory has a funny way of rearranging itself in the face of tragedy. I was up to date on the latest interview techniques, but to be perfectly honest, I hadn't tried them out on anyone. My last run-in with drug dealers notwithstanding, my cases mostly called for following suspected cheats to racquet ball and Ashtanga yoga classes. Still, I knew that these men had just lost two friends and, while likely to cooperate, might not recall the information I needed, handsy customers and suspicious lurkers alike.

"Whatever you need, Miss Stone. You can have." She pulled my mask out of her pocket and pushed it into my hand. It had lost a few sequins, but I put it on anyway until I was calm enough to go back inside.

⟜

The police had arrived by the time I returned to the waiting area, and Ellis was busy questioning a blonde teenager who was biting his nails with intense focus. Ellis wouldn't be assigned the case—it would go to an explosives expert—but he had been on the scene. The NYPD wouldn't waste a warm body. Even from across the room, I could tell Ellis wasn't getting much useful information from his subject. One word answers, if any. I asked Big Mamma about the youngster.

"Bobbie's boyfriend."

"He's a kid."

"Mmm-hmm, so was Bobbie. Nineteen. That one's trouble, mark my words. Manhattan born and raised, slinking into all the clubs with batted eyelashes and a fake driver's license."

Not one to call the kettle black, I approached the boy with a cup of coffee. His eyes were bloodshot from a combination of tears and booze. The tears I could verify; the booze was an educated guess. He was wearing artfully ripped jeans with a plaid button-up and leather boots. From far away, he might have looked like a thrift store addict, but up close, he reeked of designer threads even more than clove cigarettes. Either a kleptomaniac or someone's beloved son. I glanced at Ellis before I began speaking.

"Ms. Burstyn asked me—"

Ellis put up his hand to stop me. He got up from his seat and gestured for me to take his place. His graciousness came from frustration, but I take what I can get.

"Good luck. Kathleen, this is Martin. Martin, Kathleen."

Ellis approached the nurse at the front desk, rubbing the space between his eyebrows. I held the Styrofoam cup out to Martin, but he didn't take it and turned his attention to what was left of his pinky nail, ripping at his cuticles. His index finger was bleeding around the edges, and it was unclear how the others had survived their assaults.

"I'm so sorry," I started. "You and Bobbie were together awhile?"

Martin shrugged, and I sat back in my chair, estimating how long I had before his parents arrived, lawyering up their son if required. *Long enough to give the kid a minute to collect himself,* I decided.

How many Pink Parrot employees had been present? Mamma Burstyn could give me the exact number, but I was thinking around eight. Six performers on and off the float, plus the man driving and Big Mamma herself. Which performer had left after hearing that his coworkers had died, I wondered, watching the others give their statements to various police officers.

"Where'd you meet?" I tried again, receiving another shrug in response.

"Ah, I see. A romantic. Doesn't want to blab his story. I can appreciate that." Martin sighed, and I considered any response a small victory. "Not the ending I would have wished for you."

That elicited another sigh, and the boy sat up straighter, tucking his hands underneath his pants. The thing about being nondescript is that people don't tend to be suspicious of you; you don't remind them of anyone else, not a cranky aunt or a loathed hall monitor. They might as well be talking to a ghost, and a ghost can keep a secret, let me tell you.

"I wasn't in love with him," Martin said so fast that I couldn't be sure that he had said "wasn't" as opposed to "was." I didn't interrupt to verify. "I mean, I'm seventeen. We weren't getting married or anything."

He dropped into another silence, sliding a hand out from under himself and eyeing the nails again. I resisted the urge to grab the offending digits and let him self-mutilate instead.

"But he was fun, you know? And fucking cute."

The boy's voice broke on "cute," and I found myself having difficulty breathing again. For a moment, I forgot to ask anything at all.

"I'm here with Dolly," I said.

"I know. I saw you two together. After."

I was afraid to push my luck, but needed to. "Did you see anything else, Martin?"

"Some asshole shoved the juggler. I wish I could kill him," he said, and I had a sinking feeling Martin—with or without knowing it himself—was playing two truths and a lie with me. One, he wasn't in love with Bobbie. Two, the juggler wasn't to blame. Three, revenge wasn't unthinkable. Problem was, I had no clue which statement to trust. I wrote down my number and told him that he could call me if he needed anything. "Or remember anything," I hinted. I would be lucky if he didn't throw it away.

With two exceptions—the one who had left and Dolly, still receiving treatment—the entertainers present at the parade were finishing up their statements. I asked them to repeat a few answers after the officers had left.

"Too loud to hear anything—"

"Flames everywhere, you know?"

"What death threat?"

It seemed Big Mamma had been keeping some secrets herself.

CHAPTER THREE

M y assistant Meeza—fast on her way to becoming a private investigator in her own right—was sprawled on my couch when I got back to the office late that evening. She looked like nothing so much as a coed, from her skinny jeans and tank top to her long sleek hair pulled into a high ponytail. She was chewing gum and starting intently at her laptop screen.

"Physics homework?" I teased, dropping my mask into a drawer filled with whiteout, candy wrappers, pushpins, and other useless junk.

"I wish," she said, closing her browser window and moving the computer aside. "Jimmy's got swim class at 9 A.M. Who takes swim class as a college freshman?"

Jimmy Holliday was our client's son. Mrs. Holliday wanted to make sure that she wasn't throwing away money on college tuition for her offspring to gallivant around town, a legitimate concern for an eighteen-year-old from Iowa let loose in New York City for the first time. I wasn't sure that she would be much more pleased with swim classes; those are some expensive butterfly strokes.

"You know, you don't have to attend every class," I said.

Snagging a college I.D. for Meeza had been one of my more challenging feats. Thankfully at least a few undergrads are still unaware of pickpockets, and hey, I'd returned the wallet. I would survive my remorse at the young woman's grateful face when I ran after her shouting, "I think you dropped this!" I could even imagine her telling the family at Thanksgiving: "No, you're wrong. Everyone's *really* nice in New York City."

"Yeah, but he's more likely to skip the early ones, you know? I wish I could sit idly in a lecture. Medieval history would be nice. Or Greek drama maybe."

If Meeza wasn't surprised to see me strolling in at 10 P.M., I confess that I was surprised to find her working so late and not only because she was expected in a pool lane the next morning. Meeza still lived with her parents in Queens, and they fretted if she didn't at least check in. These days she had to check in with her boyfriend V.P. as well, and it was clear he didn't like her new profession. She had once been an under-utilized floor secretary for our building, a safe job that had all but bored her into the decision to join me on a case. It wasn't long before she'd turned in her resignation and rustled up her own customers.

In an effort to keep an eye on her, V.P. was pestering Meeza to become the office manager for his car rental business, a shady enterprise that trafficked in stolen vehicles and catered to criminals. And people like me. I didn't like to use my real name for anything I could avoid. My office was leased to one Katya Lincoln, and my apartment to Kate Manning. V.P. didn't ask for names, let alone proof of insurance. No credit card, no problem. It had worked out well for me until my sweet assistant had her head turned by his so-called ambitions. As if he knew I was thinking ill of him, Meeza's phone beeped.

"*Mujhe jaana hoga*, I was supposed to meet Vincent five minutes ago!"

She began throwing her belongings into an oversized bag while I leaned against the door and watched her fret. It didn't strike me as normal to stress over being late to meet your boyfriend. Couldn't she text him that she was running behind? "He can wait for a few more minutes."

"It's rude to keep someone waiting," Meeza said in the sing-song voice she adopted when I was being unreasonable. Still, I knew that if she was really unhappy, she would make a clucking noise, so I was in the clear. When I rubbed my eyes, she stopped her frantic packing, and I knew that I was being observed, curious about what tactful phrase Meeza would use to describe my bedraggled appearance. At least a quick stop by the bathroom had gotten most of the smoke residue off. It wasn't that unusual for my job to take me behind garbage bins and onto tar-filled rooftops. She'd definitely seen worse than scrapes and smelled worse than the electrical tang clinging to my sweater. Meeza settled on "a bit tired."

"You were at the parade?" she asked quietly before her eyes widened. "The man you know from the bird club?"

"He'll be okay," I said quickly.

Meeza paused to consider my assessment. I could see rival impulses flash across her face as she decided whether seeking more information would be appropriate or prying. "Did you get what you needed?" she finally asked.

I blanked at first, picturing Dolly's perfect skin slashed in pink, then remembered my clandestine meeting for information about Salvatore Magrelli. It wasn't often that I forgot about the man I considered Lord of the Underworld. I'd only given Meeza hazy details, and thankfully she hadn't pressed me.

"Yeah, I've got a whole file of possibilities. My own homework."

Meeza gave me an appraising look and a quick hug. When she rushed out the door, I took her place on the couch. I had my qualms about her new relationship to say the least. But V.P. and I had an unspoken agreement. He wouldn't mention my past life, dragging Meeza into worry she didn't deserve. I wouldn't share his rap sheet, a laundry list of misdemeanors begging to be bumped up to felonies.

When I sat up on my knees, I could look out the window into the alley below or the empty offices next door. Neither view was particularly exciting, not even a rat in sight. That made it easy to turn my attention to the stack of papers Ellis had given me. I glanced at the first page, feeling torn. I could hear Big Mamma's statement that she wanted someone's undivided attention. *Should I postpone my investigation while I look into the explosion?* It seemed indulgent to pursue what could be called a vendetta in the right light when a friend was in need.

I had trained myself not to think about the most harrowing days of my undercover work, using psychological tricks I'd invented myself. My actual department-assigned shrink had wanted me to relive each and every fear with the notion that visualizing the trauma would help me come to terms with it. I didn't think much of his methods and preferred to visualize shooting the heart out of a target anytime my mind wandered down an unpleasant path. Totally healthy, I know.

That night, however, I was too tired to war with my memories and found myself thinking back to the day I refused to shoot a teenager who had found out about a cocaine shipment. When Salvatore Magrelli had pushed a gun into my hand, I had shoved it back. I didn't run away fast enough to miss the sound of bullets being fired into the boy's head. You'd think something like that would be enough to build a case against the monster, but no. The boy's younger brother had taken the fall with promises of riches when he was released from juvie.

I don't know about riches, but I'd checked on him. He was dealing pot and getting into the kind of trouble you'd expect from a kid who'd watched his sibling get murdered—assault, vandalism, harassment. He didn't look like a kid anymore in his latest mug shot, but I could still picture the first one, his watery brown eyes haunting me when I let my guard down. Like now.

I spread out the papers from Ellis and began reading at random. Almost all of the evidence collected against Magrelli over the years was circumstantial. Associations with criminals, his name on shady bank documents, a photograph showing him leaving a crime scene. My own testimony against him was missing, but I can't say that I was shocked. His case being thrown out implied connections higher than I could safely imagine. Judges, senators—I doubt very many people have access to "Get Out of Jail Free" cards. Not being able to take him down had shaken my faith in the NYPD. My official discharge papers had some mumbo-jumbo language about anxiety on the job, and I'll admit to being easily spooked. "Disappointment" might have been a more accurate description. Was there an exit interview box to check for that?

Magrelli had prided himself on wise investments. While reticent on most subjects, he could bend your ear about the tobacco farm he'd picked up in Celaya, Mexico, for nothing. A few grand. He would describe the soil's smell with the language of a sommelier, hints of lavender and onion. Coca leaves looked plain enough to me, but he could make them sound like emeralds glinting in the afternoon sun. Of course, money does have a certain sheen to it. It wasn't just land; Magrelli was proud of his recruits, too.

His core group numbered no more than six, and he had kept his party-hungry brother as far away from the center as possible. Frank didn't seem to mind. He preferred the spoils to the action. The other men—always men—were Ivy League educated and Golden Retriever loyal. I thought of them as "papered." The next circle in his version of hell included his fiancée Eva Costa, but none of her relatives. Eva had been working hard to change his mind, wanting to bring her whole family up in the world with her. He'd always responded with "I'll keep an open mind," but he didn't take on fools. Her sister Zanna—the person I'd befriended as a way into the scene—was allowed to play lookout from time to time, but I doubted her presence was necessary those nights. Mine certainly wasn't, but Zanna wasn't good at being alone, and I never whined about the weather. We were usually kept far enough away to miss anything that might have aided my investigation, and I had longed for binoculars like I'd never longed for anything before.

My night's burst of energy had been replaced with a headache and sore throat, so I tossed everything aside and laid down, pulling an afghan over my legs. Three years ago, I thought that I had built an airtight case against Salvatore, his brother Frank, and one other dealer named de Luca. Now Frank and de Luca were serving thirty, and Salvatore was helping his new wife pick out nursery furniture. I shuddered at the thought of the devil having babies and reprimanded myself for not doing more, anxiety and disappointment be damned.

When I swore off the violent underbelly of the city, I had meant it. Catching adulterers was easy, and I'd never gotten worse than a paper cut as a private investigator. That is, not until last month when a small-time drug dealer had pulled me back into the fray. I couldn't bring myself to feel grateful for the blows I'd suffered, but the case had forced me to look at what was polluting my city. And it wasn't philanderers. Maybe I was a reluctant vigilante, but better late than never. *I can juggle both cases*, I thought, then laughed at my choice of words. It wasn't a happy sound, and I was glad nobody was around to hear.

CHAPTER FOUR

The next morning I spent a few futile minutes wishing the previous night's events had been a bad dream, then texted Dolly to check on him. He replied before I finished brushing my teeth in the shared office bathroom, saying that he'd been released and wanted to see me that afternoon. I told him I would meet him at The Pink Parrot, then turned my attention back to the Magrelli file. The contents were scattered over my worn, beige carpet, and I crawled down to meet them at eye level. On my stomach, I flipped through photographs and receipts, tax forms and phone records. I was trying to be thorough, but itched to skip straight to Ellis's tip about the restaurant. The Skyview wasn't any old noodle shop; it was a members-only dining club situated in a high-rise office building near Central Park South. The website brought up an application form, but no additional information. Those in the know know, I guess.

To say that I wanted to see inside was an understatement, and I downloaded the application form. In tiny print at the bottom was the usual legal spiel about a non-discrimination policy, and to be fair, it didn't seem that race, gender, or sexual orientation made a wink of difference. Cash, on the other hand, was king. In addition to tax forms, the application required three references and a sponsoring current club member. They also requested a 1,000-word summary of accomplishments and a blood sample. Okay, no blood sample, but I would watch out for mouth swabs in the ladies' room.

I Googled "*Vanity Fair* and The Skyview" to rustle up some member photographs. Surely the hotspot had hosted its lion's share of charity events. Raising Awareness of Tennis Elbow or some such. And I was in luck. A summer mingle gave me glimpses of Dolce & Gabbana dresses showing off the city socialites to their best advantages. Tuxedoed and tanned escorts mugged for the photographers. I didn't recognize anyone at first, but it wasn't my crowd. I jotted down all the names I could find, pausing when I got to one Lars Dekker, Jr. Moving my finger along the images, I matched the name with the face, and—*Hello, handsome.* That mug wasn't easy to forget.

Ellis picked up on the first ring, and I told him what I wanted as quickly as possible. That request amounted to using his brother's highfalutin' connections to get me through the front door of one very exclusive address. I could find the back rooms all by myself.

Ellis didn't respond right away, mulling over the ramifications of getting his kin involved in an unendorsed investigation of a drug cartel leader. I knew the brothers weren't close, but Ellis was dutiful. I'd once heard him refer to himself as the rescue dog in a kennel of pedigree pointers. I could almost sense his encyclopedic brain looking at all the possible scenarios of my favor, zooming in and out on the worst ones. When he settled on "calculated risk," he answered, still holding back.

"I'm not sure if Lars is a member. He's never mentioned it."

"You said yourself it was members only, gala or no gala. Would you mind checking?"

Ellis hung up without answering, but I was feeling good about my odds that he'd come through for me. If the answer was "no," he would have said as much. I clicked on a few more photographs, then stopped on one of Salvatore's one-time fiancée, now wife. She wasn't draped on anyone's arm, but standing by herself under a tasteful sign stating the restaurant name. Underneath, if I squinted, I could make out a few more words: Est. 2013, Eva Costa Magrelli, Proprietor.

———

The last time I saw Eva Costa, she had handcuffed her sister Zanna to a radiator. There was enough slack for Zanna to keep from burning herself, but she was so high that she screamed, pushed, and pulled against the metal until her hand and forearm were littered with small, cocoon-shaped marks. Her mother sang in the kitchen, trying as she always did to ignore the family business. She didn't even ask where her eldest daughter had acquired handcuffs—standard issue, not novelty with purple feathers.

I was halfheartedly trying to talk Eva into giving me the key. I wish I could say that it was tough to watch my friend injure herself, but I was as high on hope as Zanna was on blow. Zanna wasn't being punished precisely, but being prevented from ruining a large Mexican shipment scheduled to arrive the next morning. In her drug haze, she had been ranting that she knew all about the deal and wanted a cut in exchange for not telling the police. Shoddy blackmail at best and more likely to get her throat slit than get rich, which is why her loyal if not exactly loving sister had shackled her.

Where Eva was the neighborhood goddess, fawned over from morning to night, Zanna was the neighborhood loose cannon, a fighter not a lover. When the NYPD had suggested I befriend her, only my half-comatose state could have made me agree. After my parents' death, I had been a winning combination of numb and fearless. As Big Mamma had so recently argued, anyone looking out for my best interests would have suggested a less taxing assignment. I would have been aces at crime scene photography, for instance. But there was nobody except my concerned friend Ellis, who didn't have any authority at the time despite his obvious potential. So I rented the apartment next door to the Costas and slowly wiggled my way into Zanna's confidence. It wasn't that hard. Even loose cannons get lonely.

Two years later, I was no longer numb and pretty well scared of the Magrellis and the Costas. If Zanna said enough, I could walk, hence my ambivalent concern about her burns. At the time, I thought I could walk and never look back, but I was nothing if not naive. Orpheus hadn't meant to turn back to the underworld either. He'd even been warned, but turn back he did, losing his beloved in the process. I was still taking inventory on what I'd lost.

"Eva, she's bluffing," I had suggested. "How could she even know enough?"

I pulled my jet-black hair off the nape of my neck, sweating from standing over the radiator steam. Zanna was sweating, too, dripping onto the 1980s carpet that probably hadn't been cleaned since installation. The Costa apartment was dingy to say the least, and all three children—Eva, Zanna, and the baby Nino—wanted nothing more than to get the hell out. Only Eva had a shot, as far as I could tell, and she kept surprising me with her family allegiances. Why let them keep dragging her down?

"I brought her with me yesterday, to Salvatore's. He was on the phone, and—*¿Qué te pasa*, Zanna?"

I needed two measly pieces of information for my extraction dreams to become a reality: ship name and port name. Did my contact know that much? I wasn't sure, and I was trying to avoid the mistakes that come with desperation. I didn't say anything, repeating "ship name and port name" in my head. For something to do, I walked into the kitchen and poured two glasses of water from the tap. I doubted Zanna would take even a sip, but Mrs. Costa grunted in approval.

"They're both good girls," she told me in Spanish. I had my doubts. About the girls and Mrs. Costa's sincerity. Her persona was that of a devout, Venezuelan housewife—a model matriarch—and she had a repertoire of signature dishes to prove her status. But when she looked at me, the smile stopped at her eyes. Always suspicious. And sometimes in my nightmares, it's not Salvatore Magrelli or even Zanna who corners me in an alley with a baseball bat, but rather Signora Costa blowing my brains out with a .45, then stopping for groceries on the way home.

＊

Six-feet tall neon flamingos stood on either side of the Pink Parrot entrance, guarding the place along with a bouncer—excuse me, a security professional. Both birds were unlit, and Earl was nowhere to be seen. In fact, even when I peered into the windows, I couldn't see anyone. A small handwritten note said closed until further notice. It startled me to see this New York institution closed. I didn't believe anything could shake Big Mamma, and it was an effort to knock. Whatever was going on inside, I didn't want to disturb. When the door cracked open, it wasn't the owner but Dolly's red-rimmed eyes that greeted me.

"Hey, sugar," he said. "Come on in out of the rain."

I glanced up at the crisp, blue November sky and shook my head, following Dolly into the dark and latching the door behind me. Wearing jeans and a University of Florida sweatshirt, he looked like a different person than he had the night before. He navigated the room gracefully, missing the assorted chairs and tables while I banged my elbows and shins. It hurt to look at the stage, still decorated with silver streamers and disco balls, but deflated somehow, as if covered with a month's worth of dust, not a day's. Dolly's dressing room was better—lamps on at least—and when the tea kettle whistled, I relaxed enough to fix us both cups of chamomile. I could have used something stronger, but calming seemed like the right choice for Dolly.

"Ms. Burstyn asked me to look into the fire," I said, not wanting to mention the deaths, yet. I didn't need a police report to tell me that the explosion hadn't been an accident. I'd done some research, and those floats are designed to keep combustible materials away from all generators. And the wiring must meet strict standards, or the float's banned. No exceptions. If a makeshift explosive was on board, it must have been left after the event started.

"I told her last week that she should have hired you," Dolly said.

"She told you about the threat?"

Dolly put down his tea cup, careful not to tear the wraps on his hands. His forehead was bandaged, as well, and he didn't look at his reflection when he stepped toward the vanity. I was glad that his wounds seemed to be limited to burns, although I knew they must ache. He pulled out a decorative wooden box from the top drawer. I wasn't holding my breath for love letters, but when he opened the lid, several red envelopes fell out.

"Threats plural. We all got them. These aren't all wishes for imminent demise. A few from fans, as well." He picked up the smallest envelope and handed it to me. Inside was the same wedding stock paper that Big Mamma's threat had featured, and the invitation was basically the same. "You know what's funny," Dolly continued. "The memorial really will be at St. Mark's Church. It's where all the artists are dying to go."

CHAPTER FIVE

Dolly attempted a hand flourish, but the gauze made the gesture look painful rather than funny. I brought my attention back to the square paper, rubbing my fingers along the embossed words.

"I don't know much about printing, but this seems nice. It could be something for me to check out."

"For *us* to check out."

I considered protesting but realized that it was pointless. Dolly had lost his friends and wouldn't be dissuaded. Plus, I could keep an eye on him if he stuck close to me. Not quite a twenty-four-hour bodyguard, but a step in the right direction. He was still a target. And I could use his help, starting with background information about the victims. As a three-year headliner for the club, he must have known the other performers well. After a long enough pause for him to think that I was resigned rather than eager, I pulled a legal pad out, uncapped a pen, and faced my friend.

"Let's start with the deceased. Roberto Giabella?"

The direct approach worked well, and Dolly filled me in on Bobbie, starting with his audition and ending with his seventeen-year-old boyfriend Martin. There wasn't much to tell, since Bobbie had been working at The Pink Parrot for less than eight months. Two as a waiter, five and change as a performer. A rapid rise, according to Dolly. The other victim, Taylor Soto, wasn't even on the float when it blew up. He and some other members of the waitstaff were walking beside, and he was hit in the head by a support beam. Knocked instantly unconscious, the doctors had said, if that was any comfort to the family. Even though Taylor wasn't listed on the funeral invite, Dolly told me what he knew anyway. Busboy turned bartender with hopes to be in the show.

I asked about the performers who had been threatened specifically, and Dolly settled into his role as informant, zeroing in on what secrets might be most relevant. In Juniper Summer's case, he went by Jake Summer while visiting his family and girlfriend in Utah. Yep, girlfriend as in a twenty-year-old matriculated at Salt Lake Community College waiting until her wedding night for sex with her high school sweetheart.

"That's not likely to end well," I said when Dolly stood up to grab some photographs from his mirror. He pointed out Juniper, whose pale complexion was almost ghoulish in his stage makeup.

"You're telling me, but Juniper's not even the biggest Pandora's box. We've got a senator's son and an honest-to-Cher drug dealer. You didn't hear either of those from me."

I jotted down "Sen. son" next to Carlton Casborough, and "drugs" next to Herman White who sold, you guessed it, coke. In small quantities as far as Dolly knew. A little side income, not a lot of risk, though I'd seen enough coke dealers slide from small-time to shit-deep without noticing. Ravi Sethi and Aaron Kline weren't nearly as scandalous. Ravi was married to his long-time partner and owned a 5% stake in The Pink Parrot, his ten-year career anniversary present from Big Mamma. He didn't perform as much anymore, preferring his new management role to the spotlight. And Aaron was everyone's favorite, guests and coworkers alike. The one you called in an emergency if you needed your dog walked. Aside from sexual orientation, the men didn't have much in common, and I was pretty sure we were looking at a hate crime. There was always a possibility that the club itself was the target, and I wrote that in my margins as well.

"I need to talk to Ms. Burstyn, too. Can you write down anything else you think of?"

I handed over my legal pad and squeezed Dolly's shoulder before heading toward the bar, where I figured Big Mamma would be waiting for me by now. She didn't disappoint. Dressed in a three-piece pin-striped suit, she looked ready for a courtroom, and I couldn't blame her. I knew from experience that she'd be lucky if her only visitors today were from the police department and insurance agency. She was as likely to hear from Bobbie's family lawyers, funeral home directors, and newspaper reporters.

"The service is tomorrow," she said without looking up from the files she had spread on a cocktail table. "You'll come?"

"I'll be there. Kind of ballsy to have it at St. Mark's, no?"

Big Mamma chortled. "Balls or ovaries—that's all I've ever had, Miss Stone. You, too, if I'm not wrong about you."

I wanted to argue, not for my sake but hers. My assets were few and far between, and I'd long thought of this woman as one of the top entrepreneurs in New York City. Eva Magrelli was a shadow of a shadow in comparison. I bit my tongue before I asked my host about The Skyview, wanting the dirt but knowing it wasn't appropriate to get off topic. Day 1, and I was already tempted to blur the lines between my two cases. Not a promising start. I glanced at the files on the table and saw dozens of resumes and headshots.

"Looking for replacements?" I asked.

"These are for you. All the ones we didn't hire."

I could see where Big Mamma might think of these men as suspects, but I didn't buy it. Not getting a gig is no reason to kill people, and I said as much.

"Think of it this way, Miss Stone. We're the University Club for drag queens. This isn't a gig, it's a family and a damn well-connected one at that. Salary and benefits? Icing. Some people look around and see nothing but a seedy club, but these are A-list performers."

Dolly, her Aist of A-listers, was perched in the doorway watching us. I guess he hadn't thought of anything worth adding to our notes.

"I can think of better uses of your time, Darío, than scowling," Big Mamma said. She still hadn't looked up from her files, but I was sure she knew what expression to expect from using Dolly's legal name. If I avoided Kathleen Stone as much as possible, Dolly avoided Darío Rodriquez like it was his job. I suppose in a way it was. No one came to see Mr. Rodriquez on Saturday nights.

"Any rivals that I should know about?" I said, partly to change the subject.

"There are a few club owners downtown who'd like to compete with my lineup. They're nowhere near this echelon, but I'll give you the names. And you'll take these."

She collected the photographs and papers, shoving everything into a folder as the house phone rang. She pulled it over to her table and checked the caller I.D. before answering in a stern voice: "About time I heard from you." She waved her hand, signaling to both Dolly and me that we were dismissed.

Kennedy S. Vanders wasn't the easiest woman to inhabit. For starters, I didn't know what the "S" stood for. Perhaps a maiden name: Starkweather or Samsonite. I mouthed "Starkweather" into my bathroom mirror then watched my face morph into someone more worldly. My jaw tightened, and I penciled in darker eyebrows until they arched into perpetual disdain. I tucked the silky red strands of my wig behind my ears in order to insert large cubic zirconium studs. In the The Skyview's sure-to-be flattering light, no one would know the difference between real and fake. A lady could hope.

I had spent the afternoon running Google searches and background checks on the thirty-three Pink Parrot rejects, but aside from a few slaps on the wrist, the men were clean. And mostly impressive: a Rhodes Scholar, an award-winning journalist, a painter rumored to be in the Whitney Museum's next Biennial exhibition. While I was sure they were disappointed by not being hired at Manhattan's most exclusive drag club, I was equally certain that they would find work elsewhere. Revenge didn't strike me as the right motive. Not this time. Not for this brand of castoffs.

When I wrapped up my day's work on the Pink Parrot case, I had just enough time to prepare for a glamorous albeit perilous night out. Ellis's brother Lars Dekker had been more than game to help an industrious P.I., even if he probably didn't remember meeting me. The weekend that I'd spent at his family's Long Island estate was a speck in my rearview, as well. His eagerness confirmed my long-held suspicion that it's boring being rich. At least that's what I always told myself to get through the morning commutes.

On the cab ride to midtown, I considered what I knew about my alter ego Kennedy. In a previous incarnation, she had been the wife of a wealthy businessman, but now I thought she was probably divorced, maybe looking for Victim #2.

I smiled when I thought of that detail, and I had to admit that I liked this character. Over the years, that had become a pattern—identifying with my personas more than myself. On the surface, Kennedy Starkweather Vanders and I had nothing in common, but there was always something to grab. A perverted sense of humor. A fondness for Monopoly. In this instance, her red hair was supplied by my favorite wig. It had once been brutally mussed by a NYPD evidence bag, but after ministrations from hairpiece guru Vondya Vasiliev, it was a survivor. Like me. See? There's always a connection.

That night, my doppelganger grabbed the attention of my cab driver, and he didn't try to hide his curiosity. "What's a woman like you doing in the Heights?" was his opening gambit.

I kept my gaze on the Hudson River, admired the twinkling lights off the George Washington Bridge, and wished the driver would focus more on the traffic. Instead, he weaved with one hand on the wheel, both eyes on my face in the mirror.

"My sister," I responded curtly, trying to check his enthusiasm. It wasn't my lucky night—unfortunate, since I hoped to play a little poker. A hastily scrawled note on The Skyview brochure among Ellis's papers hinted at a secret (until you asked the right questions) table. Illegal, yes, and also likely where I'd find Magrelli's high-rolling associates, the ones I believed would lead to the ringleader himself.

"No shit," the driver replied. "My sister lives up there, too. You and me, we could be related."

In the backseat window I could see Kennedy's wry expression, then an undercurrent of nerves that I didn't want to be visible. I'm good at blending, but maybe this was too much of a stretch. I thought I knew how the monied acted, but maybe in private, there was a whole other language to master. I pulled my attention to the driver. There was no need to be haughty. Yet.

"We could be," I agreed. "Where are you from?"

In most cases, it's rude to assume that people are from anywhere but New York City—everyone wants to be a genuine New Yorker—but many are. It's a transplant city, my parents the exception rather than the rule. And the driver, Eliasz Brzezicki, according to the certification displayed on the back of the driver's seat, didn't seem to mind.

"Poland, you know where that is?"

"Yeah, I know."

He pointed to a photograph on his dash that showed two little girls with wide, oval eyes.

"My girls, they're from here. Born in Queens. They're not Polish."

I knew what he meant, though I hoped they appreciated their heritage. I like to call myself a mutt, but I knew my parents' histories, the unexpected combinations that produced a daughter indistinguishable in a crowd.

"They're pretty," I said. "What grades are they in?"

"First and third. Best of their classes, too."

"I bet."

The driver laid on the horn as a black SUV tried to pass on the right. He shifted toward that lane, and the other driver slammed on the brakes. I braced myself against the door, but nothing happened.

"Math. They like math."

I removed my hands from the door handle. "Good for them."

When we got off Riverside Drive, there was more traffic and more honking, but we made our way past the theater district and down the street I needed. Normally, I would never cough up the cash for a taxi, but I didn't want anyone to see me coming up from the subway. Maybe I was being crazy, but these were high stakes. I wasn't sure what all I would lose if I lost. My stomach flipped at that thought, and

I rummaged around in my purse so that the shaking in my hands wouldn't show.

"You sure this is the spot?" the driver asked. We had pulled up in front of a tall office building, and it looked deserted except for the lobby attendant. That was part of the allure, I knew. Anonymity and a hint of intrigue. More than a hint in my case, but I wasn't turning back. I handed the drive two twenties and told him to keep the change. He turned on the interior light to make a note on his clipboard. With one last deep breath, I forced myself to turn the door handle and slipped out.

"Good luck," the cabbie called before I slammed the door behind me. Did he say that to all his fares? Or was I giving off a smell of desperation? I waved my thanks through the glass and pulled my fake Chanel bag onto my shoulder. I'd dealt myself a hand. There was nothing else to do but play.

CHAPTER SIX

I had spent the afternoon stressing over the level of security required of a private city club, but in the end, an assertive walk and laminated I.D. were all I needed to be waved through the gates to the elevator bank. If all went according to plan, Ellis's brother would have vouched for me, pushing my trial membership through the usual red tape. My net worth may have been exaggerated, my political connections inflated. Then again, why shouldn't I winter in the Riviera? I put my bikini on one leg at a time like everyone else.

The maître d' looked a lot more formidable than the building's lone guard I had spotted roaming the lobby. I knew that hosts and hostesses at swank places like this were often restaurateurs in the making, able to list every customer's quirks and—more importantly—accommodate them. I wouldn't be able to stroll in un-noted, and as expected, the woman greeted me with the right amount of welcome and suspicion.

"Good evening, ma'am. So nice to see you tonight. Are you joining us?"

Membership at The Skyview had a six-month to a year wait time, and the most likely reason for my appearance was that they had recently lost a member. I could almost see the woman hoping that meant someone had died rather than someone had been dissatisfied with the service. Her more pressing hope was that she hadn't been kept out of the loop on purpose, a sure indicator of an imminent coup. To summarize, I'd unnerved her a little, which might not be a bad start to our relationship. She came around the podium to shake my hand, and I noticed silver stilettos peeking out below the hem of her tailored trousers. Here was a woman used to the pain caused by an eight-hour shift standing on needles. Tough, I surmised, and grasped her outstretched palm.

"Kennedy Vanders. I've been positively dying to get into this vault," I began, showing how much I respected her work, then shifted gears to show my own influence. "I may have leapfrogged the line, I'm afraid, but I really couldn't stand the thought of waiting until I got back from Portofino next month."

"Of course not. Would you like to sit at the bar while your table is prepared?"

"Oh yes, thank you."

I followed her gesture to a marble slab where two women in understatedly expensive dresses discussed the Met's new season, lamenting the lack of Puccini over their rieslings. I sat far away from them, not wanting to test my opera knowledge over chitchat, and pretended to study my phone's planner. I ordered a champagne, waving off the question of brand with "whatever you recommend" and tried to study the landscape discreetly. I'd read that FIFA referees practice eye exercises to improve their peripheral vision, and I envied their range. Could I find a sight trainer? If any city in the world had such an occupation, it would be New York. I typed a few random words on my phone to look busy, then took a less furtive look at my surroundings.

The space was larger than I would have guessed, taking up the building's entire floor—not all of it visible, of course, but Ellis had pulled the floorplan for me. There was a kitchen nearby, but not a single crashing pot could be heard in the dining area. The thirty or so tables were spaced far apart to give the illusion of privacy. When I accidentally made eye contact with a once chart-topping singer, I turned my attention to the view of Central Park. As myself, I would have blushed, but Kennedy wouldn't care about a has-been, no matter the still-healthy balance on the warbler's bank account. Anyway, I was more interested in the velvet curtain designating a VIP room or party space.

Getting a table was my first hurdle, and I knew that Miss Hostess wasn't really preparing it, but rather scouring her data-base for my name and history, puzzling out who on staff had phoned in a favor. Only the owner had that much authority, so when my name appeared (fingers crossed), she would have to accept my presence and start buttering me up. Speaking of buttering, from my brief perusal of the room, the lobster looked divine, and I was looking forward to the menu even as the thought of spending a hundred dollars for dinner made my skin crawl. Scrimping on costs would be a giveaway, though. Plus, a generous client had handed me a bonus that I didn't deserve on my last case. I planned to invest it in making the city safer, and if that meant choking down some chocolate soufflé, call me a martyr and add me to the society page. Under a pseudonym, please.

When the hostess came back into view, there was no trace of frustration on her perfectly unlined brow, but she must have felt slightly off-kilter by my reservation. *When had it been added*, she was asking herself. She was probably the same age as Kennedy, early 30s, only a few years older than my actual age, and I couldn't help but be impressed that she kept this high-end of high-end establishments running smoothly. When I smiled at her, it was mostly genuine. I wasn't as sure about her returning beam. The white sheen off her canines seemed more bleach than genetic.

"Right this way, Ms. Vanders," she said, gesturing toward a corner table that would allow me to survey the entire room. That is to say, a prime spot, and I silently thanked the Dekker family for their influence.

"Please, Kennedy is fine. I didn't catch your name," I said, turning to fully face her.

"Bethany Rosen. Beth. We hope you enjoy your visit. It's not every day we get to entertain a new guest."

"Really? I knew the waitlist was long, but someone must be plucked from the maddening crowd from time to time."

"From time to time, yes." Beth handed me a wine list, recommended the steak tartare, then vanished, hopefully to worry about something besides me. Maybe there could be a shortage of truffles. A celebrity meltdown? I surveyed my fellow diners to see who might be in need of a Valium.

Aside from the singer, I didn't recognize anyone. I'm sure another perusal of *Vanity Fair* would have revealed a few well-known faces, but I didn't keep up with the Manhattan socialites. I slid into my chair and eavesdropped on the chatter of the nearest two tables. I admit to being slightly disappointed by their banality. Sure, their diamonds were real, but their conversations would have worked as well on the bus. I caught snippets about postponed vacations and sick children. A couple debated the merits of the latest blockbuster, *The World Ends Again*. When one man started boasting about his portfolio, I almost sighed with relief. See? They were different than us.

I was so caught up in my casual judgment of strangers that I almost missed the appearance of Eva Magrelli. And she's hard to miss. When I had first met the eldest Costa, she had favored bright nylon dresses and stacked heels. Even then, she had a poise that set her apart from the other young women in the neighborhood. It wasn't simply that she was prettier—and with her long, tan legs and matching mane, she definitely was—but that she oozed a certain peace with the world. As if she knew she wouldn't always live in the cramped Bronx apartment that her mother filled with the scent of grilled onions by noon each day. Seeing her now in designer slacks and a cardigan didn't seem like a total transformation. Rather, the other Eva, the Costa girl, was a role she had been playing, and didn't she deserve her statue now?

Eva handed Beth a small slip of paper, patting the hostess on the arm in a way that implied they were friendly if not friends. Both women glanced over at a man who had sat down at the bar, and I guessed him to be a member without a reservation. When Eva approached him with a sad shake of her head, I thought we might get to see some entitled anger in action. Instead, the man shrugged in defeat and accepted the complimentary cognac the bartender served him. I couldn't hear at my distance, but the scene was easy to interpret. "It was worth a shot, yada, yada, yada." My server cleared his throat to get my attention.

"Good evening, ma'am. My name is Gustav, and I'll be taking care of you this evening. Would you like to start with another glass of champagne?"

I paused to consider the questioner. Not the young, attractive actors employed at lesser establishments, but a seasoned professional who could easily take home five hundred dollars a night here. There weren't any prices on the menu, but I guessed that the businessmen at the table across the room from me would spend a cool two grand alone.

As I asked for a recommendation and glanced over the list of wine names, I lost track of Eva. I willed myself to be patient as I accepted Gustav's first choice. He approved of my decision and disappeared as someone else brought over a complimentary *amuse-bouche*. I nibbled at the cheesy edges of the delicacy, sipped my sparkling water, and snuck glances at the velvet curtain, desperately wanting to know what or who lurked behind. The green fabric color choice wasn't lost on me, and which sad Oz character was I? I wasn't feeling brave, but then again, I hadn't asked the cab driver to turn around and take me home. That left me without a heart or brains. Hell, maybe I was some sort of tin lion hybrid. Somehow, I doubted the wizard behind this partition would be inclined to help me.

I was concerned that Eva might recognize me, but not overly scared. My face is unmemorable; the bones seem to shift, depending on the light. Plus, I had been passing for Puerto Rican when I lived next door to her family. With my recently sunscreen-protected skin, I was at least three shades lighter. Add the red wig, and a census worker would check "Caucasian" or "Of European decent." Not completely inaccurate, if you considered Russia part of Europe, but not the whole story. Since when did a race box tell you the whole story? I thought back to my Polish cabdriver and hoped my great-grandparents weren't rolling in their graves at my flippancy.

The meal was uneventful. I ordered as extravagantly as I dared, knowing that a larger check would make my request to join the VIP action a bit more palatable. With that in mind, I selected items from every category, despite not being a first course kind of gal, not wanting to waste valuable stomach space on soup or salad. The dessert wasn't a burden, and I was scraping up the last of the *crème fraîche* when the waiter came to check on my progress.

"Everything was wonderful, thank you."

"I'm glad you enjoyed your meal. We hope to see more of you." Gustav bowed slightly—not obsequious, but respectful. His gold wedding band was the only indication of a life outside this room. His auburn hair was gray around the edges, and I speculated on his past. The Skyview had only been open for a year, so had he been unemployed like so many others in this city? Lost in the shuffle when a prior stalwart of the restaurant scene closed its doors maybe? What did he know about the proprietor's shady connections? I wouldn't get a chance to find out, although I doubted he would break under interrogation anyway. A server of his caliber would be old-school loyal. A talent for keeping your lips sealed was a valuable commodity in any industry.

"Oh, I'm sure you will," I replied after a beat. "I've been told you have entertainment for anyone so inclined." I paused to make sure that he understood my meaning. He did, but double-checked anyway.

"Yes, there's live music every Saturday. This week a trio from the Mannes faculty will be performing."

"Delightful. I was thinking of something in particular for tonight. Cards," I finished bluntly.

He bowed again. "Of course, ma'am. Let me find out for you."

He left the bill on the table, and I managed not to gasp when I peeked at the total. It was worse than I expected. I didn't want to think about how many pasta and jarred sauce meals were in my future to make up for this evening's splurge. And it wasn't finished, yet. I was counting on the club's vetting process to be good enough to grant me access to the game, but was still surprised when Gustav returned so quickly to tell me that the group would welcome a new face. I figured that they had actually said "new target" or "new sucker," but I thanked him, handing over exact change. I can fake a lot of documents, but credit card fraud isn't on my resume.

Gustav tucked the leather holder into his apron, then gestured for me to head toward the curtain, which seemed to grow more mysterious with each step. I hoped for something otherworldly behind it—sword swallowers or contortionists at the very least—but found merely a long oak-paneled hallway with metal doors, much more sedate than the dining and bar area. Behind the last door, the sound of poker chips piling onto each other could be heard over muffled conversation, and I went in before I lost my resolve.

As my eyes adjusted to the dim light, I knew that I would be sized up. I imagined the chuckles the men repressed when they saw me. Some stereotypes work in your favor if you know how to use them, and I was sure every last one of the four players would assume a woman wearing diamond studs and carrying a Chanel purse wouldn't know her way around a deck of cards. That included the lone other female, cracking open a new pack and eyeing me over the rims of her thick reading glasses. I nodded at her, a possible ally if I needed one. She nodded back, and I announced myself to the others present.

"Kennedy Starkweather Vanders. Pardon the intrusion, but may I join you?"

CHAPTER SEVEN

L ars Dekker rose to greet me with a kiss on the cheek as we had agreed upon over the phone, appropriate for an old family friend. It had been more than six years since I'd met the notorious playboy. He'd been lounging by the backyard pool, sipping a martini and reading David Markson. My urge to laugh at his monogrammed swim trunks had been squashed by his friendly demeanor. We weren't going to become best buds, but he was likable, politics-ready you might say, despite his obvious attempts to seem more adult than his twenty-four years. He had grown into his role as next in line to a fortune with panache. Tonight he had draped the jacket of his suit over his chair, but somehow his shirt was as smooth as if it had been ironed only minutes before. His gold cufflinks read "LGD," and I paused to consider what the "G" might stand for before getting a good look at his face. He wasn't a "Most Eligible Bachelor" according to the gossip rags for nothing. His translucent blue eyes weren't hidden behind glasses like his brother's, and his darker hair made them even more noticeable.

I settled myself into a free leather chair and glanced around, confused by the spare accommodations. Sure, the table and chairs were nice and I appreciated the mood lighting, hoping it disguised my age a bit, but it was frankly hard to see. Not only were there no waiters, there weren't even windows, and I pitied the claustrophobic gambler who might wander into a game expecting Vegas-style luxury. Drinks were serve yourself from a rolling cart. It dawned on me that these were serious players, not just bored millionaires. Why else would they put up with this room? The thought didn't make signing a note for $10,000—the entirety of the money I had received on my last unusually lucrative case—any easier. I hoped Lars hadn't steered me wrong when he suggested the amount. For all I knew, the stakes included Bentleys and summer homes.

A respectable but by no means staggering amount of chips appeared in front me, and I used every last drop of my talents to keep my face neutral. I had no intention of losing all this money, but seeing my entire life's worth in round plastic coins was humbling. I twirled a five hundred on the green felt and inquired about the ante, corrected at once that in Texas Hold'em, the first monies are called "blinds." I swear I could sense my new pals licking their chops. Nothing like fresh meat. I waited for the inevitable adrenaline to kick in. It couldn't come fast enough and when I threw the chip, a thrill slid down my spine. *Here we go.*

"Drink, honey?" asked a woman who introduced herself as Sybil while pouring me a generous gin and tonic before I had time to reply. She slid the glass toward me as the baby-faced dealer gave everyone a pair. I took a sip before peeking at the cards: two jacks.

So as not to give anything away, I shifted my focus to the birdcage in the corner, the room's sole decoration, if you could call it that. It was a plain, square container, not much bigger than a carry-on suitcase, but the birds were something. Parakeets maybe. Their blue feathers glittered in the light, especially when they flitted from perch to perch as if to get a better view of us. I was trying not to let my nerves show, but when the dealer winked at me, I thought perhaps I had given myself away. I tucked strands of my red wig behind one ear, letting my cubic zirconium studs sparkle. *Finches*, I thought, keeping my focus on the fluttering in the corner rather than in my stomach.

"Parrotlets," said the man to my right. He must have caught me staring because he pointed toward the cage.

"You must be joking. Such a darling name for such darling creatures. No, surely you're teasing me," I answered, putting my cards back down on the table. I wasn't likely to forget a matching pair.

"No, ma'am. Those are cobalt parrotlets, Miss Eva's prize possession."

I turned toward the man who had uttered the magic word. Not "parrotlets," but "Eva," the sole reason I was sitting around that table, pretending to be a socialite with a gambling addiction. Well, Kennedy wouldn't call it an addiction. Proclivity. I spun my five-hundred chip again and didn't try to hide my once-over. The gentleman was the one player to look like he might be a professional. He wore a wide-brim Stetson, perfectly reasonable for San Antonio, but we were in a midtown Manhattan high-rise. In his sixties, he was the oldest player, too, and gave off an oil-tycoon vibe. To his right was Sybil, a foul-mouthed, whiskey-drinking forty-year-old who, if I had to guess, had earned her money rather than inherited. It was hard not to compare her to the polished pinstriped fellow who had grunted at me instead of introducing himself. I'd dubbed him Mr. Manners. When it was his turn, he called, and everyone followed, waiting to see what the communal cards offered.

The dealer was skinny as a piece of lettuce, but undeniably handsome. His back was to the parrotlets, and they seemed to like him, alighting on the rung closest to his chair most often. When they chirped, he called back to them in a soothing voice, *"mis dulzuras."* He was well-dressed, his shirt crisp and tucked in, but didn't seem like a high roller himself. Someone on his way up, but not up.

The flop pulled my attention away from my companions, and I noted the three, ten, and additional jack. My heart sped up at the last card, and I realized that I was having fun, though fun was hardly the point. Mr. Manners didn't call this time, but raised the bet by a hundred.

"Will this be a one-time visit, Mrs. Vanders?" the Texan asked. He'd been reticent to share his name, too, and I tried to weasel a proper introduction from him.

"Please, call me Kennedy." I waited for him to respond in kind, but was disappointed. When the pause stretched on too long, I tried a smile just shy of flirtatious. "I hope this isn't my only appearance. I'll raise you five hundred." I threw my chip in, and the Texan met me. So did the others, and I prayed my wager hadn't been too small. I was fairly confident that this hand was mine, and a few extra thousands would make the evening easier.

"Is this the usual crowd?" I fished. I was thinking about Eva, looking for more than a casual name drop. Her husband had been her ticket out, and she had made the most of it. The restaurant was clearly hers in more than name and doing very well at that. At least now when Signora Costa said her children were in the restaurant business, she wouldn't have any lies to confess at mass. Even so I would guess Signora Costa was pretty close-lipped, even with Father Ignatius.

"There are a few others who stop by when the mood strikes them." Lars glanced at his cards again, and I decided he probably didn't have anything promising. It's easier to remember your hand when it's good. I looked at my own for show and watched the dealer flip over a ten for the turn. That card made the game a little more interesting, but even if someone had a ten already, my three jacks would win. I added another five hundred, and Lars folded as expected. The Texan did, as well, which was a bit more surprising. I probably wouldn't be able to read him for awhile, if ever.

That left Mr. Manners and Sybil, who paused before matching my bet then refilling her whiskey glass. She could reach the bottle without being accused of card snooping, and I decided she chose her seat with that goal in mind. It would be a shame to leave a glass empty for a whole hand.

Now that he had folded, Lars was downright chatty, asking me about my fake neighborhood and fake career. I thought perhaps he was playing with me, testing the extent of my rehearsal. Perhaps he didn't realize how dangerous my exposure would be. I was grateful to Ellis for not giving him the full details. And a brother who would do a favor without needing an explanation? That was sibling loyalty I could get behind. Most nights, I improvised my characters, but I'd given Kennedy some thought, so his inquiries didn't unnerve me much.

"Charity work mostly nowadays," I said in answer to Lars's latest question.

"Like handing over your money to us," Mr. Manners said too loudly, his first contribution to the conversation. He guffawed, and I felt myself bristle as he tossed his chips to the middle.

"Like stray kittens and puppies, but I could be persuaded to support other lost causes."

Only Sybil laughed, but I caught Lars smiling. Mr. Manners didn't respond, but the dealer joked about everyone playing nice. Then he threw down the last card of the hand, a young-looking lad sporting an axe and a funny hat. It was the fourth jack.

Only years of practice kept me from revealing my disbelief. I knew the odds of getting four of a kind were ridiculously low, four in something like two or three million. When I hazarded a glance at the dealer, he squinted his left eye in a sort of half-wink. He had set me up, but why? I raced through the possibilities as quickly as I could manage, stalling as I considered my bet. Part of me wanted to fold rather than face the fallout, but then the dealer would know I wasn't there to play poker. Or at least not to win. Was that his job? To suss out spies? That meant The Skyview had something to hide beyond a small, illegal gaming room, a slap-on-the-wrist crime as likely ignored as prosecuted.

"All in," I finally said, shoving my pile into the center and carefully avoiding further eye contact with the dealer. It was an apt metaphor for my life. All in. I could taste vomit in the back of my throat. There was no way anyone had a better hand than me based on the five visible cards, but more importantly, if everyone folded, I wouldn't have to show my cards. What could go wrong?

Sybil whistled, and the Texan took off his hat to wipe his brow. His bald spot was sprouting a few stray hairs, and I knew that the hat wasn't intended solely for intimidation. Mr. Manners seemed downright pissed, grumbling about inexperienced players. It was the worst time for Eva to make her appearance, but in she marched.

"Hello, lovies," she began, squeezing Sybil on her shoulder and smiling broadly at the Texan. She paid the most attention to the dealer, draping her arm around him before kissing him on the temple. She whispered something into his ear, and he flushed. "Everyone have everything they need? Ms. Vanders?"

The moment of truth had arrived, and I played my part with as much aplomb as Mrs. Salvatore Magrelli.

"Oh, quite. Your guests have been welcoming to say the least. I think they're about to give me their shirts."

"Beginner's luck?"

"Something like that."

When she smiled, I let out the breath that I had been holding. She whispered into the dealer's ear once more, sliding her hand up his chest, almost as if making sure we knew he belonged to her. It was a possessive gesture, but the young man didn't seem to mind. The parrotlets twittered, jumping from rung to rung in their excitement.

"If you need anything, please don't hesitate to let me know. I'll have some champagne brought in, shall I?" Eva asked.

The "shall" signaled what I already suspected; she had erased her past life. I wondered briefly if Salvatore had Eliza Doolittled her or if this was the role she was born to play. Part of me envied her full immersion. I wanted a character of my own to keep, too.

Eva slipped out of the room, presumably to alert a staff member then maybe visit her office. That was the behind-the-scene location that interested me the most, but moving from dining room to gaming room in one night wasn't bad. How many more visits would it take to slip unnoticed through the hallways? Of course, I doubted I would be welcome back at all if I laid down my jacks. The dealer might be fired, as well, unless he was in cahoots with his boss. *With his lover?* Maybe they wanted me gone and fast.

"What'll it be," I prompted. Sybil threw in the towel, and I turned my attention to Mr. Manners, who popped some Nicorette gum into his mouth. He shook his head slightly and pushed his cards away while I managed not to faint in relief. I was pretty sure that I had just cheated some very powerful people, but I wasn't about to complain about my extra three grand. Besides, I needed it more than they did. *Oh, Kennedy, how many falls have started with such a thought?* And, yet, that wasn't a Kennedy S. Vanders thought so much as a Kathleen Stone one. I didn't know who was playing whom at the moment, which was dangerous. The Dom Pérignon arrived as I raked my winnings toward me and tried to decide when pleasure became a problem.

"To the winner, the spoils," Sybil said, handing me the champagne to uncork. My life hadn't given me many opportunities to open a three-hundred-dollar bottle of anything, but I knew that hosing down the crowd was for NASCAR and strip clubs. I twisted the bottle slowly until I felt the cork pop out, then filled the '20s-style glasses that the waiter had set out. Had it been Gustav? He had moved with such precision that I had hardly noticed his presence at all. Mr. Manners shook his glass away, and Sybil gamely grabbed two, passing one along to the dealer.

"Drink up, kid," she said, swallowing a gulp. I held my glass toward him to express my thanks for the cards, and he did one of those half-winks again. This time, I was almost sure Sybil saw him, but all she said was, "Fast before I change my mind."

The young man grinned and drained his glass before moving it out of his way and breaking open a new deck. *A new deck for each hand?* I wondered if the group had reason to be mistrustful. Or was wastefulness part of the appeal. How long would it take to become bored with a life of luxury? My idea of a night out involved a whole pizza to myself as I sat in the back of a rented Honda Civic. And I wasn't sure what people meant by "a night off."

"Refill, Kennedy?" I blinked back into reality and glanced at my now empty glass. Lars was already pouring the last few drops into it, and I thanked him aloud for his effort and silently for snapping me out of my daydreams. Of course, I would have been brought around soon enough when the dealer started shrieking. He was foaming at the mouth, clutching his throat while his face turned from pink to red. When blood mixed with the foam, terror filled the room. I jerked out of my chair as did everyone at the table, the Texan taking charge as if he'd been elected to the post.

"Call an ambulance," he said to Lars, who slipped his cell phone out and dialed. I was jostled toward the back of the room, but when I suggested they loosen his collar, Sybil reached down and undid his tie and top few buttons. Eva swooped into the room and immediately went into hysterics. She fell to her knees beside the dealer, shouting "Ernesto!" repeatedly. When she looked wild-eyed around the room, I could see the streaks of mascara running down her face. *"Esto es mi culpa,"* she mumbled, wiping snot from her nose, then grasping the hand of Ernesto. *This is my fault.*

CHAPTER EIGHT

Sybil was absentmindedly patting my back when the police squad arrived. Her attempts at comfort had more or less the same effect as the emergency room kitten from the night before. Not calming, but appreciated. Paramedics pronounced Ernesto Belasco dead on the scene, and his body was covered and carted away. Not through the restaurant, of course, but down the building's service elevator. No cognacs were disturbed in the process. I imagined that Sybil was actually the one needing comfort since she seemed to have known the victim, but I couldn't think of what to say beyond platitudes. I wasn't even entirely certain that we should call him a victim, although what could cause such a reaction other than poison?

"I don't think they'll keep us long," I said to fill the silence.

"Oh, honey, I don't care about that."

It was unnatural for me, but I forced myself to hug Sybil. She was the only one who didn't seem annoyed about the delay. After failing in his self-appointed life-saving duties, the Texan had deflated then shook off the loss. Mr. Manners was now chewing two pieces of Nicorette simultaneously, and Lars had taken to pacing the small conference room. We were being kept for questioning along with all of the restaurant employees, though they were allowed to continue their work until last call at 2 A.M. None of the waitstaff seemed especially disturbed by Ernesto's death, and I figured he wasn't a regular W-2. Eva wouldn't let her side dish mingle with the hoi polloi. I couldn't imagine that Eva would be much help unless she'd dramatically improved since the last time I saw her. She hadn't returned since walking out with the EMTs.

Detective Dekker, Ellis, barely glanced at me when he arrived. I had texted him the basic scenario, warning him in essence. I didn't want him to be disciplined for supplying me with information about The Skyview, but if he was assigned the case, it would be less awkward. His colleagues down at the station weren't exactly fond of me, although a few had apologized for thinking I had once murdered two people. It was a start.

Ellis approached Lars, and they shook hands more formally than seemed necessary. On the other hand, I didn't think that they had spent much time together since Lars graduated from high school and went off to Princeton. Seeing the brothers side by side was a sort of experiment in lifestyle choices. While both men were attractive, Lars's looks were less worn-out, more ready-for-Hollywood. The few wrinkles that lined his brow looked distinguished unlike Ellis's heavy ones, the severest of which divided his pale eyebrows. He also had a scar that started at the corner of his lip and snaked up to his hairline. I had yet to get the scoop on that mark. He had seen the six-inch slash on my inner thigh. Maybe one day we would swap stories. Ellis caught me examining his face, and his frown deepened. Maybe not. He signaled to an officer who announced that all the poker players, "guests" he called them diplomatically, would be questioned separately.

"Miss Stone?" the officer called out, checking his notes.

I glared at the back of Ellis's head before raising my hand. Sybil made a strangled noise beside me and moved away. Mr. Manners and the Texan turned to stare. Two hours from start to finish. My fastest blown cover to date. At least it probably wouldn't end with my body being thrown in the Hudson. Shark food had never been my life's ambition.

The young officer—"Officer Reynolds, ma'am"—led me down a dimly lit corridor and into what was certainly the boss's office volunteered for the occasion. "Out of sight" seemed to be its selling point. Officer Reynolds politely asked if I needed water, then disappeared the way he came. I had been hoping for a sneak peek of Eva's lair and here was my chance. It made me forgive Ellis a little as I studied the huge canvas portrait of Eva and Salvatore hanging on the back wall. In it, the bride was wearing a white wedding dress with a train that disappeared outside of the frame. She beamed into the camera while her husband stared at her cheek, not quite adoring but content. It was the kind of photo one might find in a bridal catalogue, a little too staged, maybe, but the gorgeous models made up for the lack of love. At first glance, it evoked envy, but I knew better. While I wasn't positive that Eva and the deceased card dealer were romantically involved, I would wager this month's rent that their relationship wasn't entirely professional. Of course, that was assuming I was able to recover my money. Maybe the others wouldn't miss ten grand, but I sure as hell would.

When I heard Ellis open the door behind me, I straightened up in my chair and waited for him to begin. When he didn't, I looked behind me to see that he was also studying the picture.

"He doesn't look like the devil," Ellis said.

"Not even if you squint? Imagine a couple of horns?"

Ellis shook his head grimly. I was feeling rather grim myself. The photo was a little too big and life-like, flooding my system with abject fear. It was possible that Salvatore was in the building right this minute, stalking the restaurant's hallways, looking for his wife. There seemed to be a pretty good chance that he had caused the distress, too, and I explained as much to Ellis.

"You think she and the boy were lovers?"

"She caressed him," I said, not wanting to go on the record, but trusting my gut. "And said it was her fault. See what the others say."

Ellis raised his eyebrows at me, and I knew what he was thinking. It was a little game we played where he said he wouldn't share information then I pulled it out of him.

"What do you know about Eva?" he asked.

I thought about our last encounter, Eva stomping around her family's apartment, ignoring the threats and curses of Zanna, who never really calmed down after being handcuffed to the radiator. After an hour of so, she had passed out, and I was able to move her exposed skin away from the metal pipes. I had asked for the key again, but Eva had shook her head. She had turned her attention to her younger brother, Nino, who had overheard Zanna spill some valuable details. Ship name and port name. I had heard the information, too.

I had been desperate to get outside so that I could place a call to my police contacts. I had ten hours before the Maritime Sapphire, a tanker carrying 25,000 tons of oil and one unmarked crate of cocaine, arrived at Port Jefferson, but organizing a raid didn't happen quickly. Nino and I had always gotten along fine, but at the moment, I was pissed at him for stalling me. He was whining to Eva about her decision to take Zanna rather than him to see Salvatore. I didn't think either choice made sense, but then I'd never had siblings.

Nino had struggled to get past a fifth-grade reading level, content with intimidating younger kids. He was a bully and not a very good one at that. Kids wouldn't make fun of him to his face, but as soon as he left the room, they would make cracks about his spiked hair and habit of saying "Easy, man" for no reason, almost as if reminding himself. Eva wanted to bring both her siblings with her as she ascended into wealth and comfort, but unsurprisingly Salvatore wasn't convinced. His business savvy had made him a cartel leader, the Hades in their midst, and Eva's fussing didn't faze him. To Zanna, he had given certain minor responsibilities, but Nino wasn't allowed to so much as fetch coffee. After he once bragged about knowing a drop-off location, Nino wasn't even allowed in the room when plans were discussed.

Ellis was waiting patiently for me to sort through these memories, pick out the information I thought might help. "She's loyal," I finally said. "And usually level-headed," I added. "She lost it when the dealer started choking."

"We're running a background check now, but his license says he's Ernesto Belasco, twenty-two, lives in Brooklyn with his parents."

"He let me win. Four jacks on my first hand. I thought he was a spy maybe, for the club. An initiation of sorts. See how players react. Do you think he knew I didn't belong here?"

Ellis didn't like the question. His posture stiffened, and I knew that I had hit a nerve. "You belong here. Everyone belongs here. It's a restaurant."

With a members-only list, I thought, but remained silent. In a funny way, I found class discrepancies less bothersome than Ellis. I guess it's easier when you don't now what you're missing. Of course, Ellis could call it a day and join his brother at lawn tennis whenever he wanted. I watched Ellis inspect Eva's desk calendar day by day and decided that wasn't likely. If anyone was born for this thankless pursuit of criminals, it was him. He seemed entirely focused on his job, if not on interrogating me.

"Anything unusual?" I said. Ellis glanced at me then opened the desk's top drawer. "Did I notice anything suspicious?" I started again. "Yes, thank you for asking. If Ernesto was cheating on behalf of other players, I would imagine he'd have some enemies. I've heard these games can get ridiculous— people puts their Rolexes in the pot, their cars."

"What would you have done if you lost everything?"

"What does anyone do? Start over. It wouldn't be the first time. I bet it even gets easier with practice."

Ellis stopped riffling and looked at me intently. "It gets harder, Kathleen. Trust me."

Every time Ellis used my real name, I shivered. It was like he was summoning a ghost, and she wanted to respond. I could feel her under my ribcage, but she was good and trapped. I tucked a strand of my red wig behind my ear and stood up. If he was going to riffle, so was I. As Ellis opened another drawer, I slid in front of Eva's computer to open a browser and inspect her history. Gmail, USA Today, Craigslist, a wine emporium, and a Google search on parrotlet diets. No "how to mix poison with champagne" or even "how to leave your lover." But I wasn't really looking for something to link Eva to Ernesto's death. I was looking for traces of her husband using this restaurant for his gain somehow.

"You know that's illegal, right? Without a warrant?" I pointed at the papers Ellis was photographing.

"I was told to search the premises."

In the end, our NSA-worthy spying didn't matter. Aside from the wedding photograph, there was nothing at all objection- able in Eva's office. She might as well have been a poster girl for making it in America with hard work and a little luck. They could put her bootstraps in a museum display.

CHAPTER NINE

S t. Mark's Church is one of the oldest sanctuaries in Manhattan with a rich history of worship, but it's better known for its artist-friendly events. Patti Smith read her poems there. Richard Foreman put on his avant-garde plays. I had never set foot inside and, despite the mythology, wasn't looking forward to my first visit. Watching a young man die the night before had left me feeling flustered, but I knew I couldn't skip the dual memorial for Bobbie Giabella and Taylor Soto, even if I hadn't been looking into their deaths. Dolly needed the support. He hadn't said as much, but he'd texted me directions despite the fact that I was the one who'd gotten my fourteen-year-old belly button pierced at The Rose Petal in the East Village. I doubted the tattoo parlor was still in business, but I wasn't likely to get lost either.

Dolly walked a few steps in front of me, greeting nearly everyone by name, introducing anyone he thought I needed to meet. That had been our arranged code. He would ignore me if he didn't expect someone to have anything of value for our investigation. I was glad to see that there were a few cops and at least one plainclothes detective milling about. Despite the NYPD's early dismissal of Mamma Burstyn's concerns, they were taking the explosion seriously. A woman in a bulletproof vest was leading a German Shepherd around the building periphery.

Interrogating people at a funeral is awkward, to say the least, but I did my best to gather information without being insensitive. One of Taylor's friends told me that Taylor had been looking forward to the Halloween parade. It was the first time he was participating, and he had taken extra care with his neon pink mask, even sewing on some extra sequins and feathers that morning. Bobbie's parents hugged me, mistaking me for a friend, and making me feel like a cockroach, especially when I asked if their son had mentioned any threats. When his mom started sobbing, Bobbie's boyfriend from the emergency room, Martin, caught my attention and grimaced. I tried to follow his movements through the crowd, but it was as if he disappeared. There were over two hundred guests, not counting the media circling like vultures at the back.

When the minister made motions to begin, I sat down next to Dolly. He didn't want to be up front with Big Mamma and his coworkers because he didn't fit in. They had gone all out—cocktail attire with imposing, black lace veils and costume jewelry. In comparison, Dolly could have applied for a job as a small-town accountant. His black suit was worn at the elbows and knees, and his dark brown shoes didn't match. I squeezed his fingers when the first eulogist, Carlton Casborough the Senator's son, a.k.a. Cassandra when on stage, approached the podium. Dolly leaned close to my ear.

"Word this morning is that he was fooling around with Bobbie. I don't think the teen heartthrob knew."

I craned my neck over the rows to see if I could spot Martin again, but didn't find his disheveled hair among the masses.

He could have left without anyone noticing. I had never met Carlton, but a lot of violence has been committed in the name of love and even lust. He seemed genuinely broken up as he talked about meeting Bobbie for the first time, bonding over their mutual Paul Simon fandom. But I was well-aware that a seasoned performer could squeeze out a few crocodile tears in the line of duty.

"Sometimes when I was feeling low, he would call me Al," Carlton paused. "It would make me smile every time." Someone sang out a few lyrics from the song, and everyone murmured in approval. "So, Betty, if you can hear me, know that you're missed."

Carlton blew a kiss toward the ceiling and returned to his seat, hugging the second eulogist before they switched places. It should have made my eyes water at least, but Carlton had gone from sympathy to suspect in two minutes flat. That was when the chanting started from outside.

The noise was faint, but since Dolly and I were sitting near the exit, I could make out their awfulness. The picketers hadn't been too vocal on our way in, waving their "America Is Doomed" signs. I guess they were waiting for the most inappropriate time to interrupt. As another performer, Aaron Kline, led those inside in an a cappella version of "Candle in the Wind," shouts of "Better off dead, better off dead" echoed through the front lobby. Carlton slipped down my suspect list, and I scooted out of the pew and pushed past the reporters into the gray Saturday afternoon. The protesters had swelled in number, and I was shocked to see twenty or so people in matching "Better off dead" T-shirts shouting from Second Avenue. A spontaneous counter-protest was growing and would soon outnumber the organizers. I hustled down the stairs before the haters could be surrounded and disbanded by hot-tempered New Yorkers. I needed at least a few names.

"Excuse me," I shouted, elbowing past an imposing, bearded biker who was shaking his helmet and telling the protesters something that started with "You have no right—" and ended in imaginative expletives. He moved out of my way, and I found myself face to face with a fit thirty-something handing out anti-gay pamphlets. I took one and was welcomed to Mount Olympus Retreat, "Where Normal Is a Wish Away."

"Thank you," I said, holding out my hand. "Karen Connifer, *New York Post*." I was improvising and crossing my fingers that he didn't ask for any sort of credentials. A few real reporters had followed me out, and I hoped that the rest would stay inside until after the ceremony. I didn't want my photo in the papers, especially not anywhere close to this group of nut jobs.

"I sawww you go into that hellhole. You're a sympathizerrr, as backward as the rest of them."

He spoke in a surprisingly clear, but slow manner as if searching for each word. The tone was as flat as any Midwestern dialect I'd ever heard, and I adjusted my own speed to match his. It seemed possible that he had a mental deficiency, which could explain how he got mixed up with this lot. Beaten up at school? I knew I was reaching, but I kept going anyway.

"Trying to be fair and balanced. May I have your name?"

He pointed to the back of his pamphlet, and I read "Leader Cronos Holt." Leader? I couldn't imagine this man leading so much as a shoe-tying mission. And, yet, here he was, surrounded by more than a dozen followers. Their shoes must all be velcro. Leader Holt was now lethargically shouting obscenities at the motorcycle man, enunciating each foul syllable, and the crowd began to push closer. I ducked down and off the sidewalk to avoid being caught in the inevitable brouhaha.

I could creep back into the church, but didn't want to interrupt genuine mourning, so I turned toward the cemetery and found a park bench instead. It wasn't peaceful with the shouts from the street, but it was discreet. Nobody would bother me, a grieving widow perhaps, in my black dress and black jacket. I pulled my scarf tighter against the wind that was knocking around dead leaves and read the three-paneled, glossy brochure. It advertised the Mount Olympus Retreat, an "immersion program for mind recalibrating," which I translated to mean one of those gay conversion camps. "Find the gods inside you" was an unfortunate tagline for a homophobic hate group. I didn't like *The Iliad* lines on the back panel any better: "There are no binding oaths between men and lions— / wolves and lambs can enjoy no meeting of the minds— / they are all bent on hating each other to the death."

If the brochure was printed at the same place as the funeral invitations, I would have pretty good circumstantial evidence against the group that called themselves the Zeus Society. Not endorsed by any governing body, I could safely assume. An oddly named operation given the ancient Greek acceptance of romantic relationships between older and younger males. Maybe that was the point?

The Zeus Society boasted "thousands of men and women saved from an eternity of unimaginable torture." Despite being unimaginable, someone had decided on flames and manacles as decorations. Each page was half-covered in fire, but there was still plenty of text from Leader Holt. Not one actual verse from a religious text. Not even more lines from *The Iliad*, although what else would they use? Zeus praising Ganymede's beauty?

At the bottom of the last page in small font was a logo for a Manhattan print shop, The Fountain. It was a place to start, and I took out my work cell, a cheap flip phone with a blocked number, and left a message with the manager. They were closed until noon, so the group must have picked them up yesterday. Or had them lying around for whenever the hate bug hit them.

I suppose it made sense to have a print shop on the ready. With eight million people in New York City, there are plenty to hate.

My personal cell started vibrating from my purse, and I groped around until I unearthed it. Since only a few people had the number, I answered without checking the I.D., suddenly worried that Meeza was in danger. Ever since she had started dating a car thief she was at the back of my mind, one step away from a misdemeanor in the name of devotion. It wasn't Meeza, but a vaguely familiar voice inviting me to dinner.

"I'm sorry, who is this?"

I switched on the recording device I kept ready to go and hoped that the incoming number was traceable. My heart sped up, and I looked around frantically to see if anyone was watching me. The angry mob couldn't care less about a woman sitting by herself among some tombstones, and I stood up to get a better view of the passing pedestrians. No one looked particularly threatening, at least none more so than usual in this part of town.

"Kathleen, it's Lars. Lars Dekker? I wanted to talk to you about last night. Get your perspective. Maybe hire you? Something." He paused, and my heart returned to its normal rhythm. "I guess I'm a suspect. I didn't even know Ernesto."

I walked over to a quieter corner, away from the street noise. Lars didn't sound like the confident tycoon from The Skyview. He sounded like, well, like someone who'd watched a person die in front of them.

"How'd you get this number?"

"Ellis gave it to me. He's not thrilled about the idea of me hiring you to work independently, but you're the only private investigator that I know. The only one I've ever met actually."

I didn't doubt that was true. His kind didn't mingle with mine. It was curious that Lars wouldn't trust his brother's abilities, but maybe he didn't know how capable Ellis really was.

"Your brother's been assigned the case. You don't have anything to worry about."

"Dinner, please. I'm not asking for a commitment."

"I'm working another case right now." Which was true up to a point. I had no intention of giving up on Magrelli, but I didn't want anyone else involved in my vendetta.

"Don't say no until we talk."

I stared at the stone facade of the church, moss clinging to the crevices. Not all of the people inside could have faith, an unwavering belief in righteousness. But it meant something that the hate mongers weren't sitting in the pews, that sanctuary was given to those most in need of comfort. I thought of Big Mamma waiting to sell her version of peace to a dedicated flock.

I knew that if I said yes to dinner that I would be using Lars in some way and, by extension, his brother. I wanted to know what he knew about the Magrellis, and I wasn't as interested in clearing his name. Ellis would never consider us suspects, not really. There was still time to turn back, say no to this dinner, focus on who caused the Halloween explosion and leave Magrelli for another time. But how many people would he hurt while I was waiting for the perfect timing? Big Mamma was right when she said I was a kid when I went undercover. But I wasn't a kid anymore.

CHAPTER TEN

T here was a time when I thought V.P. looked harmless. His grin was too big for his face, his hair too shaggy to mean serious business. Seeing him leaned up against my apartment door made me question my earlier naivety. It wasn't the worn leather jacket—we all had one of those—but the look of pure hatred that he reserved solely for me these days. I hadn't given him my address, of course, but he had used the GPS tracker in one of the cars he lent me. As far as I knew, he'd only given the location out to one other person, my former lover Marco Medina, but I couldn't be sure. It was enough to make me consider giving up my apartment, but it was rent stabilized. It takes more than a few close calls with the Grim Reaper to make a New Yorker give up her reasonable monthly payments.

"To what do I owe the pleasure," I began, slipping my keys between my fingers. As a do-good, law-abiding, "No trouble here, Officer" citizen, I no longer carried a gun, but I could take out an eye if I caught him off-guard. Not the kind of thought you want to have about a friend's boyfriend, but there it was. What could I say? Meeza deserved better.

"Ah Kat, Kaaat, Kaaatttt. Do I really need a reason?"

I ignored his grating tone and unlocked my front door. No sense upsetting the neighbors, most of whom wouldn't call the police for anything less than a three-alarm fire.

"Thanks for the Kia last week. I appreciated the ride on short notice."

V.P.'s illegal car rental catered to anyone who didn't want traceable tags—mostly criminals, but I knew there was at least one other private investigator on his roster because Meeza had told me. I hoped that other P.I. wasn't getting personal house calls, too. They usually meant an outstanding debt and busted knees, but I was up to date. I knew I wasn't dealing with Zipcar.

"For you? Any time. Did you catch a killer?"

"I nabbed a husband with pants around his ankles. You know, the usual."

V.P. helped himself to a beer from my refrigerator, shaking his head at the scant supplies. I basically kept drinks and condiments. Anything else tended to go bad before I had a chance to consume it.

"Quite the glamorous life you lead, darling." He put on a drawl for "darling," but Vincent Patel was from the Bronx. I had checked.

"It has its upsides."

I dropped my bag onto the bed that took up most of the space in my studio. I did not, on the other hand, drop my keys even when I opened the curtains to let in the fading light. Instead, I shoved my hands into my jacket pockets and waited for whatever it was V.P. had to tell me. In person, no less. He played it cool, sprawling out on the loveseat, his long legs draped over one of the arms, dirty boots barely touching the upholstery, but touching nonetheless. I rocked back on my heels and tried not to show any emotion. The last man to sprawl on my sofa had been the one that V.P. had directed to my place. But Marco was long gone, an exceptional cop taking a well-deserved break. I could have joined him on that break, but then where would I be? Enjoying the white sands of Bali when I could be chatting up homophobes and thieves?

"I'd like to hear about these upsides, Kat, I really would," V.P. finally said. "I'd like to know what's in it for my beloved Meeza. You know, aside from the late nights and early mornings, shit pay and no benefits."

I may have chuckled at V.P.'s concern over benefits. I doubted his company offered 401Ks. And I'm pretty sure his medical meant a guy in the back doing stitches with whiskey for anesthesia. Of course, laughing wasn't the best response, and my visitor became unhinged. He flung himself up and into my face, spitting his threats.

"Don't fucking mess with me. She's changing, asking where I am when I don't call. Who I'm with. Who I'm with is my business. Mine."

I probably shouldn't have antagonized him, but there are ways I like to be addressed and ways I don't. "Fucking mess with you," I started. "Don't you mess with Meeza. She's a good girl—no, she's a damn peach. Running around with scum like you. I think it's time you left her alone."

I stepped even closer, wrapping my fingers around the keys until one of them cut into my thumb. V. P. didn't back down, and I didn't expect him to. The smell of coconut hair gel combined with sweat—mine or his, I wasn't sure. We were both giving into the adrenaline, spoiling for a fight.

"I'm not the one dragging her into God knows what situations."

I was itching to shove him, but didn't want to be the one to make things physical. "She works her own cases," I said.

"That may be, but I know you're getting your hands dirty again. Those bruises last month weren't from the neighborhood softball league, and if anything happens to her—" He cut himself off, but I knew the rest.

"Out." I pointed toward the door, and he walked toward it, chugging his beer. When he grabbed the knob, he turned to look at me again.

"You hear me, right? If anything happens to her. Anything."

He shut the door behind him, and I flipped the deadbolt. My thumb started to throb, and I sucked on it. Between this and the scrapes from the parade, my hands were starting to resemble discounted Halloween props. Sliding down to the floor, I tried not to admit that he had a point if not the best delivery. Meeza didn't belong in either of our worlds and would probably be better off marrying one of the various taxidermists and lawnmower salesmen that her parents used set her up with. Probably.

My neon pink Band-Aid didn't match the outfit I had cobbled together for chichi dining. Circo is the so-called casual offshoot of Le Cirque, but I defy you to spot a pair of shorts. The circus-themed drapery and sculptures were visible from where I waited at the bar, but the blue hairs at table six were the real show, and everyone was sneaking glances at them. I couldn't place their faces, but I was betting theater legends. Their laughter was robust, and the room seemed to lean toward their warmth. I wasn't immune and found myself smiling in their direction.

"I didn't recognize you until you smiled."

I turned to the man who had sat down on my left, worried at not being more aware of my surroundings. It seemed like the kind of place where nothing could go wrong, but that assumption would get a lady in trouble.

Sans wig, nails, and affectation, I was probably hard to spot, so I didn't hold it against Lars even if he had met me—the real me—years ago. He looked the same as the night before, down to the pinstriped suit, though the shade may have been a touch lighter. More navy than gray? I had a sudden urge to run my fingers down the lapel and forced myself to meet his pale blue eyes instead.

"You wouldn't be the first," I said, then blushed slightly in the long pause that followed. As Kate Manning, Kennedy Starkweather Vanders, or Kiki (No Last Name), I could be confident, brazen even. As myself, I mostly felt out of place. And I hadn't bothered Dolly with helping me prepare for this business meeting that felt like a date, so my short hair wasn't exactly glamorous, and my dress would have looked better with black heels. Even I knew that much about fashion. I stuck my hand out before my thoughts meandered too far down that road. "It's nice to see you again, Lars."

He shook my hand, holding on a moment longer than necessary, then settled my tab despite my feeble protest. It was one glass of wine, but it was more than I usually spent on an entire bottle.

The hostess could have been a carbon copy of the one at The Skyview, Bethany "Beth" Rosen. Not in appearance, but in efficiency. It was clear she knew Lars from previous dinners, but she welcomed me, too, with a gracious gesture toward a table in the back corner. It was near the kitchen, not the pick of the litter, but also noisy enough to discuss some private matters. Lars and his co-conspirator maître d' knew what they were doing. As we walked over, I imagined what other private conversations Lars might have had there.

He held my chair out for me, and I tried to gracefully manage the half-squat required for him to scoot me up to the table. It went off better than expected, and I smiled, surprising myself again. Perhaps these high-end restaurants mixed a little Zoloft in their drinks.

"Should I order for us?" Lars asked, picking up the wine menu. I liked that he asked and nodded in agreement, thanking the waiter who brought over some complimentary pâté, though I wasn't inclined to try the cat food–looking stuff, delicacy or no.

"Surely you don't mind the carbs," Lars said, laying the menu down in order to scoop some up onto a piece of bread.

"No, just my gag reflex."

Lars laughed, and I was glad that he didn't mind my non-cosmopolitan attitude. I tried to tuck a strand of hair behind my ear in the silence that followed, but I wasn't wearing a wig and there was nothing to tuck.

The meal wasn't as comfortable as ones I'd had with his brother, but there was a tingle of excitement in learning about someone new. He wanted to know perhaps a bit too much about my past, and I gave him the client version: B.S. in Criminology from John Jay College, two years undercover, three years running my own business. References? I've got plenty.

He held up his hand at this last part. "Not necessary. Ellis vouched for you. Listen, Kathleen. Can I call you that?" I liked that Lars asked that, too, and I mentioned that clients usually called me Katya or Ms. Lincoln, but Kathleen was okay, given the circumstances.

"Great," he said. "Kathleen. I'm not sure how much trouble I'm in by being in that poker room. Ellis says the people around the table are the most likely suspects. We opened the champagne."

"I opened it," I corrected him.

"Someone in the room could have slipped the poison in."

"Who? A magician? I think we would have noticed someone mixing a little cyanide into our glasses."

While Lars mulled this over, I shared another theory, that the poison could have been on the glass. I remembered the waiter—*was it Gustav?*—sneaking in and out.

"And you can find out who, right? I'll pay your going rate."

Mr. Manners had refused his glass, but Sybil had been the one to pass it along to Ernesto. Either could have been in cahoots with Magrelli, jealous of Eva's relationship with the young, good-looking card dealer. I took a bite of my crème brûlée and weighed how unethical it would be for me to take money for a case I was going to pursue anyway.

"Listen, I'm looking into this already," I said. "And your brother will probably have the perp in custody before we finish our nightcaps."

I doubted even Ellis Dekker worked that fast, but it vexed me that Lars didn't appreciate his brother's reputation. Lars ignored my comments, and I had a feeling that he was used to getting his way.

"I've got my lawyer on retainer, too. You can give her everything you learn."

Well, you couldn't accuse me of swindling the man. I leaned back in my chair and watched a server carry a two-tiered cake toward a large group. They didn't sing, but someone—the birthday girl's father maybe—was giving a speech to a young woman. She looked decidedly happy, no second-guessing for her. The life in front of her was all icing and presents, holidays in the Alps. I shook myself. No one escaped tragedy, no matter the balance of their checking account.

"Do you know anything about Salvatore Magrelli?" I asked, finally getting around to the real reason I had agreed to dinner. At least, that's what I was telling myself. That I enjoyed the company was a bonus.

"I know he's Eva's husband. I've met him once or twice." His voice held a certain amount of hesitation, and I didn't blame him for speaking carefully. I never wanted to be on the man's wrong side again either. And it looked like I was heading in that direction.

"I knew him. In a former life. I don't think he'd take kindly to his wife screwing around." Meeza would have known a more polite euphemism for cheating, but Lars didn't balk at my change in tone or the venom that dripped into my voice when I talked about Salvatore.

Lars folded his napkin onto the table and signaled for the check. When the waiter disappeared into the kitchen, Lars leaned toward me, his eyes searching mine for something I couldn't name.

"Not her lover," he said, his eyes darting to my lips then back up. "Her cousin."

CHAPTER ELEVEN

D olly didn't say much after we boarded the Q train at
42nd Street, heading south toward Brighton Beach.
That was fine; I didn't much feel like gabbing anyway.
Dolly rested his head on my shoulder, and I thought back to my
unsatisfactory conversation with Ellis early that morning. He
had known about his brother's intentions, of course, but didn't
seem pleased about my involvement. "I know it's your case,"
I had said, adding "officially" in my head. "I won't interfere."
But we both knew I probably would, best intentions aside.

Ellis didn't say much about his interviews with the other
players or with Eva. It would have been too risky for me to
question Eva directly, so any information I gleaned from Ellis's
one-word answers was important. The gist was that she felt
guilty about something, but it wasn't murdering her cousin.
Seeing how affectionate she'd been toward him, I didn't buy
her as the one pulling the trigger—or lacing the champagne
either. Ellis confirmed what I had discovered via a quick
Google search. Poker dealing wasn't Ernesto Belasco's livelihood, or at least not his primary one. He worked at a hair salon

in Prospect Heights, Brooklyn, which is where Dolly and I were headed—right after a visit to my own favorite hairdresser, wig aficionado Vondya Vasiliev.

Dolly had insisted on going with me, and I was grateful. Vondya was a force to be reckoned with, and her attitude toward me was—let's call it "volatile." I was the prodigal daughter one moment, the beyond-hope daughter the next. Dolly, on the other hand, was her best customer and, yes, more like a son. He spent most weekend afternoons in her shop, treating it like his own personal living room. That's how we had met, me promising to come see him perform, him knowing I was lying (even when I didn't know that I was lying).

It wasn't my conversation with Ellis that had me on edge. I hadn't returned to Vondya's shop since I had been attacked nearby at Coney Island on my last investigation. James Clifton was a surprising drug trafficker—a former grocer who had gotten in over his head, then liked that feeling of drowning a little too much, the sweet choke of release. He could keep it, and he probably was, serving thirty to life for felony murder and conspiracy to commit. Even knowing that he was behind bars, I didn't feel safe. A small part of me still worried that he had been working for a much bigger fish. Another small part of me still worried that he had whispered my name to that shark. Or perhaps to a young card dealer named Ernesto Belasco? Could that poison have been intended for me? I shook off that notion as paranoia, that old so-and-so, and woke Dolly when we got to our stop.

The doors dinged open, letting bracing air into the subway car. I hugged my bag to my stomach. Dolly stretched, letting his gray T-shirt rise up to reveal a tan, almost concave stomach. It made my eyes well for a split-second as I thought about what he must do to keep so thin.

Dolly and I carried the silence between us as we walked from the station and up a single flight of steps to the wig shop. There was a tiny shingle with her name on it, practically invisible from the street, and a bell jingled when we stepped inside. The owner's hum cut off abruptly, and she didn't sound happy to be interrupted when she called, "Give uz a minute." She muttered something in Russian under her breath, then appeared smelling faintly of incense.

"Sorry to bother you," I began, but was cut off by a bear hug, Vondya patting my ass in a grandmotherly if not entirely appropriate manner. She pulled me away from her, then wetly kissed both my cheeks. I wanted to wipe off her spit, but forced my arms to remain at my sides, smiling weakly at this woman. She didn't respond in kind.

"*Moy dorogoy*, what do you meaning, scaring me like this? Huh? What? Your gun have no cell reception." She laughed heartily at this last notion, even dabbing at the corners of her eyes before batting her eyelashes at Dolly. He winked back at her like a perfect accomplice, and I didn't tell either of them that I was sans weapon these days, a teetotaler of firearms. Who was I to spoil their fun?

Vondya was making cooing noises at Dolly, expressing her sympathies over his lost friends. "All my friends died, too," she added. "A different generation. Good, working ladies. Not like these Xes and Zes and what not. These, what you call them? Mill-in-in-ills."

She shot me a look on Millennials, and I shrugged, not sure what my birth year had to do with anything. I had turned twenty-seven in May, but was about as far-removed from the youth movement as a person could get, especially in the red pageboy I saw sitting on the counter. It added at least five years. Vondya saw me staring at it and finally smiled. She had every right to be proud of her work, from the genuine human hair to the meticulous dyes and cuts. I hadn't seen her listed on any who's who lists, but she was an artist.

"I knew you'd be back. That's why I no call at first. Then a month?" Vondya had left me a message that would strip the paint off a house. I was to come right away, or she was throwing my property away. She may have been bluffing, but I didn't want to find out. She gestured for me to sit in one of the salon chairs arranged along the wall, and Dolly plopped down on the couch, idling flipping through magazines. I could tell he wasn't really reading "How to Seduce Your Husband with Microwaveable Meals," but he was sufficiently distracted.

"There's no need, Vondya. I know it fits." Vondya huffed as she secured the hair to my head with dexterity that belied the hints of arthritis she sometimes exhibited. I knew once the wig was in place, it wouldn't go anywhere. This was the hair of a previous incarnation of Kennedy Vanders and one real estate agent named Kathy Seasons. After my favorite red hairdo was taken for evidence, I had compromised with this less flattering look. It did the usual tricks of transformation. I pulled an orange-red lipstick from my bag and smeared it on. Vondya handed me a brown eyebrow pencil, and I obediently filled in dark lines. Kathleen Stone vanished. Call me an addict, but I felt better already.

When not hobnobbing with Manhattan socialites and making sure the right cards landed in the right order, Ernesto worked as a janitor and errand boy at a salon in Park Slope. It was about the same size as Vondya's, put there was no secret back room filled with bags of human hair. In this place, the hair was on the floor, a lot of it actually, and a man started apologizing before even introducing himself.

"You're telling me, sweetheart, but what can we do? You tell me? We put the 'Hiring' sign out, but everybody thinks they can cut hair, that sweeping is beneath them. Yours is gorgeous, by the way. The color."

I moved out of the way before the stylist could grab a strand and thanked him, holding out my hand between us. He clasped it briefly, his eyes flitting appreciatively over Dolly even if his hair was shorn off—not a potential client. To his credit, his eyes barely lingered on the forehead gauze that covered the worst of Dolly's burns.

"We're working for—"

Dolly cut me off. "Ernesto was a friend."

The salon owner's eyes filled, and he hugged us both spontaneously. Between Dolly, Vondya, and the as yet unnamed stylist, I had been touched more in the past two hours than in the past two months. I wasn't sure that I would get used to it.

"You're not—no, I guess not. I'm Antonio by the way." He released us and assessed Dolly again. "No, though there is a likeness."

I'd noticed the resemblance between Dolly and Ernesto, as well, but thanked my lucky stars that my friend wasn't a Magrelli cousin.

Antonio gestured toward the last station, and we followed his rhinestoned jeans to that corner. Its contents were unsurprising, a blowdryer and a jar of that blue sanitizing liquid favored by hairdressers nationwide. No combs floated inside the jar, and Antonio explained that Ernesto had recently been promoted, but he'd never gotten to cut so much as a single bang. Dolly ran his finger along the photograph of Ernesto, his armed draped over a handsome man smiling broadly at the unseen photograph. They were dressed similarly in tight band T-shirts, and their hair was gelled into fauxhawks. Ernesto looked nearly unrecognizable from the young, buttoned-up man I'd met at The Skyview. But who was I to throw stones?

"Did you know him, too?" Antonio said, his eyes filling again, as he gestured toward Ernesto's boyfriend.

"I met him once," Dolly lied. "I can't recall his name."

"Bomber, that's what everyone called him anyway. Between you, me, and the blowdryer, I haven't seen Ernesto as much since they started dated." Antonio's tears disappeared and were replaced with a hint of—what was it? Irritation? When he saw me look at him in surprise, he hurried to explain. "I mean, he missed work shifts. Three in the last few weeks alone. And this was *after* I told him about the imminent promotion. I'm not going to speak ill of the dead, but you know what, I wouldn't *not* say ungrateful."

"Did he say why he's missed work?" It sounded too much like a cop question, so I added, "Has he been sick?"

Dolly played along beautifully, mentioning that Ernesto had looked tired the last time they'd been together.

"Oh, I'm sure he did. That boy spends more time at tongue than anyone I know. And I know some people."

"At tongue?" I asked, confused.

"Tongue," Dolly said, snapping his fingers. "Yeah, that's where I met Bomber. Quite a club."

Antonio sniffed, putting his hands on his hips. It seemed to be a sign that we had outstayed our warm welcome, and I thanked him for letting us stop by. He busied himself with the appointment book as we stepped onto Seventh Avenue. My mind was having a hard time processing this new information, but at the very least, I knew that Salvatore Magrelli wasn't likely to be jealous of Eva's gay cousin. Scratch that motive off the list. I felt deflated then embarrassed by my reaction. What kind of P.I. thinks a murder case is going to be simple, a trail of cookie crumbs leading right to the witch's cottage.

As we walked back toward the train, Dolly didn't say much, letting me work over the existing evidence. Was it a coincidence that three young, gay men had been killed in one week? Probably, right? Or could the Zeus Society be trying to update their status from wacko group to terrorist cell? It seemed like a long shot that slow-talking, velcro-wearing Leader Cronos could find his way into The Skyview, but I texted Meeza to compile a list of all attacks and murders in the last month, highlighting any that could even vaguely be classified as hate crimes. I glanced at my friend who was shuffling along, hands balled into fists at his sides. I was glad to see that they weren't wrapped any longer. Those burns would heal quickly.

"That was great," I said, and Dolly shrugged. "Listen, you don't have to help me with this case. You don't have to help me with *either* case, if you don't want to."

"I want to. You're helping me find the bastard who tried to kill me."

"Yeah, and Big Mamma is paying me to do so."

"You would do it anyway," Dolly said, ending our discussion. Was that true? Sometimes it seemed like Dolly knew me better than I knew myself. I spent so much time pretending to be other people that I wasn't sure what Kathleen would do. I knew it mattered, whether I was the kind of person to help a friend or not, but I couldn't think about that right now. The Zeus Society, huh? Maybe they were looking for new recruits.

CHAPTER TWELVE

Before deciding on which of his dresses looked most homophobic, Dolly and I had one more Brooklyn stop to make. It was the stop I was dreading most, but Ernesto's parents could give us some personal details. Their brownstone was old—"established" Dolly called it—bricks flaking from the last paint attempt to hide the mold and general decay. The wires for a vinyl awning waved over the front door, but there was no awning, just a plastic grocery bag that had migrated from the street and mocked us with its happy face.

I pressed the buzzer for apartment 15, mentally rehearsing the speech I thought would let us up, but the door clicked open without so much as a required password. I'm pretty sure the word was "gloom" anyway, as in the day, the mood, the dimly lit stairwell that protested each of our steps with a loud groan. The whole building might shake given the right winds, and I wondered how it had fared during Hurricane Sandy. It was still standing, so that was something.

Apartment 15 was on the fifth floor, and we made our way up as quickly as possible before the tenants changed their minds and kept their door locked to pesky private investigators. I'd only been one for three years, but let me tell you, very few people are delighted to see us. Even our clients would rather communicate via phone or, increasingly, email. That suited me fine. I'd yet to meet a people-person P.I. Not that I attended the annual Cheating Spouses Convention or anything.

The apartment beside the Belascos had the door cracked open, chain still latched for security. I thought about telling the elderly woman staring at me that a ten-year-old could break one of those, but we all need our illusions. The woman harrumphed, mumbling something about "damn kids and keeping it down." So much for an ally.

Even before I met them, it was hard not to worry about Mr. and Mrs. Belasco, who had left their front door wide open for whoever had rung their bell. I knocked on the frame and waited for an invitation to enter. When none came, I poked my head around the door and helloed. Didn't these folks know that their in-laws were criminals? Or maybe that was the point. No one was going to mess with a drug dealer's Escalade, keys in the ignition or not.

The living room reeked of stale cigarettes, not necessarily smoked recently but absorbed into the wood-paneled walls and green carpet. The rose-printed couch was covered in plastic as was the matching recliner. There was something whimsical about the green carpet and red roses, as if the flowers were growing up from the floor in an abandoned Wonderland. When Mrs. Belasco hurried into the room, I expected something eccentric—at least colorful nails or a "Queen of the Kitchen" sweatshirt. Instead, she was in jeans and a collared shirt, hands with a tray of iced teas as if she'd been expecting us.

"*Pase, mis dulzuras*. Friends of Ernie's, yes," she asked, switching to English after she looked me over.

"Yes, thank you for welcoming us into your home, *señora*. You must be tired of company. Have a lot of us been stopping by?" Dolly asked, taking charge as if he'd dealt with plenty of grieving parents before. Maybe he had. We hadn't gotten to the talk-all-night sleepover phase of our friendship, yet.

Mrs. Belasco gestured for us to sit on the sofa, and as we did, it squeaked under us. I found myself sliding back on the plastic, unable to stop until my back hit the cushion. Dolly didn't crack a smile, and I must admit that I was impressed. With his professionalism, yes, but also with his choice to make us friends rather than hired hounds. Not that I would have barged in announcing that I was working for one of the suspects, but a reporter cover could have worked.

"So many," said Mrs. Belasco in response to Dolly's question. "Most I recognize, but some like you, are new. It's nice, you know, that he was so loved."

I glanced around the room. Posing as a reporter would have made it easier for me to ask questions, but Mrs. Belasco might not have answered them. Instead, I took in the framed photo of Ernesto with his mom. It was a high school graduation, and the new adult beamed, convinced that his dreams were in reach. He had looked similarly confident the night I met him. I doubted he worried that he was about to be killed, especially if he was as well-liked as his parents believed.

"Mostly *muchachos*," Mrs. Belasco said, breaking my train of thought. "May I ask your name, miss?"

"Kathy Seasons," I said, using my real-estate alter ego name if not occupation. "I actually met him at The Skyview. I'm a waitress there?"

At "Skyview," the mother's eyes widened, and she reached out to take my hand. "Ah yes, of course. He met some people there, he said."

"I actually don't know him that well," I started, embarrassed by her sympathy. "I'm not even sure why I'm here, I just, you know, he was so nice? When Dolly said he wanted to pay his condolences, I tried to—I tagged alone," I finished, hoping that I sounded sheepish and sincere.

"Of course. When we decided not to have a funeral service, we knew there'd be visitors."

No funeral service? I nodded, but was thinking, *now that's odd.* Was I stereotyping too much when I assumed the Belascos from Venezuela were Catholic? I glanced at Dolly then back at Mrs. Belasco, letting a new, horrifying possibility sink in. Unless they didn't think a religious ceremony was appropriate for their gay son. I knew I was jumping to conclusions—leaping really—but I still felt something harden inside me. I took a sip of tea to see if the knot would loosen. It didn't.

Mr. Belasco hurried in, his hair still wet from the shower. He was more reserved than his wife, but still didn't make us feel as if we were imposing. I guess they really were used to receiving visitors.

"We went by the salon today, too. I didn't know he'd been promoted. You must have been proud," I said.

"Yes," Mrs. Belasco responded, so softly I almost missed the word. "He was always talented," she continued. *At hair,* I wondered. *Or cards.* You'd have to be pretty slick to cheat a roomful of high rollers. Maybe someone hadn't liked being taken in by a kid from Bed-Stuy.

"I met Bomber recently, too," I said, and Dolly nudged my knee. Yes, I was going too far, but I wasn't sure if I'd have another chance to rustle up any useful information. "Do you know where I could find him? I'd like for him to know—I'd like to tell him—something."

The awkward routine seemed to be fairly convincing, but the parents still glanced at each other before answering. It was why witnesses were always questioned separately; never let them get their stories straight, pardon the pun.

"He's not been around," Mr. Belasco said and shrugged. "Maybe his friends know." He gestured toward Dolly. I started making motions to leave, not wanting to be found out if they asked Dolly anything too personal about their son. We offered our condolences and headed back out into the gray afternoon. It had started to sprinkle during our visit, and I pulled an umbrella from my bag. I'm not fastidious about my appearance, but the wrath of Vondya is enough to make me keep my wigs dry at the very least. Dolly stood thoughtfully staring up at the Belascos' window.

"Were your parents supportive?" I asked. A small grin appeared on his face, the first real one that I could remember seeing since the explosion. It creased the tape running around his gauze, which probably stung. I'd had my fair share of injuries, and there's not much more painful than burns.

"Mom threw me a coming out party, complete with a Dolly Parton cake and soundtrack. I was sixteen, popular, and everyone came. Don't go feeling sorry for me, kitty cat." He reached out and touched my forehead. "At least not about that."

The gesture was intimate enough to make me uncomfortable. I glanced up and down the avenue for something to do. That was when I spotted the unmarked cruiser, and no one I recognized taking our photograph.

———

Paranoid. Perhaps not the first trait that you would list on a personal ad, but I didn't plan to be dipping my un-pedicured toes into the online dating scene anytime soon. I would cop to paranoid any day of the week. And obsessed while we were at it.

When my personal cell phone rang, I jumped and Dolly squeezed my hand. I flipped open the screen and squinted at the unknown number with a Manhattan area code. I stopped

Dolly and kept my eyes on the cruiser when I hit the answer button.

"If I say I could kill you, will you take it the wrong way?" Ellis asked.

"Probably," I answered. "Why are you having me followed?" There was a long beat, and I knew I had asked the wrong question. "Wait, you mean you're watching the parents?"

That question was also greeted by a pause, and I knew I was right.

"I'm not confirming that."

"Gotcha. Would you confirm a possible link between Ernesto Belasco's murder and the Halloween explosion?"

"No, I would not."

Ellis had never been an adept liar, letting me talk us into bars underage and garner pity from our professors the next day by pleading sinus infections. I shouldn't have been surprised that our class valedictorian was a step ahead of me, aware that The Skyview victim was gay and, if I interpreted the nuance correctly, looking into any hate crime connections. There were definitely moments when I wished I were still on the force if only to be in the loop, but the macho office politics I could leave behind.

"Thanks, pal. You've been helpful."

"I know you're not going to drop this, and I won't tell you to," Ellis started, begrudgingly. "But be careful."

He'd said those three words to me a lot lately and still my throat constricted for a moment. I flipped the phone closed, staring at the scratched surface.

"You know, a badass spy like you should really have an iPhone."

"And be tracked by the NSA? Disposal living is the life for me," I sang, making Dolly smile again even if it didn't reach his eyes. "Come on. Let's go find some hate mongers."

It was after 6, and all I really wanted was a shower, but Dolly had been a good sport to accompany me all day. The least I could do was look into the print shop that made the brochures for the Zeus Society. As we waited on the A train platform, I asked Dolly to fill me in on Carlton Casborough, Bobbie's dish on the side. Almost everyone I've ever met would have asked, "Do you think he's behind the float sabotage," but Dolly wasn't predictable. Instead, he told me about their first meeting after Dolly had been hired. Dolly described him as an equal-opportunity flirt, always a compliment ready and never back-handed like some of the others.

"He would never say, 'I love how you make those extra pounds work for you' or something like that."

Dolly was trying to keep an objective tone and mostly succeeded, but I guessed that he liked Carlton.

"Is he fake?" I asked, knowing it was at least a slightly offensive question, if not easy to misconstrue. I wasn't talking wigs and eyeliner, though. Dolly considered for a moment. His attention seemed to be absorbed by a mangy-looking rat that was nosing around the tracks, looking for loot. After a minute, Dolly shook his head.

"No, I don't think so. Maybe unaware. A few of the other performers and waiters had crushes on him."

"Which ones?" I asked. The train lights appeared in the tunnel, and the rat scurried into an opening in the wall. I stepped back from the platform edge a few inches before the first cars screeched by. It was too loud to hear over the noise, and Dolly waited until the doors dinged open to answer. He couldn't be sure of anyone but Aaron Kline, describing him as "puppy doggish" when Carlton was around.

On the thirty-minute ride, Dolly filled me on a few other details: where Carlton was born, when he moved to New York. I wanted to ask Dolly if he knew who had stormed out of the emergency room after the deaths were announced, but I thought that a question better left for Big Mamma. Dolly had still been in an exam room at the time.

My head hurt by the time we pushed open the door to The Fountain, and I realized that I hadn't eaten anything since breakfast. Of course, I had stuffed myself the night before at Circo, so maybe it all evened out. I flushed thinking of dinner with Lars, which made my head pound even more. The smell of toner and ink didn't help much.

It was a small, high-end shop, appropriate for the increasingly posh West Village. The walls were lined with stationary, and I longed to compare the death threat note to the samples, but figured I had best talk to the manager first. She was blonde, pony-tailed, and efficient, sizing me up even before I'd said so much as "hello." I wasn't worried because Charlotte—according to her blue name tag—wasn't sizing me up, but Kathy Seasons, who usually lived on the Upper East Side but for the evening's purposes was a West Village neighbor, irate about a pamphlet she'd received earlier that weekend.

I pushed the offending literature from the Zeus Society toward Charlotte, who opened it and flicked off a piece of lint that had attached itself to a corner.

"I left a message yesterday. I suppose no one saw fit to return my call. Do you find anything wrong with this?"

Charlotte didn't glance at me, but instead studied each panel for a few seconds before flipping to the back and repeating the process.

"No ma'am. This seems to be of excellent quality, per our usual standards. Would you like to see our price list?"

Part of me marveled at her moxie. This girl couldn't have been out of college for very long, if at all. She could be fully matriculated down the street at The New School for all I knew. I could tell that Dolly wasn't pleased by her nonchalant response. He didn't say anything, but stiffened beside me.

"So this establishment supports hate speech," I stated, trying to get a rise out of her, but she looked back at me calmly. "I'm sure a few online forums would be happy to know. It deserves its own hashtag, really. Maybe #thefountainbigots."

"We don't judge the content, ma'am, just print it. Stylishly," she added, her confidence disorienting.

I paused to regroup, acknowledging that if she wasn't concerned about bad press, Charlotte had the power here. She had the intel I needed, too.

"In that case, we'd like to print our own materials to balance this filth. I will take a look at that price list after all."

Charlotte acted as if she knew that would be my answer all along and grabbed a mint green sheet from behind the counter to discuss my options. "The eight by four flyer is nice on stock paper, if you want something to distribute that won't be as likely to end in the gutter. We can print it right now for you if you'd like. We're open until nine on Sundays."

I glanced at the clock to see that it was nearing seven, then took out my legal pad to make a quick design. Drawing's not my forte, and I hadn't drawn so much as a heart doodle since freshman year of college, but I traced a quick jack-o-lantern and wrote in capital letters: INFORMATION ABOUT THE HALLOWEEN EXPLOSION WANTED $$$

"Let's start with 500, shall we?" Charlotte asked, not batting an eye over the fact that my flyer wasn't related to the Zeus Society brochure I'd been railing against. I've always valued a discreet doctor, but a discreet printmaker might be equally valuable. "What number would you like listed?"

Charlotte was already typing up a prototype for me to approve, and I gave her my office number. While Dolly and I waited, I texted Meeza that all office calls should go to voicemail. I doubted we'd get anything other than pranks and drunks, but it was worth a shot.

Dolly had yet to say anything since we'd entered the store. We were too close to the parade site for this to be a comfortable outing.

"We'll get them," I said, the words catching in my throat as if my brain disapproved of how trite my mouth was being. But Dolly nodded.

"You bet your sweet angel ass," he said.

CHAPTER THIRTEEN

Mother's bindi, what is that?" Meeza exclaimed as I scooted past the new floor secretary, Meeza's not-so-efficient replacement, and into the office. I assumed my assistant wasn't referring to the bag of bagels squeezed under my arm because she took that from me and helped herself to a garlic and onion. And she probably wasn't referring to my blonde "Kate" wig, a bob I thought of as soccer-Mom chic, because she'd seen me in it on multiple occasions by now, including our very first stakeout together. No, it had to be the gray flowered dress that I'd picked up from a thrift shop. Turns out, Dolly didn't own anything that screamed "I hate gays, too!" so I'd popped into a Washington Heights Salvation Army and picked up this winner. I held it out in front of me, trying to decide whether the black flowers looked understated or goth.

"It's not so bad," I began, noting that it was pilled in a few places and seemed to have a (fingers crossed) coffee stain along one seam. The lace collar had probably been white in a past life.

"That thing needs to be de-loused."

I agreed that a quick tumble in a washing machine wouldn't hurt, but there was no time for such luxuries. According to the woman I spoke to after calling the brochure number, there was a Zeus Society meeting today at a Brooklyn warehouse. The phrase "Brooklyn warehouse" brought back too many unpleasant memories to think about, so I pushed them away and focused on wardrobe. Seriously, did anything good ever happen in a Brooklyn warehouse? Even the art openings often had sub-par bathroom situations.

"Is Kate too blonde, you think?" I asked Meeza, turning toward her. Preoccupied, I had neglected to notice how tired she looked. There were circles under her eyes, and her usually neat hair was sloppily gathered on top of her head. If I wasn't mistaken, she was using a scrunchie. Did they even make those anymore? I tossed the dress down on my desk and gave Meeza my full attention. "You know, you really don't have to go to the 8 A.M. classes," I said as gently as possible.

"The diligent lad hasn't missed one, yet. The teacher, on the other hand, is starting to doubt my cockamamie story about the registrar's office. I'm not sure I'll make it through another week without being tossed out."

She laughed, and some of my worry about her eased. I opened my mouth to say something about V.P., then stopped. I'd never meddled with a relationship before and wasn't sure I deserved to try now. What did I know about a healthy romance? Marco was the last thing I had resembling a boyfriend, and we had lived in a sort of fantasy land—a dark fantasy land, mind you—between my undercover assignment and his. The subtext on that one was clear: It would never last.

"Anyone call about the flyer?" I asked, saving the pity party for a later time. The Fountain manager Charlotte had been a vault, refusing to give us even the slightest hint about whether the brochure and Pink Parrot death threats were both printed on site. I'd slid them onto the counter side by side, but she might as well have been looking at postcards from Oregon. "Good quality," she had said. "If it doesn't have our logo, I can't say if it was printed here." She admitted that most customers preferred the logo-free option even though it was more expensive, and did we want to upgrade our order?

Not ready to admit defeat, Dolly and I had wandered up and down Sixth Avenue handing out all 500 of the newly printed cries for help. Plenty were indeed thrown into the gutter despite the quality paper Charlotte had sold us, but others offered high fives and fist bumps. I wouldn't overstate our welcome amongst the other pushy flyer folks, but some locals at least were grateful that Dolly and I were canvassing for something other than strip clubs.

The West Village at night was my favorite neighborhood growing up. As a teenager, I would wander around with my gaggle of girlfriends, trying to talk our way into dive bars and usually succeeding. Everyone we passed looked like a poet or a photographer, and we were going to be muses and models. I guess that was our version of a princess fantasy, although I've seen enough strung out women during Fashion Week to know runways are no palaces. It's funny, I can't remember my friends' faces very well. I'm sure they've forgotten mine by now.

"A few, nothing promising. One climate control conspiracy theory and three men asking how much we'd pay for information," Meeza said, checking her notes on the calls.

"Do I want to know what a climate controller is?"

"Katya," Meeza said, as she flipped through our meager assortment of mail. I peered at her quizzically, not sure why she was using one of my aliases. Maybe there was a bill addressed to her? "Katya Lincoln. That ugly brown wig will read as down-at-the-heel crazy person. That's what you're going for, right?"

"It's not so bad," I said, but it was more like a Pavlovian response by now. I knew the permanently bunned style wasn't flattering, but my reluctance to wear it didn't have anything to do with vanity. I met clients as Katya Lincoln and liked to keep that identity separate. It was the one I used most often. When I dreamed, I was usually dressed as Katya, sensible Katya who lived a long way from my former, rat-invested Bronx apartment. For years, I'd lived in fear of being recognized by one of my drug dealing associates and had gone out of my way to make sure my hair was never that jet black or same length again. I slathered on sunscreen lest my tawny skin get too dark, and sunglasses were *de rigueur*. What can I say? I'd choose safe over glamorous any day of the week. My high school buddies would be ashamed of me.

In the end, I tied a scarf around the Kate wig, so that only a few blonde strands were visible. The dress smelled faintly of fish, and I tried not to think about who might have died in those threads. The one upside was that no one sat next to me on the train. I was left in peace to think over my conversation with Big Mamma. I'd called to ask who had fled the emergency room and got a funny feeling when she said Aaron Kline, the man who acted like a puppy when Carlton Casborough was around. Had Aaron known that Carlton was sleeping with Bobbie? Could he have wanted to get rid of the competition badly enough to sabotage the float?

While the hate group seemed more likely to send a funeral invitation in advance, I was determined to leave no stone unturned. I'd made that mistake before. And why was Aaron at the parade anyway if he wasn't performing? Big Mamma hadn't talked much after answering my questions, and I remembered Dolly saying that Aaron was everyone's favorite. Maybe that was all there was to it. He was distraught to lose his friends. If he needed an excuse to flee the harsh lights of an emergency waiting room, he certainly had one.

Today was a solo mission, Dolly's ability to pass for straight not exactly in question, but better not to take any chances. When I emerged from the subway, I spotted a 99-cent store and a Chinese takeout joint on a busy thoroughfare. I hoped the meeting was nearby, so that someone could at least hear my screams if need be. A part of me thought it might be a good idea to let Ellis know my plans, but the Halloween explosion wasn't his case, and I didn't much feel like working with whoever had been assigned to what was being treated as an accident—a suspicious accident, worthy of investigation and caution, but still an accident. Nobody could have predicted that a juggler would trip badly enough to send a flaming baton toward the Pink Parrot. I imagined the NYPD would keep the case classified as an accident until absolutely necessary to announce otherwise. A terrorist cell was no less frightening for being homegrown, and they wanted to avoid hysteria. They'd be using the term "wiring malfunction" unless someone leaked the bomb squad report. When one of my cell phones vibrated, I was startled, worried that Ellis had psychic abilities to go along with his prophet eyes. But it was the other Dekker, and I let it go to voicemail with some regret. I didn't need the distraction.

The warehouse was farther away from stores than I would have liked and about what you would expect. Aluminum siding, razor wire on the roof. The door's padlock was undone, and I slipped it off and into my cloth grocery bag. I didn't want to be locked inside this ramshackle facility. When I opened the door, the creak echoed, and I was confused about what I was seeing. Although the space was mostly empty, there were rows of metal shelves with matching metal containers that looked sort of like small trashcan lids, if trashcan lids were regularly polished. They gleamed in the lights. There were large windows at the top of the space, but the overheads were on, as well. If anything, it was too bright for my liking. I had to enter anyway.

The concrete floor was busted in a few places, and I side-stepped some larger pieces. I glanced down a few aisles, but there didn't seem to be anyone around, so I slid one of the containers off the rack. It was dated with a piece of masking tape: July 7, 1996. There was no dust to corroborate that assertion, and I felt certain these were handled regularly, whatever they were. I pried the top off and found a film reel. Holding a few frames up and squinting at them, I could make out a busty, naked brunette kneeling in front of an erect penis. I didn't need to see the rest. I'd taken plenty of salacious photographs of adulterers, but this was a different sort of cash game. Why was the Zeus Society meeting in a garage full of porn?

Footsteps were approaching from another room, and I rapidly stuffed the film back into the container and replaced it as gently as possible. It still clanged into place, and the footsteps paused. The sound of a gun being cocked made me freeze, and I found my voice as quickly as possible.

"Halloooo," I called out. "Is anyone there?"

The footsteps hurried in my direction, and I wasn't surprised to see Leader Holt turn the corner. The Winchester pointed directly at my head was a whole other story, and I ducked. To his credit, Cronos lowered the barrel toward the ground when he took in my unintimidating figure.

"Ma'aaam," he said, tipping his head in my direction. "Thiiis is private property."

"Leader Holt? The Leader Holt? I've been wanting to meet you for so long," I gushed. "You saved my nephew, flat-out saved him. He hasn't acted on his—" I paused as if looking for the right word. "Well, I don't even like to talk about it, but praise be, if I'm not talking to Leader Holt."

I wasn't sure if I was pouring on the religion too thick. A quick glance at Wikipedia had confirmed that the Zeus Society wasn't recognized by any governing organization. With their name, they were more likely to have pagan rather than Christian ties. Their brochure was heavy on Greek mythology, a curious choice given the stories of Zeus and others engaging in homoeroticism. I'd been trying to piece together this discrepancy, but so far had no theories. I was equally baffled by their meeting location, keeping my fingers crossed for some quick revelations. The leader seemed placated by my zeal and smiled a lizard smile, shouldering his weapon.

"Yes, ma'aaam, that's me. Are you here for the meeting perhaps?"

His slow way of talking didn't seem like an act, but it was disconcerting. The desire to finish his sentences for him was strong, and I had to squash that rude impulse. I'd hate to be kicked out before I met the rest of this merry band.

"I am indeed. I don't have much money—"

The leader held up his hand. "Allll are welcome," he said with no apparent sarcasm. Bile rose up in my throat. The fish smell from my dress wasn't helping.

Cronos led me out of the main storage room and into a smaller, white-walled space. It was as bright as the rest of the building, and I squinted around at the folding chairs. They were all filled, but a stocky man in the back stood up so that I could sit. I thanked him and pulled my bag close to my chest. The padlock was heavy, and I hoped I wouldn't have to swing it at anyone.

"No shame in the maaan, shame that does great harm or driiives men on to good," the leader began. Murmurs of affirmation followed, and when I glanced quizzically at the woman sitting next to me, she reached into her purse and pulled out a copy of *The Iliad*. It looked battered enough to have seen actual battle. Without much effort, she flipped open to the right page and showed me the verse Leader Holt had quoted. He was still talking, but I hadn't missed much in my distraction. "Good afternoon, citizens," he was repeating. "We are gathered here to praise the efforts of our outreach group who touched many souls at Saturday's orgy."

It took me a minute to translate, but they were congratulating themselves on protesting the memorial service of Bobbie and Taylor. I nodded along with the crowd, my head heavy.

"Aaaand," Holt continued, the word sounding like a drumroll. "We have yet another new face in our midst. Two in one day, how about that? Would you stand up, ma'am, and introduce yourself."

I swallowed hard as thirty men and women turned in unison to face me. I found myself staring at their pupils, looking for serpentine slits. Snake handling hadn't been exposed in New York City, but there are all kinds spread throughout the boroughs. Lock up your adders with this group around, that's all I'm saying.

"I'm Kate Manning, and as I was telling the man there," I paused to gesture toward Cronos Holt. "You all saved my nephew. He was going down a, well, a vile path, and now his family's at peace."

A few members of my audience grunted, satisfied, as they turned back toward the front. My heart was pounding, and all my senses were telling me to run. I would never escape this crowd if they got angry. My working knowledge of Greek myths was limited to one freshman English class that I'd shared with Ellis, but I knew sometimes people were torn limb from limb for no apparent reason. I sank back into my chair, and a hand patted my back. I turned to acknowledge the stocky man who had given me my seat and paled.

I hadn't recognized him at first without his Stetson, but this man was most definitely the Texan I had met at The Skyview. I faced front again quickly, hoping that he wouldn't recognize me. *He wouldn't, right?* I was kicking myself for not taking more care with my disguise, keeping the Kate wig on in fear of overusing Katya. *Stupid.*

A gray-haired woman was sharing news about increased donations, and I was too panicked to be disgusted by the figures. Who were these anonymous folks? Couldn't they be satisfied with blog trolling? I was willing to bet that one such backer was amongst us now. I'd seen his fancy watch and wad of cash.

My goal went from reconnaissance to survival in a flash, and I could barely focus on the speech. If I had been fully present, I would have wanted to find out why donations had increased. Was the influx of cash due to successfully killing two maybe three members of the gay community in one week? And was the assassin sitting right behind me? His presence couldn't be a coincidence, so there must be a link between this hate group in a smut-filled warehouse and the gamblers from Eva's highfaluting club.

When the remarks concluded and plans were made to meet at the same time next week, I eased up from my chair, planning to disappear into the crowd. Instead, everyone wanted to shake my hand, welcome me to the fold. I was invited to a support group and a tupperware party in the same breath. Leader Holt seemed smug as he watched his followers greet me. I kept myself from hissing at him, but barely. When the Texan stepped in front of me to introduce himself, I cringed but shook his hand. There was nothing else I could do. He didn't seem to know me, and I turned to accept well wishes from six or more smiling faces. As soon as possible, I slipped toward the exit and into the storage facility again.

I kept myself from running, knowing the old dress shoes I'd donned would boom on the concrete floors. When I was sure that I was out of sight, I slipped one of the metal containers off the rack and tried to wedge it into my bag. It was too big, and I had to put it back, cringing again at the sound. I headed toward the door, looking frantically over my shoulder to make sure that I wasn't being followed. Turns out, I should have been more anxious about who was in front.

CHAPTER FOURTEEN

I f I had been looking where I was going, he never would
have been able to pull me into his chest and clamp his big
hand over my mouth. I tried to bite, but there was no loose
flesh. When the Texan made soothing sounds close to my ears
as if I were a stubborn horse, I could feel the bile rise up in my
throat again. I swallowed hard, not wanting to choke on my
own vomit. There are more dignified ways to meet your maker.

"I reckoned I might see you here," he said, his low drawl
sounding downright sinister. He dragged me toward a back
room, my heels scrapping futilely in the process. I was afraid
to go with him and afraid to make noise. My odds of besting
a 250-pound man in a tussle weren't high, but they were
better than my odds of surviving a bullet from the leader's
rifle. When the Texan tossed me into a windowless space and
locked us in together, I started to doubt my decision. Why is
it so hard to choose the lesser of two evils?

I expected instant violence, would have preferred it, to the
slow stalk the Texan did around the room as if looking for my
vulnerabilities. There were plenty, I wanted to tell him. No
need to be picky.

"The cop said you're one of the good guys, but we have our doubts."

"What cop? Who's we?" I said, folding my arms in front of me to keep them from shaking.

The Texan shook his head. "Should I call you Kennedy or Kate?"

"Katya," I said, adjusting to the unfortunate fact that I'd been recognized. I slipped my scarf off my head, not wanting the material used to choke me. It hadn't served its purpose anyway.

"How about Kathleen Stone, former undercover cop for the NYPD who still thinks she's hot shit."

"That'll do," I said, not wanting to quibble with the presumed bravado. My moments of self-confidence were few and far between and usually didn't happen under the name Kathleen Stone anymore. If he'd been warned about me, that would explain how he recognized me at least. It was a relief to know that I wasn't losing my touch. But a small relief. I twisted the scarf into a long chord, thinking any weapon was better than none.

"The problem is that your reputation isn't stellar. Your last client's husband was killed on your watch."

True, I thought.

"Your main suspect was shanked behind bars."

Fair enough.

"And there's some speculation that you might be in cahoots with one Salvatore Magrelli. Name ring a bell?"

My mind was reeling, trying to process how he could know so much about me. My response to Magrelli's name was to shiver, but otherwise, I remained impassive. "Don't give anything away" was my life's motto. I doubted any designers would put it on a T-shirt, but it worked for me.

After an interminable pause, the Texan pulled out a badge from his blazer pocket: John Thornfield, DEA.

"Drugs," I said. Of course. I wouldn't be the only person to think of getting to Magrelli through his wife. I considered how long Agent Thornfield must have been undercover at The Skyview to be so chummy with everyone, then didn't marvel at his open hostility toward me. I had put his operation in danger, if not him personally. More relaxed but still confused, I unraveled the scarf and folded it into my bag. "I'll apologize if you want me to, but if you think Ernesto Belasco's death is drug-related, why are you at this meeting?"

It dawned on me that Agent Thornfield was the other new member that Leader Holt had mentioned, and I asked how he had found his way here.

"Ernesto Belasco's funeral didn't get as much press as the Drag Queen Disaster—" I cringed at the insensitive term that had been floating around in some of the sleazier newspapers. If Agent Thornfield noticed my reaction, he didn't acknowledge it. "But there were a few Zeusers at the burial."

"His parents said that they didn't have a funeral."

"No service, a graveside for immediate family members. Damned if I know how the Zeus clan found out about it."

"How did they even know he was gay? I figured that out yesterday."

"They keep a database, Star of David-style, except in an Excel sheet." He spat on the ground before continuing. "They set up Google alerts for each name that they have on record. It's incomplete, but impressively thorough."

"Impressively?"

The Texan shook his head at my irritation. My attitude was apparently less impressive than a target list.

"I'm not sure if there's a drug connection, yet, but it's worth checking out. If I can bring down a hate group in my spare time, hell, that's a fine day's work."

"What about the porn?" I asked, mulling over this new development. I leaned against the wall, my knees weak since the adrenaline was leaving my system. Agent Thornfield hadn't threatened me to back off his case, so I was feeling okay about my odds of seeing this investigation through. And vigilantism is overrated. If the DEA brought down Salvatore Magrelli all the better. I'd rather keep my head on my neck, thank you very much.

"No kiddie stuff that I saw, but I'll look into the production companies. Probably a storage facility. A few extra bucks a month to keep some men's habits from their wives."

I was lost in thought, staring at the flaking paint on a cinder-block wall when John continued talking. "Which brings me to you, Miss Stone."

I stood up a little straighter, ready for the lecture. It wasn't the one I expected.

"You're working for the Dekker fellow, right?"

"Yes. Lars," I clarified.

"And his brother's the cop?"

"The detective, yes."

John grunted. "Alrighty then. Let's see what shakes out."

The Pink Parrot had reopened, and customers were packed in, vying for drinks and seats. The benefit performance wasn't until Saturday, but that didn't stop the locals from paying their respects in the form of large cash tips. Carlton Casborough was on stage as Cassandra when I entered, and I paused to consider whether the man wearing cowboy boots and a red halter dress looked like a murderer. It was easier to believe that a hate group had been behind the explosion than a jealous lover, but statistically speaking, you're more likely to know your killer.

I glanced at my phone to check the time and remembered the voicemail from Lars that I hadn't checked. It was too loud to hear when I pressed the phone to my ear, but he had texted, as well: "Dinner 2morrow nite?" I texted back "sure" before I could chicken out and ignored the anticipation that settled in my stomach. At least I could update him on what I'd found out from Thornfield. Otherwise, my trip to the viper's den had been something of a bust. All I'd really found out was that the Zeus Society had been at the graveside service for Ernesto and the memorial for Bobbie and Taylor. It was a link, sure, but cobweb thin.

I squeezed through the sea of bodies, murmuring apologies for stepped-on toes, and ducked backstage. Dolly's dressing-room door was closed, but he was expecting me, and I entered after knocking. Dolly wasn't gussied up for performing, and I wanted to know if he ever would again. The burn was exposed and covered with scabs that seemed infected, though I'm no expert. I mentioned something about antibiotics, and my friend pointed at a Duane Reade bag tossed beside old lipsticks on his vanity.

"The doc says the wound needs to air out, so I've been taking it out for strolls in Riverside Park," Dolly said.

"How romantic."

"No other murders," he said, turning his computer screen toward me, so that I could see the NYPD's graphic. "But three gay men killed in one week doesn't seem like a fluke to me."

Meeza had already told me this information, but I wanted Dolly to think he was helping. And he was. In fact, I wouldn't have been at The Pink Parrot if I didn't need some serious help.

"I still consider Tongue worth checking out," I said, thinking again about killers usually knowing their victims. I wanted to talk to Bomber, Ernesto's boyfriend who hadn't yet shown his respects to the grieving parents. Dolly hadn't complained about me juggling two cases, but I think he wanted them to be connected. To be honest, so did I. I was with DEA agent John Thornfield on this one: Why not take down a hate group when you can?

"*Bien sûr, ma chérie.* I wish I could go with you," Dolly said, examining his burn in the mirror. "Trust me when I say this face wouldn't go over well."

He made this declaration in a matter-of-fact tone. Dolly may have chosen a drama-filled career, but he carried his burdens lightly. It was possible that his star turn was over, not to mention the ubiquitous longing glances I'd seen thrown in his direction. Not that he still wasn't beautiful to me, but I may have been biased.

"I was thinking I might go as Keith," I said after a pause, and Dolly laughed. The sound was spontaneous rather than mean, and I found myself laughing, too, even though I hadn't been joking. Maybe I hadn't thought this one completely through, but I sometimes passed myself off as a teenager named Keith by slipping into some skater clothes and slicking down my boy-short hair. It was one of my favorite disguises, a sure-fire way to be left alone.

"Not if you want to get into the place. It's gayboy bunny or nothing."

By the time I teetered out onto the street, Dolly had worked some witchcraft on me. I sported the long, platinum curls I thought of as Kiki and a black, sequined dress that hit a scandalous-length above my knees. Dolly had conceded to my plea for tights, but they were silver and sparkled. I had my Kate Manning ID with me, just in case, not that I resembled a soccer mom in the least, but I doubted anyone would card me. With caked on foundation and fake eyelashes, I looked older—if not washed-up at least trying-too-hard. Maybe under stage lights this getup would scream "alluring," but here in the flashing neon in front of The Pink Parrot, "garish" came to mind. So much for my usual plan of flying under the radar. I raised my hand, and two taxis squealed to a stop.

CHAPTER FIFTEEN

The house music was hypnotic after awhile, or maybe the 7 & 7 I'd ordered was too strong. In any case, I was sleepier than I should have been on a reconnaissance mission. "Go do that badass spy shit that you do," Dolly had said when I slinked (okay, tripped) out of his room. So I was trying. The Zeus Society convert dress I had worn that morning may have left something to be desired, but at least it didn't pinch my sides if I turned too quickly. Tina Turner must have superpowers to shake and sing in similar outfits. Thinking about my run-in with Leader Cronos Holt and his devotees made me feel more tired, but I ordered another drink (light on the Seagrams) and surveyed my surroundings.

The club was tamer than I imagined it would be, but it was a Monday night after all. No one was taking advantage of the dance floor, and the disco ball made rainbow-colored patterns on the floor as it spun. The tables around the edges were mostly occupied. My story, which I shared with the uninterested bartender, was that I was waiting on someone. I wasn't the only woman in the place, but the only other one was with a group, some sort of celebration I deduced from their occasional cheers. They seemed to be toasting a friend who covered his face every time at their declarations of love. "More, more" disguised as "Stop it, you guys."

I tossed back my drink, so that I could order another. *What would Tina Turner do*, I asked myself. Well, Tina wouldn't hang out on this barstool by herself, that's for damn sure. Bomber's Facebook privacy settings had been severe, and even jealous-ex-worthy cyberstalking hadn't turned up a photograph. I was hoping that he would look familiar from the snapshot at Ernesto's salon workstation. It was probably like picking out your suitcase from the luggage carousel. You couldn't describe it in a police report, but when it slid into view, you'd know to grab the handle. Fingers crossed. The bartender acknowledged me when I caught his eye, but finished his conversation before sauntering in my direction. He either thought I wasn't likely to be a repeat costumer or was too cool to care.

"I'll have another, although it looks like I've been stood up," I said. He raised a perfectly plucked eyebrow, then turned to pull the whiskey from a shelf. "Hey, you don't happen to know if Bomber's here tonight. I can at least say hi and not call this whole night a bust."

The bartender looked at me curiously as he added Seven Up to my glass, then gestured toward the birthday party in the corner.

"Well, I'll be! How could I have missed him?" I slid a twenty onto the bar and said he could keep the change, hoping a five-dollar tip read as grateful rather than desperate—or worse, suspicious—and headed toward the group in question. The woman noticed my approach, and she didn't seem welcoming, her smile replaced by a thin, tight line of pink lipgloss. *May she get it on her teeth for scowling.*

"So sorry to interrupt," I began. "My pals are late—really late, like rude-level late—and I'm bored to absolute tears. Do you think I could join you? I'm Kiki, by the way."

The group tried to communicate telepathically, but in the end, the first to speak got his way, and he muttered "sure." I slid in beside him on the pleather bench, maneuvering my short skirt in as lady-like manner as possible. I wished the man had a luggage tag that I could check, but I was pretty sure that I was sitting next to Bomber.

"I've seen you here before," I began before anyone could start questioning me. In my periphery, I could tell that the bartender noticed my acceptance into the group, and I was glad that he was well out of earshot. Actually, the other occupants of the table were basically out of earshot, as well, given the bass line pouring from the speakers above our heads. I yelled my opening line this time, "I've seen you here before!"

Bomber leaned close to my ear. "I should hope so! It's my place," he shouted and laughed, pleased with himself. The others laughed, too, although they couldn't have heard him.

"Well, shut my mouth, no way," I said. "That is too dreamy. This place is wild." I poured on the compliments thick and hoped he caught some of them. In Ernesto's photograph, he had looked barely old enough to drink, but up close, I could see that he was probably in his late twenties, baby-faced but with faint lines on his forehead. It still seemed crazy that such a young guy would own a Manhattan nightclub. The rent payments alone on this place must have been astronomical, and good credit can only get you so far. Color me impressed.

I was less impressed by his easy manner, his total lack of obvious heartache. His boyfriend had been killed three days before; shouldn't he be at home wallowing? I thought about Mr. and Mrs. Belasco's tart response to Bomber's whereabouts. Maybe what I had mistaken for homophobia was a dislike for their son's choice of partner. And if Ernesto hadn't been showing up for work, did that mean he planned to get serious with this budding mogul? Maybe Bomber wasn't much into having a trophy husband.

I took another drink of my 7 & 7 and looked up at Bomber's friends with an over-the-top pout on my lips.

"I can't believe I've been STOOD UP." They expressed various amounts of sympathy. It was clear that I had disrupted their levity, and all they wanted was for me to leave them alone. I wasn't quite finished, and turned back to Bomber, cupping my hand around his ear.

"Where's that handsome beau of yours? I've seen him around here, too."

The music didn't screech to a halt, but it might as well have. Bomber must have made some sort of signal because a bodyguard appeared to suggest I retake my seat at the bar. No velvet ropes in sight, but that area was now "V.I.P." I waved good-bye to the group as if accustomed to being shuffled out of sight and sauntered back over to the bar with my glass.

"I guess I'm calling it quits for the night," I said to the bartender. He barely looked up from the flirtatious conversation he had struck up with the older gentleman who had taken my spot. I tucked my tail and headed out in the brisk night. A taxi pulled up before I even raised my hand.

"Home, Jeeves" is something I have never said. I had the driver drop me at Columbus Circle, then took the subway home where I carefully placed Dolly's wig on a mannequin head then fell asleep in my dress and makeup.

⸺

I've felt worse, but I didn't feel human when I woke up the next morning. A quick glance in the mirror told me that I didn't look human either. An overlooked bobby pin had lodged itself in my cheek, leaving a two-inch mark, but that was nothing compared to my raccoon eyes and cow-licked bangs. I put the whole mess in the shower and felt better after a few long inhales of steam. Occasionally the water would slip to scalding without warning, but the tub was wide enough to avoid the spray until it resumed a bearable temperature. With hot water included in the lease, I wasn't about to complain. I wasn't a water waster, considering how much time I spent sleeping at the office, but I wasn't winning any showering speed races. By the time I emerged, my skin was pink, and I nodded at myself in the mirror as I would a stranger. A savvy stranger since she had being doing more than shampooing; she'd also been brainstorming.

Wasn't motive as likely to be love as hate? Bomber's callous behavior had made me reconsider the possibility of violent lovers in both my cases. Did Ernesto ask too much of his club-owning paramour? And did young Martin know that his fella Bobbie was fooling around with co-worker Carlton? What are teenagers if not reckless, and maybe Martin didn't expect the float to explode, only catch fire, teach his boyfriend a lesson. *Romeo and Juliet* is no way to live a life.

At the office, Meeza pulled up Martin's Facebook page, complete with school information: The Holy Cross of the Upper East Side, an all-boys institution known for its pageant of alumni luminaries, including at least one Supreme Court Justice and an A-list movie star. I glanced through the photographs that were public and didn't see anything too alarming. No beer bottles or shirtless poses. Smart kid.

"Jimmy Holliday, too," said Meeza, referring to the NYU undergrad she'd been paid to tail. "Hasn't missed a class, yet. I, on the other hand, have gotten the boot from swimming. 'No roster, no diving board,' the instructor said. As if I wanted to jump off that death trap anyway."

It was the most I'd heard from Meeza in days, and I laughed at her bad imitation of the swim teacher.

"Italian," I guessed.

"No, *arð baapa rð!* British."

This made me laugh more, and when V.P. poked his coconut-smelling head into the office, we were both wiping our eyes.

"Working hard or hardly working," he asked.

This made Meeza laugh harder, but my sense of humor must have slipped out when he slipped in. I could easily add V.P. to my growing list of suspicious lovers, making the whole romance thing pretty unappealing, Lars Dekker's pretty blue eyes notwithstanding.

If V.P. noticed the glares I shot in his direction, he didn't seem to mind and kissed Meeza before holding out his hand to me. I shook it and didn't flinch when he painfully tightened his grip. His rings pressed into my almost-healed scrapes, but macho isn't that hard to fake. I didn't even stick my tongue out at him, winning some major adult points.

"I thought my girl might like some breakfast."

Meeza glanced at the bagel I had brought her, and I shook my head at her reluctance to offend me. "No, you crazy kids have fun."

"You sure?" Meeza asked, but V.P. was already ushering her out. I could hear her uninhibited laughter through my office's thin walls. I shared the floor with other loosely called entrepreneurs, a ragtag bunch of mostly lawsuit attorneys. I didn't see them very much, and the floor secretary who replaced Meeza had yet to speak to me. Maybe she didn't recognize me in my various getups, but more likely, she didn't care. If I wanted to run a one-woman call girl ring, who was she to object? Sometimes on my way to the bathroom, I could hear snippets of conversation as she held her cell phone between ear and shoulder to leave her hands free for computer solitaire, but otherwise, she might as well have not been there.

I scrolled through Martin's Facebook page again to make sure I hadn't missed anything, then jotted down the address of his school. He didn't strike me as the extracurricular type, so I was betting I could find him smashing his tie into his backpack at 3:01 P.M. In the meantime, there were a hundred or so "tips" to hear from the flyer Dolly and I had distributed. I dialed the voicemail number and slumped down on the futon, resting the phone base on my stomach and expecting to be entertained if not enlightened. A woman's voice said "hello" then hesitated. "I don't want to get anyone in trouble," she began then hurried on. "But I think I saw someone push that man throwing the fire."

CHAPTER SIXTEEN

The tipster had called me from a pay phone in the Union Square subway stop. When the trains screeched into the station, I couldn't hear her, but the gist was that she didn't want the juggler to be arrested, never mind about the reward. Her story matched Martin King's, which made me think the juggler really wasn't involved. I knew he'd been questioned by the NYPD on the night of the explosion, and they hadn't arrested him. But they hadn't so much as detained a single person. Had the juggler seen who pushed him? If so, he probably would have told the police, but I didn't want to cross out the possibility. In fact, I wanted to rush straight to the circus school that had been a parade entry, but the remaining messages weren't going to hear themselves.

Meeza could take over when she got back, but it seemed unfair to leave this entire tedious chore to her. The other calls were from, by and large, conspiracy theorists. I doubted the parade organizers had links to Egyptian princes wanting revenge for tomb robbing. Come to think of it, I wasn't sure Egypt even had princes anymore. The caller fingering the

Masons had used a voice disguiser, but that wasn't half so frightening as the man who believed that all the fake blood sold in Halloween stores is from test lab animals. He ended his rant by asking about the reward and leaving his number. I didn't write it down.

Two hours later, and Meeza still hadn't returned. Perhaps she had gone straight to NYU to tail Jimmy Holliday, but I doubted it. V.P. seemed pretty determined to keep her away from me, and I hated to admit it, but maybe he was right. The fear of Salvatore Magrelli I had felt when I testified against him had been replaced with anger—the deep, simmering kind that might lead to an explosion. Anyone near me was likely to get hit with some debris.

There were ten or so messages left to hear, so I took a break and exited the building, unhappy to find that the temperature had dipped since the morning. The sidewalks were littered with leaves that crunched when I stepped on them, and the sky threatened snow. As I walked around the corner for a sandwich, I tried to sort out the possible suspects in my head for both cases, letting the Zeus Society hover above everything, a charming murder-minded umbrella.

While listening to the more innocuous messages, I'd multitasked by researching hate groups and wasn't happy with what I'd found. For one, KKK membership rates were on the incline, with Louisiana a veritable rattlesnake's nest. Other parts of the country weren't winning any Nobel Peace Prizes either. If drug dealers scared me, white supremacists made me want to build myself a fallout shelter and live off beans until the apocalypse took care of a few bloodlines. But I knew thinking big was the wrong way to solve a crime—two crimes to be more precise. I've been out of school for awhile, but I still knew to start with the details.

The bodega cat meowed at me as I added potato salad to my order, and I bent down to scratch his ears. He purred and rubbed his body over my hand, petting himself. Not particularly ferocious, but I guess I would feel differently if I were a mouse.

For Ernesto, there were five other people in the room when he died: John "The Texan" Thornfield, Glenn "Mr. Manners" Dalton, Sybil Sheridon, Lars Dekker, and me. I paid for my meal and thought about what other names should be added. A Google search had yielded an alarming amount of information about poison residue that could be left on a glass undetected until ingested by a victim. There were even substances that could be dormant in the body for a few hours before mixing with something else and causing a deadly reaction, sometimes accidentally so. That meant adding other folks Ernesto might have seen that day, including his non-grieving boyfriend Bomber and other Skyview staff members.

On the other side of this chaos, lay the bodies of Roberto Giabella and Taylor Soto. Poor Taylor. Not even the center of attention after being killed. Had any of the eulogists mentioned him? Not while I was there. I waved to the floor secretary as I headed into my office, but she didn't glance up from her computer screen. I may have glimpsed a queen of hearts being moved to a king of spades.

Poor Taylor or not, Bobbie seemed to be the target, or one of them at least. Dolly had shown me all of his hate mail letters, but none were as explicitly threatening as the funeral invitations. Awful, yes, but not the "I want to eat your organs" type. Dolly affirmed my guess that the other staff members looked up to him. He wouldn't go so far as to say "idolized," but I would. What was perhaps more surprising was that he didn't consider any of them close, and I wondered if that could be significant. Could someone have been vying for Dolly's spot as headliner?

"Who are your friends?" I had asked, assuming there was a gaggle of smart, well-dressed men to accompany Dolly to art openings and benefits. "I work hard, kitty cat" was his reply. I didn't think Dolly and I had much in common, but maybe I was wrong.

Once back at my desk, I pushed my sandwich to the side and brought out a legal pad. I turned my mental list into a real one, making a column for Ernesto and a column for Bobbie. Under Ernesto, Bomber was at the top followed by Mr. Manners. When I'd called to request an interview, he'd taught me some new euphemisms that I wouldn't be repeating to anyone. Sybil had been more polite if not more forthcoming, understandably suspicious of my swift change from hoity-toity philanthropist to unknown P.I. She'd asked me to direct all questions to her lawyers, a couple of sharks named Winston & Winston. I put Sybil in the Ernesto column, although my heart wasn't in it. Salvatore went at the bottom even though he didn't have a motive now and wishful thinking wouldn't create one for him.

Under Bobbie, I jotted down Carlton Casborough and Martin King to complete the love triangle. I added Aaron Kline since he was enamored with Carlton and had ducked out of the emergency room. I'd tried to set up an interview with him, but he wasn't returning my calls. The stack of headshots Big Mamma had given me yielded one remote possibility. The others were either successfully working elsewhere or long gone from New York City. I had run a background check on the one unemployed reject, and his past was squeaky clean. It seemed unlikely that a 30-year-old aspiring actor with a blog about cartoons would suddenly turn to arson, but I wrote him down, too. Looking at my names, it was hard not to circle back to my umbrella, Leader Cronos Holt holding the handle.

"What'd you find out," Ellis said by way of greeting when I called him. While an inquiry about my general health would have been nice, it was a compliment that Ellis thought I might know something useful. Of course, he also wanted me to re-join New York's Finest, and I wasn't warming to the idea, especially given their cavalier treatment of Big Mamma's concerns. Not to mention the fact that Ellis was the only who had expressed any interest in wanting me back. No one would bust out the ticker tape if I returned.

"There's a hate group in town."

"The Zeus clan. Yeah, we're working that angle."

I could hear someone hollering for Ellis's attention, but he must have shrugged them off because he didn't hang up, waiting for me to continue.

"Did you question Cronos Holt?"

"Quite a charmer that one."

Ellis's sarcasm was apparent, but I thought Cronos probably was charming, at least to his followers. I remembered the worn copy of *The Iliad* that I'd been handed and decided not to underestimate the abilities of the slowest talking person I'd ever met. His brain was moving faster than his tongue.

"Is the DEA agent legit? John Thornfield," I clarified.

"As far as I know. He's here in town for Magrelli, which means you can back off."

I'd had the exact same thought, but that didn't keep me from taking offense. Where had he been five years ago when his help—anyone's help—would have been appreciated?

"I'm wondering if the three murders are linked," I said.

Ellis didn't feed me a line about the float explosion not technically being called a double homicide, yet, which I appreciated. He also paused long enough for me to think that I was onto something.

"You asked me that already. Which case are you working on right now?

"Both."

"I've got The Skyview kid under control. I don't care about Lars's meddling."

There was an unspoken warning there, and I respected Ellis. Everyone did. But I'd accepted the case, and I'd see it through.

"I'm meeting your brother again tonight," I said. There was another long pause, and I could hear someone yell again for his opinion on something. I'd spent a few weeks of my life in the precinct office, but I didn't miss the noise, the constant lobbying for attention to your case, your clues. I'd be happy if I never heard the term "non-priority" again.

"Where?" Ellis asked.

I mentioned the name of the restaurant, and he hung up on me before I could tell him about the fire tip I'd received that morning. I'd look into it on my own, but next up on my to-do list was to pick up a kid from school.

CHAPTER SEVENTEEN

T he Holy Cross of the Upper East Side boasted wrought-iron gates that groaned emphatically when I pulled on them. No security guards came running into view, so I proceeded into the courtyard. It was Old New York nice, with a fountain statue of Adam and Eve sharing an apple. A serpent wound around their shoulders, water trickling from its mouth. It was an odd choice for a high school, but striking for its sheer size, eight-feet tall at least. Around the perimeter, there were five benches, one of which was occupied by a bored-looking dad staring at his iPhone. I'd worn my nicest black suit, but had made no efforts at disguising myself. I needed Martin to recognize me, and I warred with my instincts not to keep glancing over my shoulder.

I had testified anonymously against the three cartel leaders, Frank and Salvatore Magrelli plus one associate. But it wouldn't have been too difficult to guess that the nosy woman from next door who disappeared right after the bust was an undercover cop. The night of the shakedown had been mayhem, and I'd been handcuffed along with a dozen others. But once released,

I would have returned for my belongings, right? If no one else cared, Señora Costa at the very least would have noticed my absence. I didn't want her paring knife anywhere near me.

I took a closer look at the bored parent to make sure that he didn't look like a hired gun. He popped his gum and jabbed at his screen.

It wasn't three o'clock yet, so I settled down on a different bench. I'd bought a prop copy of *The New Yorker* at a nearby kiosk. It was the annual food issue, and the cover featured a lively restaurant scene with a family of four walking by the window with takeout. For a moment I considered why the artist had put the girl and boy in costumes, but decided it was realistic. I'd passed plenty of kids refusing to give up on Halloween, and why shouldn't a five-year-old dress like a ninja if he wanted? I flipped to an article by Rebecca Mead and tried to lose myself in the nuances of Greek yogurt. By the time the bell rang, I was hungry and ready to get on with this unscheduled chat.

A herd of teenagers stampeded into the dismal fall day, tossing papers at each other and shrieking with delight at their newfound freedom. I scanned them quickly, hoping that Martin's face wouldn't be obscured. And then my young suspect appeared, shuffling off to the side, head down, nails in his mouth. I paused before calling out to him, noting his obvious depression versus Bomber's ebullience. *Depression or guilt*, a sharp inner voice sang out. *Pay attention.*

"Martin," I called, and he looked up at me languidly. He didn't seem shaken up in the least to see me and ambled over, dropping his backpack beside me.

"Can I get a ride," he asked.

"I walked."

He laughed, a hollow sound that made goosebumps on my arms. The kid wasn't doing well, that much was clear. His hair was greasy, and there were flakes of dandruff on his blazer shoulders. He smelled of sweat, pot, and something acrid and unidentifiable. Just filth maybe. Where were his parents? When I asked, he was noncommittal, and that turned out to be our conversation's theme.

"Would you like to sit down? I want to ask you a few more questions about Bobbie."

"Roberto," Martin said.

"Roberto," I agreed.

I didn't want to be any closer to Martin, but I didn't want our conversation to look unusual either. There were a few more adults milling around now, teachers and administrators, I assumed. A few paused to examine me, but probably thought I was a social worker or a relative. Or they were too tired at the end of the day to make a fuss. I gestured to the empty spot beside me, and Martin slid into it, slumping down. He crossed his arms in front of him momentarily, then unfolded himself so that he could attack his thumb nail. The sight of his bloody cuticles made me feel sick.

"Was there anyone who would have wanted to hurt Bobbie? I mean Roberto."

Martin shrugged and rested his head on the back of the bench. He stared up at the clouds, and I stared at his dilated pupils. It didn't seem likely given the school's notoriously strict disciplinary code, but Martin King was high. Really high.

"Had he complained about anyone?"

Martin shrugged again, and I had a sudden urge to shake him.

"I'm trying to help," I said instead.

Martin mumbled his response, but it was something along the lines of "It's not help if you get paid for it."

Was that true? I wasn't sure, but I was also losing patience.

"You know you're a suspect, right? And at seventeen, you'd be tried as an adult."

"How am I a suspect?" Martin rolled his eyes until they were more or less focused on mine.

"Jealous lover? It's a pretty old story. You've maybe even read *Othello* in this upstanding establishment." I gestured toward the stone walls of the school entrance.

"*Othello, MacBeth, Richard III, Julius Caesar, Romeo and Juliet*, all the Henrys. If someone dies, we've read it." I raised my eyebrows at him. Was this sociopath curriculum or college prep? I waited for my young scholar to continue. "Jealous of Carlton Casborough? Carlty? Carl the Anteater? Bobbie was pity-fucking him. He was a good guy like that."

Martin teared up, and I glanced around to see who might be watching us. A couple of kids were arguing on a bench, but the courtyard had mostly cleared out. The bored father must have found his progeny and skedaddled.

"So you weren't jealous of Carlton? Not even a little bit?"

"Leave me alone, okay."

Martin didn't go anywhere, and I sat with him in silence. I wasn't sure about much, but I knew this kid had lost someone he loved. And I knew how that felt.

<hr/>

Lars Dekker had chosen what he called a low-key establishment. It's true there were no chandeliers, but the pinot noir I was nursing cost twenty dollars a glass, and there was a jazz trio in the corner. I tugged down the cuffs of my suit jacket and avoided my reflection behind the bar. The mirror gave me a clear view of the entire restaurant, and I surveyed the couples and friends gossiping over lobster rolls and oysters. There was a school of bronze tuna suspended over their heads, and I paused for a second to hope it didn't crash into the dining room. Then I went back to fidgeting with my clothes.

I had remained calm and collected for the first fifteen minutes of my wait, mulling over the likelihood that Martin was responsible for the parade explosion. My instincts said that he was innocent, a kid mourning his first love. And despite what he had told me in the Roosevelt emergency waiting room, he had clearly been in love with Bobbie. *Roberto*, Martin would have corrected, implying he liked the prestige that went along with dating an older man, even one only a year out of high school himself.

Eventually my sympathy for Martin turned to embarrassment for myself as I realized that I might have been stood up for real this time. After thirty minutes that "might" turned to "definitely," and I slid money onto the bar to pay for my drink. As I was thanking the bartender, a Dekker walked in, but it wasn't the one that I had been expecting.

Ellis's frantic appearance made a few people turn to gape at him. He wasn't wearing a jacket despite the bite in the November air, and he was sweating through his blue, collared shirt. When he caught my eye in the mirror, he didn't need to wave to get my attention. He might as well have been holding a placard: Bad News. My ears were ringing, and I shook my head to keep from fainting as I headed across the room. The walk seemed longer than the thirty or so steps it must have taken. It was as if I had entered a funhouse—walls closing in, pathways rocking. When I got to Ellis, the hostess was asking if he wanted a table, but I grabbed his arm and pulled him onto the street.

He didn't say anything, and handed me his phone where a voicemail message was already playing. No one was speaking, but loud popping noises could be heard over what sounded like gusts of wind.

"Gunfire?"

Ellis cleared his throat. "I got this message from Lars's phone, and he won't return my calls."

My ears started ringing again, and I concentrated to ask a simple question.

"Why are you here?"

"Where else would I go?"

CHAPTER EIGHTEEN

For a moment, I wasn't sure where I was, though the room looked familiar. Then my eyes focused on the framed *Casablanca* poster on the wall, and I sat up quickly and glanced at the digital clock: 7:00 A.M. Ellis was the one person I knew personally in Manhattan who had a guest bedroom. I'd slept off plenty of hangovers under this very duvet, but that was years ago when I was a different person. That girl would have bounced into her friend's bedroom and woken him up by hitting him with pillows, demanding coffee and breakfast. This woman was hoping that she could write a note and sneak out unseen. No such luck.

Ellis was showered, dressed, and caffeinated by the time I made my bed and walked into the kitchen. He handed me a cup of coffee and pushed a plate of toast toward me. Resigned for an awkward morning, I sat down across from him at the little cafe-style table. We had stayed up late the night before, bouncing around theories and trying to decide on the best plan of action. Ellis had filed a missing person report, but his brother wasn't a minor or mentally impaired. No search had been started.

Ellis was writing in a beat-up notebook, and I didn't interrupt him as I slathered blackberry jelly on my bread. I tried to read the expression on his tired face. By the end of the day, Ellis would look like a cop—tough and intimidating. Those traits grew at the same rate as his stubble. That morning, he was freshly shaven and looked more like the undergrad I used to know, convinced he could save the city one solved case after another like a string of sausages.

"Any word?" I asked.

Ellis shook his head, but put down his pen to look at me. For a moment, his eyes softened, worried, and I looked down at my cup. If I pretended to scrape some food from the side, I wouldn't have to look back up.

"You heard from him yesterday?" Ellis asked, even though we'd gone over this already. There must have been something bothering him about the timeline.

"Yes, he left a voicemail and texted. Both around noon," I repeated, curious about why that might be significant.

Ellis held out his hand, and for one baffled moment, I thought he wanted to hold mine. Then I dug my cell phone out, dropped it into his palm, and told him the passcode. He flipped the screen open, raising an eyebrow at my cheap choice, then accessed my messages. As he listened to his brother's voice, he closed his eyes, and I couldn't even guess at his emotions. I wasn't sure how far the bond of brotherly love went. After the recording played, he kept his eyes closed for a minute, and I shifted in my chair, trying to peek at his notes.

"It sounds more like a date than a meeting." His tone was matter-of-fact rather than accusatory, and I knew that he was switching into investigator mode. "Were you romantically involved?"

"Ellis—" My old friend raised his hand to cut me off.

"It's okay, Kathleen. I just want to find my brother."

I marveled at Ellis's ability to compartmentalize. "It was a meeting. As far as I know," I added.

"I asked you to leave The Skyview to me, but I know you haven't. What progress? Any ideas who killed the kid?"

"You think there's a link?" I did too, of course, but wanted verification. I didn't know Lars very well, and he could have been involved in any number of shady businesses. Would the Dekkers be receiving a call for ransom? Until we had confirmation, Ellis and I both refused to admit that the gunshots might mean Lars was dead.

"From what I could tell, he was rolling pretty deep. Thousands of dollars every night. He could be in debt."

I chuckled at the thought of a Dekker being in debt, then checked myself at Ellis's expression. "Ellis, seriously, there's no way he went through millions of inheritance dollars playing cards with friends."

"Partial inheritance. We don't get everything until our parents are both dearly departed."

I shrugged. They still had plenty, though only the size and location of Ellis's apartment hinted at his wealth. Dishes were rinsed but piled in the sink. The one piece of personalization was a signed Hank Aaron baseball in an acrylic container. And even that was on top of the refrigerator, collecting dust.

"He didn't seem like an addict is all I'm saying. We only played one hand, but he was good-natured about losing. Mr. Manners, whatsit, Glenn Dalton, was peeved. He could have known that Ernesto was staking the deck, but my gut says he didn't like being shown up by a newcomer. And a woman to boot."

I paused for a moment to thank my lucky stars that The Skyview had honored my chips—not the ones I had won since that hand was deemed inadmissible, but my original ten grand. It was now safely earning .01% interest in a savings account.

"Something doesn't sit right," Ellis said. "If the dealer was cheating for players, maybe he was cheating on my brother's behalf. Lars could have asked Ernesto to let you in on the deal."

It wasn't that far of a stretch except why would Ernesto put his neck out for Lars rather than be grateful to his cousin Eva for the job? And why would both Ernesto and Lars cheat for me? I idly flipped through *The New York Times*, barely registering the election coverage and prediction that Bill de Blasio would become our new mayor. Voting was one of the few occasions when I'd unearth my real I.D. from my mattress.

"Eva and Ernesto seemed close," I said. "Affectionate with each other. Would he risk losing that relationship?"

"Other theories."

It wasn't a question, but the beginning of another brainstorming session. He jotted his own gambling debt idea down, and I tried to think about whether I had noticed anything unusual during the past few days. What hadn't been unusual would have been an easier question, but not as useful.

"V.P. threatened me," I finally offered. "He doesn't want Meeza mixed up in my life."

Ellis wrote down "V. P.—Warning?" and waited to see if I had anything to add.

"Do I need to go down to the station, make this interview official?"

Dread mixed unpleasantly with the coffee and toast in my stomach, but I didn't want to make Ellis's life more difficult. He rose and rinsed his cup out in the sink. As if inspired by my earlier inspection of his kitchen, he started loading everything into the dishwasher, and I envied the luxury of having a robot clean my plates. Even if I wanted to dip into my savings, there was no room for one in my tiny studio space. *A new drying rack*, I mused, humoring myself to avoid pitying myself. I could spare ten bucks with a ten-grand emergency fund. I hadn't liked the circumstances under which I'd been awarded my monetary bonus, but I would take it. There was always the possibility that I would need to leave the country in a hurry.

Ellis's T-shirt slid up, revealing a pale stomach and blonde hairs leading into his jeans. I may have been staring when he spun toward me, so I turned my attention back to the newspaper. The words didn't make sense at first, but eventually I zeroed in on a headline about gay marriage being passed in Illinois.

"I'm off the Skyview case," Ellis said to my profile, pushing his glasses up the bridge of his nose. "As of 0600 this morning when I called the sergeant at home with questions. He doesn't think I can be objective. I'm always objective."

He had always been objective, true, but I had to side with the sergeant on this one. Which is why I found myself choking on coffee when Ellis said that he wanted to work with me instead. I was shaking my head, but coughing too hard to verbally refuse him. When I stopped, I noticed that I had splattered a few drops on page C2 and reached for a rag. That's when I saw the thin column about the Halloween parade explosion, *The Times* being too classy to call it the Drag Queen Disaster. The writer didn't have much new information, but he mentioned the hate mail that had been received by The Pink Parrot, a detail Big Mamma must have given to the press. She was clearly willing to get help wherever she could find it. If reporters wanted to sniff around, that was fine by me. I held up the page to Ellis, and he nodded, ahead of me as always and not one to be side-tracked.

"For what it's worth, you're not objective either. You like him," Ellis began, using the ultra rational voice he had developed to debate classmates in our upper level criminology courses. I should have folded then and there, but instead I wasted ten minutes trying spur-of-the-moment responses to an argument he'd clearly mapped out before I woke up. In the end, he won not only because he's the better arguer but because working two big cases at once had left me drained, especially since I couldn't exactly ask Meeza to do surveillance on her own boyfriend. Ellis offered to speak with V.P. so that I could go to clown school. That sounded about right.

———

A trapeze artist dangled by his knees as I approached the Amateur Acrobatics Club, an outdoor space along the waterfront. He was a good thirty feet above the safety net, calling out advice to a timid-looking woman on the opposite platform. She was holding the bar in her hands, but shaking her head no.

"Up and away," the trapeze man shouted, swinging gently back and forth.

It was one of those fall days that make up for the dreary ones, but I wasn't feeling any more optimistic than yesterday. Blue, cloudless skies provided a backdrop for the small drama unfolding in front of me. The woman took a deep breath and jumped up, only to come thudding right back down to her platform, a little farther away from the edge if anything. Another expert crawled up the ladder to join her on the small space, and the original trapeze man somersaulted into the air to land with surprising force on the net. He flipped over the edge and onto his feet, grinning at me the entire time. What else could I do but clap?

He mock bowed and sauntered toward me, squinting pleasantly against the sun. His tan, ripped forearms were the kind you would want in front of you if hurling your body into the air. Apparently, the student was unmoved and going for another solo swing with her trainer's encouragement.

"You can lead a horse to water," the man said in greeting.

"But you can't make her defy death," I finished.

"What must we do today to get you into a harness?" he asked, used car salesman-style.

Pay me, I thought. "It looks like a lot of fun, but I'm actually more interested in juggling."

He slipped into a sweatshirt and pulled the hood over his shaved head. The school name was on the front, but "Amateur" was scratched out and replaced with "Awesome." I handed him a card with a fake name but a real number, and he wiped his hands off before grabbing a High Flyers postcard off a registration table and introducing himself.

"Simon Simpson," he said, putting his thumb by his name and telephone number. "Reporter?"

"P.I.," I said. It wasn't like me to announce my profession, but Ellis's desire to work with me had given me some confidence. Between him and Big Mamma, they would have me convinced I knew what I was doing.

The man tugged the strings on his sweatshirt until only his nose and eyes were showing. It was crisp out, but the sunshine made it feel warmer. I hadn't worn a jacket and figured Simon Simpson didn't need the hood. "This about the parade?" he asked.

"I want to talk to him. He's not a suspect."

"Who's not a suspect?"

I shrugged. He had me there. I didn't know the juggler's name or really anything other than the fact that he was male. That's kind of hard to disguise in spandex. The woman from the hotline tip had said he was startled when someone shoved him from behind. Then horrified. He hadn't been at the emergency room, so he must have recovered fast enough to run away from the flames.

"Figures," Simon said, puffing himself out even more. "Listen, I don't have to answer your questions, and I'd rather not get my buddy worked up any more than he has been. It was an accident. He feels terrible. End of story."

"Not crying your eyes out over the dead, I see."

"Why should I be? Now if someone died here, on my watch? Then I would be upset. Some strangers downtown, what difference does it make to me? No different than that punk kid killed in Queens yesterday, over buying some dope or something."

I was uneasy with Simon's nonchalant tone, and the word "punk" didn't sit well with me. I hadn't seen that story in the morning paper, but I didn't need to. I knew that story by heart. A few bad decisions, and game over at fifteen.

"Listen," I said, trying a different approach. "I'm working this case professionally, but one of the burn victims is a friend."

At that, Simon sighed and looked up toward the sky as if asking God why he had to put up with such harassment. When he looked back at me, I thought he was grinning again, although his mouth still wasn't visible.

"Fifteen minutes in the sky, fifteen minutes with my friend."

"What's his name," I countered.

"After."

I weighed the offer while watching the student come screaming down into the net. She bounced three times before crawling to the edge and ungracefully tumbling to the ground. She lay there for a moment catching her breath, and I wondered what deal she'd made for this torture. I hoped that it was better than mine.

———✦———

The metal ladder was surprisingly warm, and I quickened my climbing pace to reach the platform some forty feet in the air where Simon was already waiting for me. If the height had looked intimidating from the ground, now it looked downright catastrophic. I started shaking before Simon winked at me in what I assumed was meant to be encouragement, but the gesture seemed to be coming from a gaping tunnel to hell. Afraid of heights? Who, me? I wouldn't have named such a phobia on my long list of fears, but come to think of it the George Washington Bridge did give me the heebie-jeebies, and why was the platform moving?

"It's not moving, sugar. Vertigo?"

He winked again, and I swallowed, expecting a biting remark about his casually derogatory nickname—"I'm nobody's sugar, you glorified squirrel" or something—but instead gagged on my own spit and had to grip one of the poles to keep from falling. It dawned on me that Simon had been giving me instructions, but all I could hear was a faint buzzing noise. He put down his hood, and I could make out the words "swing and drop." Easy peasy.

Simon brought the bar toward me, placing my hands about six inches apart, and I had flashbacks to doing pull-ups at the police academy, not my strong suit even as a fit twenty-two-year-old. What if I couldn't hold my own body weight and skidded down the platform, bumping limbs and head along the way?

"You'll be fine. Leap out," Simon was saying and by his assertive albeit calm tone, he had already said that a few times. Not one to put off the inevitable, I tightened my hold and hopped into mid-air. There was a jolt in my shoulders as they adjusted to my body weight, but then I was soaring, cruising down then tilting toward the bright sky. I let out a whoop of delight as gravity pulled me back in the other direction. My bark of laughter almost drowned out the sound of something popping in the rigging, but not quite. I looked up in time to see the metal support beams cascading toward me.

CHAPTER NINETEEN

I let go out of instinct, and the bar that I had been holding followed me down. I curled myself into a ball, ignoring Simon's previous advice to always land on your rear. And in the fetal position, I plunged into the safety net. It bounced me right back into the debris, and I shuddered as something hit me hard in the elbow. The whole mess, myself included, bounced one more time, then settled.

When I opened my eyes, I could see Simon scurrying down the platform ladder, and I rolled over, cringing at the pain in my arm. I didn't want him to get away without a fight, so I crawled toward the edge of the net and tried to dismount one-handed. Someone stopped me, and I lashed out in my panic, grabbing whatever was nearest and hurling it at the man in front of me. He was holding up his hands in the universal sign of "I mean no harm." He didn't look especially trustworthy, though, his face covered in greasy purple paint with green rings around his eyes. When he spoke, I couldn't understand the words, but I could see that his tongue was forked, split in two down the middle.

He gestured for me to come toward him, and I scooted away. I could now see that Simon wasn't fleeing but instead running toward me, and my panic increased. One freak I could handle; I wasn't sure about two.

"Lady," Simon was shouting as he appeared at the net edge beside the snake man. "Are you alright?" He gestured for me to come toward him, too, and I shook my head, tightening my grip around what appeared at a glance to be a pulley. Dense enough to cause a head injury, that much I knew.

Simon grabbed the other man's shoulder, pulling him away from the net. The snake person threw up his hands in defeat and headed back into the office, stopping long enough to cast one last disparaging look my way, then slamming the door shut behind him.

"He was trying to help."

"Help what? Kill me?"

Simon chuckled, which is when my fear took a healthy step toward anger.

"Now it's funny when clients fall from the sky," I said, bringing myself again to the edge of the net and dangling my legs over the side. I didn't trust my elbow to hold my weight, but I didn't want to forfeit my makeshift weapon either. "Step back," I said, and Simon retreated a few yards, taking the opportunity to zip and tie his sweatshirt, hiding his mouth again. I dropped the pulley to the ground and used my good arm to maneuver myself awkwardly over the side, falling the last few feet and rolling when I hit the ground. I moaned and lifted myself, scooping up my weapon in the process.

Simon stopped chuckling when he saw the angle of my arm. He glanced at the debris on the net and started to backpedal, anxiety making his bluster less convincing than before. He might have been a little off, but he'd have to be full-on crackpot to take a potential lawsuit in stride.

"We've never had any trouble with our equipment before. And you're not a client, remember? This was *quid pro quo*. And you've already wasted five of your precious minutes," he said, gesturing toward the office window where I could see a greasy face peering at me through the window. "You ready for your chat?"

It didn't seem like the best idea given my injury and discombobulation, but when would I have another chance? The NYPD hadn't charged the juggler with anything, leaving him free to run whenever he pleased. And Ellis knew where I was. What was this job if not a series of calculated risks? I waved at the window with my unhurt arm and walked toward the matching plastic chairs in front, making a small stand by not going inside to be trapped. I guess the suspect must have approved of my compromise because I heard the door squeak open seconds later. He lowered himself beside me.

"Do I need a translator?" I asked, and he flicked his tongue at me suggestively. "Cute," I said, managing not to scream. "I bet the ladies are lined up around the block."

"Righ, and I'm marsssing in a leotard for girsss."

I couldn't tell if the hissing was for effect or a genuine lisp, but I was glad that I was able to understand him. He rubbed his face in a white towel, leaving uneven streaks of purple and green on his cheeks and forehead. They didn't compliment the acne, and I guessed his age to be early twenties, maybe even younger. He was small, and a well-timed shove could easily send him flying.

"Money's money," I said, but fine. He wasn't waiting around for women. It was apparent that the tongue split was new, still puffy from the surgery, and I guessed the procedure to be a thousand bucks, maybe more. Nothing compared to the elaborate cobra tattoo that circled his forearm, each scale precisely rendered, both fangs dripping blood. Three thousand at least.

When working undercover, the youngest Costa had gotten a six-inch gold and red dragon that set him back two grand. Of course, Nino was known for being taken in by swindlers. Eva got the whole family's share of common sense.

"I wouldn hur my own kin on purpossse."

"So it was an accident. Let's say, someone paid you to start a fire, create a page six story for the tabloids, not two corpses. A jury might understand that. Especially if you help me."

I glanced in Simon's direction. He was standing too far away to hear, but I had no doubt that his friend would repeat the entire conversation. Snake man was looking at him, too, and rubbing at a stubborn spot of makeup. There was a quarter-sized patch of irritated skin, two bumps rising on the corners. He picked at them until one started bleeding, then turned toward me. "I was pusssed."

"Let's say that's true then. Let's say someone shoved you from behind. You would turn to see who it was, right? You don't seem like a pushover to me."

"Ssso many disssquises. Ssso many masssks." He stood up, signaling that my time was up, then said without a trace of a speech problem: "After awhile, who can keep track of what's real and what's fantasy?"

⟞⟝

The emergency room visit was blessedly short, and I was free two hours later with my arm in a sling and my head in the clouds. It had taken two people to reset my partially dislocated elbow, and twice as many pain meds. I had treated myself to a cab ride and was looking forward to lying down on my office futon for the rest of the day. Of course, it wasn't the calm oasis I was expecting, but instead the battleground for one very pissed off assistant.

I had never seen Meeza mad before, and in my haze, I didn't recognize the signs at first: crossed arms, tapping foot, furrowed brow. Even her first words didn't clue me in, an overly polite inquiry as to my whereabouts. I mumbled something about the ER and sank down beside her on the couch. She leapt up as if I'd thrown water on her, and an idea clicked slowly into place.

"So now I'm a suspect," Meeza began, cutting me off before I could explain that V.P. had threatened me.

"Of course not. I trust you completely." While the words came out clearly, I felt as if I were shouting down a long hallway.

"Then you should trust Vincent. You introduced us, *aare bhagvaan*." I wanted to object to my role as matchmaker since that had certainly never been my intention, but Meeza was on a roll. "Years of old widows, barely adults with fuzz on their chins, a yeller, a taxidermist, a man who laughed so loudly at his own jokes that snot would dip out of his nose. Anyone would do, according to my family. Then finally, *finally*, I meet a real winner. Sweet to me, employed. Smile as cute as a—a damn cricket." She flushed when she swore, but kept going. "You know what I think? I think—I think you're no good at being a friend."

Meeza swallowed hard, and tears filled her doe-like eyes. I stood and tried to hug her, but black spots swam in my vision. My assistant wasn't having any of it anyway.

When she left, the office looked a lot bleaker. I dialed Ellis from the office landline and paced back and forth with not quite military precision, but an A for effort. I needed to stay awake. Three steps toward the window, three steps away. Deep breaths helped, but it seemed to take longer than usual for the detective to pick up. I could hear good-natured shouting in the background when he said "hello." I wondered how he was balancing his real caseload at the precinct with the pro bono work on his brother's disappearance.

"Discretion, thy name is Dekker."

"She'll recover."

"So you knew my sweet assistant would object to your interrogation methods, but still preceded to—what—key a few cars, drop some judge names, make a nuisance of yourself?"

My lucidity surprised me. Either the walking or irritation was working. Ellis didn't respond, and I did another office lap, reminding myself that he had lost a brother, not a date. I could be more sympathetic if I made an effort.

"How'd the interview with V.P. go?" I asked.

"What'd you find out?"

The change in subject made me feel as if something was being hidden from me, but I told him about my meeting with Simon and the juggler, Indigo Ivan according to the flyer he gave me as a parting gift. "Ol' Indigo is sticking with his story that someone pushed him. Claims everyone around him was wearing masks. But Simon's protective of his friend. Can you run a background check? Simon Simpson, his card says. Indigo wouldn't tell me his real name, but I'll see if I can find out anything from the parade registration."

When Ellis agreed to the background check without argument, I knew he was keeping something from me and said as much. After a pause, he started talking in a voice of practiced neutrality.

"When I went out to V.P.'s place, there were a dozen or so visible vehicles on the premises, ranging in value from a few hundred dollars to a few thousands."

I'd been to V.P.'s so-called car lot and knew the scene he was describing. "Jalopies, right." I'd driven my fair share of them.

"Yeah, but after poking around, I found a secret facility."

The VIP garage. I was familiar. V.P. kept his nicest stolen vehicles in an air-conditioned hanger of sorts. I'd been upgraded after I introduced him to Meeza. I felt queasy at the thought, and I sat down, waiting for Ellis to tell me something that I didn't already know.

"I recognized one of the cars."

"What do you mean?"

"There aren't too many Teslas on the road. And Lars's is that color and model. Silver, convertible."

"Tags?"

"Brand new. Michigan. V.P.'s fakes are better than ever."

I paused, wondering if Ellis was overreacting. I mean, there are plenty of wealthy Manhattanites who might have, ahem, lent V.P. their $100,000 car, right? And even if Ellis really had seen his brother's Tesla, what connection could there possibly be between Vincent Patel—small-time crook with big-time ambitions—and Lars Dekker—millionaire and playboy? I'm all for the mixing of classes, but how did these two even meet?

"Could V.P. have taken him for his car?" I ventured, shaking my head even as I made the suggestion.

Ellis paused again, and I closed my eyes. I couldn't stay awake much longer, but I wanted to know the details. "He didn't deny threatening you," Ellis said, quietly so that anyone around him wouldn't overhear. I could picture him glancing over his shoulder for eavesdroppers. "He seemed proud of it really. Ready to follow through."

"But I just met Lars," I objected, my face hot as I realized that I may have put someone else's life in danger. It wasn't the first time, but it was the first time since I'd left my undercover job. Even then, I only felt mildly guilty for putting people like the Costas in harm's way. They knew that they weren't pushing life insurance policies. But why had I let myself get attached to people in the real world? *But I like him,* I thought.

"But you like him," Ellis said. I hung up and dreamed of a car filled with snakes, their mouths dripping blood, their fangs smashing into the windows as they tried to escape.

CHAPTER TWENTY

I decided that the "No Loitering" sign didn't apply to pesky P.I.s, and I leaned against the dark windows of a dress shop featuring robot mannequins. Their silver faces were twisted into garish smiles, and I vowed never to wear the sweaters they advertised even if I could afford them. Which I probably couldn't considering that I was hardly a block away from the most expensive stretch of Fifth Avenue, sipping a lukewarm coffee and keeping my eye on the revolving doors across the street. Sure, it was a long shot that Sybil would be back to her gambling habits so soon after our traumatic night together, but I'd woken up at midnight, my internal clock disoriented by the pain meds. A stakeout beat rearranging my filing cabinet.

I'd donned the Kennedy S. Vanders wig to make it easier for the woman to recognize me. She wouldn't trust me, but fingers crossed, she wouldn't pepper spray me either. I'd tried calling her Winston & Winston lawyers as directed, but the assistants had taken messages then—just a hunch—threw them in the trash. One Tesla notwithstanding, it seemed unlikely that Ernesto's death and Lars's disappearance weren't linked somehow. I wasn't sure if I was waiting to speak to a suspect or a potential victim.

Ellis had promised to contact Lars's midtown garage, see if his car had been parked there lately. He would also try to get his hands on V.P.'s phone records, but I knew that would be a waste of time. V.P. used disposables, texting his new number to clients every couple of weeks. Meeza must have been too infatuated to question this unusual practice. Or perhaps I'd set a bad example. I didn't replace my phones monthly, but I'd had three sets of personal and business lines since she'd known me. They were my yearly birthday present to myself. What can I say? I know how to have a good time.

Luck was on my side for once, because around 2 A.M., Sybil came barreling out into the night. She had an unlit cigarette dangling from her lips, and I figured I could steal a few minutes of her time before she hailed a taxi. A gypsy cab honked at her, but she waved it away, then covered her lighter to block the wind. I forced myself not to sprint toward her, but instead, waited for traffic to clear before approaching. She took in my banged up arm, exhaling smoke in my direction. "I know your type," she said. "The looking for trouble type. Not my favorite."

"Nor mine," I said, stopping a few feet from her personal space. Sybil Sheridon had been easy to research. At twenty-five, she'd bought her first local television station in California, and by thirty-five, she was a media bigwig. One of *Forbes* Most Powerful Women in 2003 and 2004. Her bio since then was a little light, but there'd been rumors about an advisory position on Hillary Clinton's as yet unannounced presidential campaign. She'd been the least polished of anyone in the poker room, save the victim, but I expected her net worth and connections would give the others, well, a run for their money.

"I'm glad that's settled then. I won't be answering any of your questions, but you can stand here inhaling secondhand smoke if that's your bag."

"I want to find out what happened to Ernesto Belasco."

"Beats me, honey. Beats me." She sounded tough, but her eyes watered. This time when she exhaled, she turned to blow the smoke away from me. At this small victory, I took a step closer and could smell whiskey on her breath or seeping from her pours. She was drunk but coherent.

"You don't have to answer any questions. Tell me about him. Whatever you remember."

Sybil thought over this offer and must have decided that it was acceptable because she mentioned that she'd been a Sky-view member since it opened two years ago. *Right after Eva's wedding*, I thought. *What a honeymoon gift.* I pondered how the rich and famous found out about these exclusive places. Was there some sort of Listserv for new yacht parties and so on?

Ernesto had been there from the beginning, too, everyone's darling. "You go to some places, and the dealer's invisible. Communicates in hand gestures like a mime. It's okay, I guess, but Ernesto was endearing. Even while he was studying us—and oh sure, he studied us—he was quick to make jokes, compliments. That sort of thing. He's the one who brought in those birds."

"The parrotlets?"

"That's almost a question, Kennedy, or whoever."

"My apologies."

Sybil grunted in acknowledgment and lit another cigarette from the tip of the first one, gaining me at least two more minutes. "But yeah, parrotlets. Ernesto said the room was too drab, and hell, it was, you know? The rest of that place is shined with gold, but we get a what I call an 'any room.' I've seen worse, though." I resisted the urge to inquire where and instead let her finish. Her gambling habits weren't under investigation. "He took them right from Eva's office. She didn't mind. She doted on him."

This time I couldn't help myself and asked what she thought that Eva had meant when she screamed that it was her fault when Ernesto started convulsing. Sybil didn't say anything, and instead threw her half-smoked butt to the sidewalk. She ground it into the concrete then glanced up the street for a ride.

"You have to find the right game," she said, raising her hand at a distant set of "On Duty" lights shining from a taxi. It moved toward us, and she turned toward me. "I think you mean well, so I'll say that. You have to find the right game."

⟫

The Pink Parrot didn't open until noon, but Dolly met me down the street for breakfast. We sat on a park bench in the middle of a busy intersection, watching the pedestrians dodge traffic, making deals and dates on their cell phones. A seemingly schizophrenic man screamed about a gas leak and imminent deaths, but on closer inspection, a blinking bluetooth could be spotted in his right ear. It wasn't quiet, but it was my version of white noise.

My mind was wandering, trying to put together the pieces of two different cases, suspecting they might be linked after all, however ridiculous that had seemed at first. I'd gotten a few more hours of sleep the night before and was feeling alert, ready. If I were honest with myself, I'd admit that traditional detective work wasn't my forte. While I had been given the title of detective after my requisite time undercover, I'd never actually worked an NYPD case beside the Magrelli brothers. And in that scenario, I was more trying to prevent crimes than solve them. It was one of the quirks of law enforcement, titles being bestowed as rewards rather than signs of readiness. Come to think of it, perhaps that wasn't a quirk exclusive to police departments.

We were a pretty pair, Dolly and me. I'd foregone a disguise, knowing that my sling would make me memorable in any getup. Dolly was always one to make heads turn, but the people who turned for a second look today were more curious about the scabbing slash on his face. Parts of it were a sickly looking yellow, but I knew better than to mother him by suggesting another doctor's appointment and more antibiotics. Big Mamma would take care of him. She would take care of him now, and she would take care of him down the road. Even if he couldn't perform, he could bartend, keep the books maybe. He was smart, that much I knew. Would he want to continue in that vein? Or would it be too hard watching the others on stage?

I took a bite of my neglected bagel, cursing when a blob of cream cheese slid onto my shirt.

"Language," Dolly scolded mildly. His own bagel looked like it had been picked at by one of the circling pigeons. There was one mangy fellow that worried me, but so far, he hadn't gotten any closer than the others.

"Laundromats are my personal hell," I said, dabbing awkwardly at the spot. Dolly poured some water onto his napkin and did a better job.

"Thanks. Can we do this every day?"

"Bask in the sanctuary glow of exhaust and smog? You bet, sugar. When was the last time you left the city?"

The last time I left the city, I had been treed by a deranged spa owner. The great outdoors had never recommended themselves to me, and I said as much.

"I'm thinking of going home." He said it assertively enough that I knew he didn't mean for a vacation. "When this is over. When you do your spy shit and nail these fuckers."

"Language." My tone was light, but the thought of losing someone else made me ache. Maybe it was for the best, if Lars's disappearance was somehow connected to me. I pinched off some of my bread and threw it toward the diseased bird. He lunged at it, puffing up his feathers so that he looked more like some sort of tropical pet, at least temporarily. If I squinted, he wasn't so far removed from Eva's prized parrotlets, even if he was ten times their size. His white feathers were pretty if you ignored the red eyes and bald patches. "Can birds get mange?" I asked.

Dolly squeezed my knee. "I'd stay in touch."

"I know," I said, though I didn't believe him. If he was running away, he wouldn't want to be followed. No one ever does. But despite his warm and fuzzy memories of his family, I didn't buy that Dolly wanted to leave. He'd made a home here and was now being chased out.

I rose, dusting myself off as best as I could, then we walked toward the club without saying much. Outside, a big man in sunglasses and a suit greeted Dolly, opening the door for both of us.

"Hey, Earl," said Dolly, blowing the security guard a kiss. He nodded, but didn't respond in kind. All business, good at his job, only showing emotion if someone calls him a bouncer by mistake.

"Hey, Earl," I repeated. "I'm—" I hesitated, squashing my impulse to lie. "I'm investigating the explosion for Ms. Burstyn. Do you think I could ask you a few questions?"

Dolly stepped back out onto the street and removed a recording device from his bag. It was so new it shined, and I wasn't sure recording the conversation was a good idea. Ideal for a courtroom, but people get nervous when they know what they're saying is permanent. No chance to deny later. Correcting Dolly and embarrassing him wasn't an option, so instead I asked Earl if he minded.

"No, ma'am. Ms. Burstyn said whatever you need." He spoke into his walkie-talkie, requesting a replacement so that he could give me his full attention. We waited until a nearly identical man arrived, and I asked if I could interview him, too.

"This is my buddy. He just started. After all this." Earl gestured toward Spring Street, but I knew what he meant. I didn't have the right words either. We walked about half a block away and learned against a brick wall. Earl surveilled the streets, so I didn't have to for once.

"I'd like to focus on the weeks before the parade, but after the funeral invitation arrived," I said, confident that Big Mamma would have informed all her security personnel about the threats. "Did you have to break up any fights? Throw anyone out?"

"No, ma'am, it was calm, same as usual. We don't get a lot of scrappers here."

"Scrappers?"

"You know the type. Prowling for a fight or hanging with the boys and too drunk. We don't get a lot of bachelor parties. Bachelorettes, sure. Need an escort out before they puke on the audio equipment, sure. But fights? Not so much."

"Sounds like a good gig."

"It ain't bad. My buddy needs the work, too. Lucky this spot came open, you know?"

"Was someone fired?" I asked, a small antennae raising in my mind.

"No, Ms. Burstyn added some staff. Because of all this." He gestured again, and I forced myself not to look toward the traffic expecting to see anything helpful.

"What about amongst the staff? Anyone get mouthy?"

Earl glanced at Dolly as if for approval. He must have liked the response because he answered. "A few cat fights, excuse me, Miss Dolly."

"No, it's true, Earl. There's always some grumbling," Dolly said, squeezing the guard's pythonesque arm. "Who gets the better song, time slot, what have you."

"Anything more than that?" I asked.

"No, ma'am. I would notice, too."

"I bet you would. Thank you for your time."

Earl escorted us back to the front door where we ducked inside. I expected Big Mamma to be waiting for us, but the smattering of people on the main floor weren't familiar. There wasn't even a waiter in sight, and I questioned the appeal of The Pink Parrot without its stage performance. It was on the clean side for New York bars, but nothing special when not lit up with neon lights and bedazzled lip-synchers. Of course, noon on a Thursday isn't a peak business hour, the advertised $5 Special on Lychee Martinis notwithstanding. The customers sipping their drinks were as likely to be there for solidarity as for fruity concoctions. The Pink Parrot inspired loyalty.

"Hey, Dolly, I meant to ask you. How come you were singing live at the parade? Everyone else pretends with the tapes, right?"

"Oh sure, it's loads easier that way. Mamma's been thinking of putting together an album, so I've been practicing. A few of us have nice voices. You'd be surprised."

"You never cease to surprise me."

Dolly smiled at that, but he was lost in thought, worrying if he would still be allowed to sing on the tracks maybe. If the much anticipated recording session would even happen. If he'd be long gone by the time his friends recovered enough to quarrel over who got "Material Girl." My stomach knotted at that thought, and I ignored the pangs. We were here for Carlton Casborough, Bobbie's former side dish.

At the funeral, Carlton had been in full costume, but we found him in sweatpants and a tank top playing on the break room Xbox. It was easy to forget how young all these men were. Senator's son Carlton was self-possessed, though, and he didn't sulk or complain when we asked him to turn the game off. I noticed he saved his progress under username Studx10. Not exactly humble.

"You're here about Bobbie, right? That we were sleeping together." He took a packet of cigarettes out and tamped them down, never actually breaking the seal. I nodded, thinking maybe he could conduct his own interview. So far, so good. "I guess everyone knew. I thought we were so clever, never arriving or leaving together. Sometimes you just know, right? Like, we probably laughed differently or something."

"I hate to be blunt, Mr. Casborough—"

"Carl, please. Or at least Cassandra. Mr. Casborough is up on the Hill, voting on a measure to regulate drone usage in U.S.-occupied territories. I just killed a zombie with a purple mushroom."

"Carl, does your father know that you perform in drag?"

"Oh yeah, adds a little excitement to Papa's life, don't you think? It's a well-kept family secret. Like House of Borgia-level secrecy. If anyone found out, it'd be blackmail city."

I tried to think of how to ask my next question tactfully, but Carl saved me the effort. "Oh, it's fine, whatever. It's not a big deal that I'm gay, but this?" He put his hand on his lips and made a kissy face. "This would cause reelection problems. You don't see a lot of Senator sons working at car washes either, so whatever. It's all part of the grand illusion. Pop likes to talk about that photo of Mike Dukakis playing catch with his daughter. Playing catch? One toss, one photograph, let's get this show on the road."

It was easy to see why Bobbie had been attracted to this one. In comparison, Martin seemed juvenile with his woe-is-me teenager attitude. Of course, wasn't a woe-is-me attitude appropriate after losing your lover? Carl had yet to show any signs of grief, though he had been emotional enough at the funeral. In front of an audience.

When Aaron Kline walked in, he didn't look happy to see me. I'd called him a few times with the number Big Mamma had provided, but he'd yet to return the favor.

"You're a hard man to pin down," I said.

"You're the first person to accuse me of that," he replied, kissing Dolly on the temple then holding my friend's face between his palms. "Scars are distinguished, don't you think, Miss Stone?"

Scars, sure, but Dolly's forehead was ready for a horror movie, and I understood why Aaron was everyone's favorite. "Totally. Listen, Mr. Kline—"

He held up his hand, and I stopped. We both knew what I needed to ask. "Mostly, I want this all to be a nightmare. I wake up a week ago, and my family hasn't been torn apart."

"We all want that. Tell her the truth," Carl said.

Aaron picked up one of the Xbox controllers, fiddling with the buttons, but not really paying attention to the menu that appeared on the screen. "I was meeting Carl," he finally said, tossing the controller down. "He was late because of these stupid games."

It wasn't an alibi, but Carl confirmed this story. His guilt seemed real as he rushed to add that Bobbie was never going to leave Martin for him anyway.

"Tell me about Bobbie. Do you think that he was the intended target?" I asked.

"Bobbie wasn't happy, that's for sure."

"What makes you say that?" Dolly interjected. It was clear that he didn't agree, and I waited for Carl to make his argument.

"I hate to be the one to admit this, but he was in love with that little private school brat. And seventeen? Bobbie despaired that he was robbing the cradle, that he couldn't take him to bars. 'Bobbie,' I liked the scold him. '*You* aren't supposed to get into bars. You're nineteen, sweet cheeks.' But he was ready to settle down, make homemade pasta for a house full of kids in blazers."

Dolly shook his head, "He never said anything like that to me."

"Pillow talk," Carl said, then softened his tone. "Everyone's a little intimidated by you, D. You know how it is."

I turned in time to see Dolly's expression cloud, but even I knew it was true. I'd been to the club enough times to notice how the other performers sighed in Dolly's wake. Dolly was top-billed on the marquee, and he deserved it. This place might not work without him. Weren't they all a little nervous?

"But to answer your question," Carl continued, "no, I don't think Bobbie was the target. The seven of us were, the ones on the invitation. And a little bit of all of us blew up that night."

CHAPTER TWENTY-ONE

I wasn't sure I bought Carl and Aaron's story, and I had plenty of time to dissect it as the C train stalled underground. There was a lot of room for jealously in what looked more like a love square than a love triangle. Shakespeare would approve.

I glanced around the subway car, studying the riders, seeing if they'd share some insights on the human condition. A teenage girl was play slapping at her boyfriend as he tried to take her iPhone away. Their shrieks were fascinating the toddler beside them, who held his hands toward them but went ignored. His mother had her eyes closed, head resting against the acrylic window, "SUK IT" scratched into the surface. Across from me, a businessman read the *The Atlantic*, letting go of his wife's hand to turn the page. She had her head leaned back, too, completely trusting that he would make sure they got to their destination. And two older men who could have just been friends, but were clearly close, sat with their knees touching, debating the pros and cons of Latin American travel. "We could go to Machu Picchu," said one while his partner rolled his eyes. "You and what mule are going to drag me up that mountain?" A woman beside them grinned, but tried to hide it. Everyone eavesdrops in New York, but pretends not to hear anything. Could bouncer Earl be suffering from the same self-imposed amnesia? How likely was it that he hadn't noticed anything out of the ordinary?

"We apologize for the delay. There's been a track fire at Columbus Circle, and we'll be bypassing that station."

A collective, resigned sigh filled the aisle, and I figured I would be at least twenty minutes late. I was curious why Ellis had asked me to meet him at the precinct, seeing as we were working Ernesto Belasco's case on the sly. Could he have found something out about the parade explosion instead? A nagging voice told me to keep looking for the connection between the two, but people are killed every week in New York City. And Lars Dekker's disappearance suggested a motive other than bigotry.

The train eventually jerked into motion, and a few strangers locked eyes in relief, but I kept my gaze on the advertisements: Dr. Zizmor's perfect skin promises and a law firm specializing in no-contest divorces. When I disembarked, I told myself not to dismiss a possible link between the cases. Coincidences are for prom dresses and celebrity deaths. By the time I transferred to the crosstown bus, I had gone back to believing the two cases were separate, and I needed to keep them that way in my head. It was going to be a long day.

The 19th Precinct didn't feel like home, if that's what you're thinking. I had been thrown undercover a few months after the police academy, female volunteers being in short supply. And I had only lasted a few weeks after returning, barely long enough to train Marco Medina and collect my coffee mug.

Marco had never resented my detective status, but others made passive-aggressive remarks when I had ducked into my mandated therapy sessions. "Wish I had time to get my head shrunk." *Harharhar.*

Sammy Carter was working the front desk and didn't seem glad to see me, though he was friendlier than our last encounter when I had been suspected of a double homicide, or as I like to call those times, bygones. He buzzed me back with a few non-committal noises, and I wondered what he had done to be given desk responsibilities. It was hard to get pulled from the streets, so it must have been bad. I passed a few other familiar faces on my way past the cubicles, but no one spoke to me either, because they didn't recognize me or didn't want to. Ellis came out of his office as if on cue. No psychic connection; he'd been watching on the surveillance screens, impatient to show me something.

Off-duty there was still a sliver of softness to Ellis that reminded me of the ambitious but good-natured undergrad he'd once been. Here he was marble through and through. I'd seen him get angrier about cases, but never softer. His shirt-sleeves were rolled up, and since he was sweating, I started to sweat, too.

"We caught Ernesto Belasco's parents trying to flee the country. They were already past security in JFK when we stopped them."

"Fleeing? What makes you think that they were fleeing, not going on vacation? You think they'd hurt their own son?"

I thought about the unmarked cruiser that I had noticed outside their Bed-Stuy apartment and begrudgingly admitted that it might not have been a bad idea. We were walking rapidly through the labyrinthine hallways, headed for the observation room.

"Family does crazy things to your head. You've seen it. One day, there's joking over the mashed potatoes, the next day blood."

I doubted the Dekkers had ever sat down to mashed potatoes, but I didn't disagree with the sentiment. What I didn't know was how much he was thinking about the Belascos and how much he was thinking about his brother. What would he compromise to get him back? I hoped that I didn't have to find out.

"They didn't like that he was gay." I tried the motive out loud. Mr. Belasco had seemed slightly uncomfortable talking about his son's boyfriend, but then again, Bomber didn't strike me as a parent pleaser, even if he did run his own business. "How are you working this case again anyway?"

"Not working. Advising since I handled the first part of investigation."

I barely heard his answer, as I considered another motive for the Belascos and their niece Eva. "Maybe they were running away from Magrelli. If any family can turn potatoes to blood, it's that one."

Ellis stopped abruptly and turned me to face him. He ducked down until he was peering into my eyes with his translucent ones. I could see myself in his pupils, the smallest nesting doll in the set, the one with nothing inside.

"We all want every crime to be committed by the Big Bad Wolf. We could be the hunters bringing grandmas back to life and girls back to nightmare-less sleep. But this line of thinking will eat you alive. There are a lot of wolves, and a lot of sheep having a bad day, making one bad mistake then another to cover it up. I don't want to tell you what to do—"

"Are you sure? Because it sounds like a big roll of advice is about to come out of that pretty mouth of yours."

His mouth was close, and I licked my lips before I knew what I was doing. *And sometimes wolves wear sheep's clothing*, I thought.

Ellis straightened up, ran his hands through his cropped hair, and continued down the hallway, walking even faster than before. Who was running now?

Behind the observation glass, I could see Mr. and Mrs. Belasco holding hands and denying everything. I didn't recognize the detective across from them, but Ellis vouched for her. It was hard not to admire her interrogation style. While a lot of detectives will jump at the chance to show off their power, Detective Cowder was making inquiries in a tone that could only be described as polite: When did they buy their tickets? When did they decide to leave? Where were they going? Who was meeting them? She could have been Barbara Walters on a couch with Amy Adams talking about her latest movie role. The Belascos were reticent, shaking their heads often and giving one- or two-word answers. Nothing about their responses was screaming "innocent."

When Detective Cowder entered the observation room to consult with Ellis, I hung back. She glanced at me, then continued as if I weren't there. I stared at the seam in her gray suit jacket, a few stray threads suggesting that the pay hadn't improved much around here since I'd left.

"They're scared of something, that much is clear."

Or *someone*, I wanted to interject, but instead took a sip of my water and waited for Ellis's theory. It seemed obvious that Detective Cowder knew Ellis had continued his investigation unsanctioned. That would be the safe bet if your cop friend's brother went missing. They probably would have been disappointed in him if he'd given up.

"There's evidence to suggest that they didn't like the boyfriend. No photographs of him around anywhere. No sign of him paying his respects," Ellis said.

"Are you suggesting that—" she glanced down at her notes, "we look at Cassidy Bromowitz?"

"He has priors."

That was the first I'd heard that Bomber had a record, but I hadn't paid to run a background check. I figured any twenty-something who could get a commercial lease was clean. He must have been paying cash. A few greased palms here and there could go a long way. The question was, where would he get that kind of money? I thought about Ernesto cheating on behalf of players at The Skyview and asked myself if he could have been cheating for himself, as well, passing his winnings along. Sybil had said that Ernesto was studying them. As role models or marks?

"I'll keep an eye on him," Detective Cowder said of Bomber. She turned toward me suddenly, and I sat my glass back down on the table as if I'd been caught stealing. "What's your theory, Miss Stone?"

She used the same gentle voice that she had employed on the victim's parents, and I found myself flattered. I glanced at Ellis before pointing my little finger at the Big Bad Wolf. I couldn't help myself. "I'd say they have some new in-laws with more than a few misdemeanors in their files."

"If you mean Salvatore Magrelli, his record's cleaner than a pre-op table. But I get your drift." She flipped through her notes again, coming to some decision. "If the never-wrong Detective Decker and the much-maligned Kathleen Stone agree on the intimidation part at least, then intimidation it is. Let's see who's holding the gun, shall we?"

She snapped her notes closed and exited with heels clicking in a steady rhythm around the corner and back into the interrogation room. The Belascos barely glanced at her, looking tired and defeated. If I had to guess, I would say that they knew this day would come. They had seemed resigned to their son's friends stopping by their home unannounced and now they seemed resigned to being here.

This time, Detective Cowder didn't ask anything. Instead, she laid out our theory that someone was threatening to hurt them, then slid a blank sheet of paper and a pen across the table for them to write down a name.

"May I have my purse, please," asked Mrs. Belasco.

"Your personal affects will be returned when you tell us who's out to get you." Neither parent touched the paper in front of them. "Mrs. Belasco, we can protect you."

Mrs. Belasco shook her head, and tears pooled in her eyes. "My purse," she said again.

Mr. Belasco wrapped an arm around his wife's shoulder, pulling her toward him. It was the first time I thought it was strange that they were being questioned together. Most likely they weren't really suspects and part of me was relieved that the NYPD didn't think that they had killed their son. I preferred my Greek tragedies in the realm of mythology.

"We have something to show you," Mr. Belasco explained. "We got something in the mail."

Detective Cowder looked at the one-way mirror, and Ellis exited the room, presumably for the couple's belongings. Mrs. Belasco cried and Mr. Belasco held her while waiting for the bag. It arrived in a cadet's hands after ten minutes. Not bad for this precinct, I thought, glancing at the wall clock. 3:30 P.M. I'd been there an hour and was feeling light-headed, wishing I hadn't wasted my bagel with Dolly.

Mrs. Belasco reached for her brown leather purse, spilling the contents onto the aluminum table. Stray coins and gum wrappers tumbled to the floor while lipstick, keys, and a wallet remained safely in view. A pristine silver card nestled amongst the mess. I stood up to get a closer look, almost panting from the sudden strain on my heart. When Mrs. Belasco picked up the invitation and handed it to Detective Cowder, I couldn't make out the words, but I didn't need to. How do you R.S.V.P. to your own funeral?

The Belascos had been invited to attend their own memorial service at none other than St. Mark's Church in the Village, formal attire optional. Both the cruelty and tackiness were beyond belief. The card was sent to forensics, and the grieving parents were sent home with a police escort. Detective Cowder instructed them to call if they received any more threats. They barely acknowledged her advice, nodding at all the empty "sorry for your loss" pleasantries they received from others in the office. I couldn't say that I blamed them. While Detective Cowder's cadence was at least solicitous, most of the NYPD employees were numb to violence themselves, hardly registering loss unless it affected them directly. The mental walls were necessary, I knew, but they still looked ugly in the fluorescents.

Marco Medina managed to make the lighting seem moviestar worthy when he walked into view, but his bloodshot eyes and loose uniform made him look more like a spirit than a man. Maybe that would explain why I was so startled. Even when he waved at me, I thought for a moment that he was in my imagination, the flutters in my stomach caused from memory. Then he was crushing me into his chest, careful to avoid my bandaged arm, and saying that it was good to see me. I snapped back into reality, not sure I wasn't better off in the fantasy. I returned the embrace, feeling the ribs through the back of his shirt. The word *shell* popped into my mind, but I pushed it away. I said it was great to see him, and in a way, it was.

When I returned to the department following my undercover stint, Marco had been my trainee, ready to be embedded with the deadly Los Guardias gang. He was a distraction that soon grew into something more substantial, someone I could love under different circumstances. Maybe if I were a different person. Then again, it's not that hard to become someone else with a little practice.

"First day back?" I asked, embarrassed when the words came out garbled, like someone talking in a nearby room. I cleared my throat and glanced down. I rarely gave much thought to my shoes but now seemed as good a time as any, and I noted that the toes were scuffed and badly in need of a polish. Without knowing why, I tugged my sling down until it was covering more of my wrist.

"Not much on my desk, yet. Everyone's afraid to push me. You know how it goes."

I looked back up at him, recognizing the strain around his eyes. His self-imposed hiatus on a faraway beach had been a smart idea even if it didn't seem to have helped him. There's only so much palm trees can do. Getting out of an embedded assignment was a relief, of course, but it was accompanied with fear and guilt and a whole swamp of big, unwieldy emotions that the counselor would try to talk out of my former lover. Marco had always been reticent, so I didn't see those sessions going very well. Of course, I may or may not have threatened my own psychologist. He may or may not have reported me.

When Marco asked me what I was doing at the precinct, I explained that my two cases appeared to be linked by a hate group. Later that afternoon, I was going to be visiting their evil lair, a.k.a. a warehouse in Brooklyn. Waiting for the diagnostic report on the invitation was likely to take days, and I didn't have that kind of time. Unless I handcuffed Dolly to me, I couldn't protect him round the clock. Even then, I can't sniff out a bomb. No, I wanted whoever was responsible for these crimes behind bars as soon as possible. Preferably today.

Marco touched the wrist I had tried to hide and asked me if I needed any help. I shook my head, glancing behind me to make sure Ellis wasn't watching us. I had told him that I was going home to rest, but the lie had sounded worse than usual. We both knew that I favored a more boots-on-the-ground approach. Or penny loafers, whatever. "Be careful," Marco said.

"Of course." I was smart enough to know a trap when I saw one, right?

CHAPTER TWENTY-TWO

Indigo Ivan, our "I was pushed" juggler, had 11,000 Twitter followers and a website that featured his "family-friendly" rates. There was even a row of five-star reviews from happy customers: "Animal balloons, too?! Indigo can do it all. Our girls loved him!" His bio mentioned that he had performed with such illustrious groups as the Candy Apple Circus and Cincinnati's Spectacular Showstoppers. Meeza agreed with my assessment that he seemed legit, although her answers were terse. I'd been in the office for half an hour, and she had looked at me a grand total of once to make sure my arm was okay and to see if I needed anything. The cold shoulder wasn't her forte, but bless her, she was trying.

"He's on the parade registration list," she said, handing me a single photocopy with Indigo Ivan's name and email address highlighted.

"What's the world coming to when even the snakes aren't evil?"

Meeza continued to flip through the registration papers, looking for any anomalies. There were thousands of names, so I doubted that she would notice anything. She was in need of an excuse to ignore me and would have nosed through the phonebook if I bothered to keep one of those relics around. I knew that she wanted to be left alone, but I felt obligated to talk to her about Ellis's suspicions.

"Listen," I said, and she bristled. One word, and I had already gotten the tone wrong. "I'm sorry. I was worried about you. Am worried."

Meeza flipped to another page, using her finger to scroll down the list. The gesture reminded me of a child learning to read. She was smart, but had somehow managed to grow up in Queens with a certain amount of innocence still intact. I'd seen her marvel at being able to see a single star from our window if you craned your neck in the right uncomfortable angle.

"Maybe V.P.'s right, and this line of work is too dangerous for you. Is there something else you'd rather be doing?"

Meeza didn't say anything, probably not considering undergraduate classes dangerous. I could imagine her in a profusion of other careers, all better paid and more glamorous. She'd be a first-class travel agent. A museum docent? Maybe she really could enroll at NYU. I was working my way up to the main event and eased into it. "I don't know how often V.P. gets new merchandise, but he has a new car. It's Lars Dekker's."

My assistant finally looked at me, her wide eyes growing wider as she took in the implications of this fact. Her boyfriend had something to do with my client's disappearance. Of that much, I was sure, and I knew she was bright enough to share the same conclusion. She was also bright enough to ask the one question without a satisfying answer: "The license plates match?"

"The plate's new, probably fake, but listen—"

"No, I see. It's perfectly clear. In a city of, what is it now, eight million people, there can only be one of Lars Dekker's car. Does he drive a diamond-encrusted BMW? Or, I know, a stretch Hummer with his name spray-painted on the side."

She was stuffing files into her bag now, and I tried to explain that Teslas are pretty rare—coincidences rarer—but she didn't want to hear me.

"No, it makes sense, you don't need to explain it to me. Of course, there's one silver whatchamacallit in all of the land." She stopped suddenly, her eyes filling with tears, and for a moment, I thought she believed me. "Thank you for everything, Katya. *Kathleen*, I mean. After my client's satisfied that her son is attending his classes, I quit. You're right. There are other things I could be doing."

She finished her speech with a clear voice, but tears were rolling down her cheeks as she waved good-bye from the doorway. "You're welcome back any time," I called to her retreating frame. For the first time that I can remember, the new floor secretary actually noticed I was alive. She popped her gum in my direction and shook her head. We must have interrupted her concentration on Words with Friends. She glared at me then glared at the elevator as the doors dinged open.

Back in the office, I opened my closet and stared without really seeing the contents. My eyes were swimming, and it took me a moment to remember why I'd stopped by my office in the first place. I reached out to touch the Kate wig and thrift store dress that I had used to create newest Zeus Society member Kate Manning. Did hate or love create the most havoc in the world? The answer should be simple, a glance at history books showing us any number of genocides. And, yet, Medea didn't kill her children because she hated them, but because she loved her husband. "Medea wasn't real," I said aloud, yanking the ugly gray monstrosity off the rack and kicking off my shoes.

By the time I had reached the train station, sadness had given way to anger, and I wanted to hit the turnstile for not reading my MetroCard on the first try. If I could prove V.P.'s involvement, Meeza would be safe. Whether she would still be my friend was another story, but that could wait. Bashing in her boyfriend's head would have to wait, too, but I didn't plan on delaying that to-do list item for long.

Before approaching the warehouse, I straightened my scarf and formulated my cover story if I ran into anyone. There wasn't a Zeus Society meeting scheduled that day, but for all I knew, converts slept amongst the reels of pornography while visions of sugarplums and lynchings danced in their heads. My story was that my nephew's ex had reached out to me for comfort, and I didn't know how to respond. Were there scholarships for the Mount Olympus treatment camp? Marco's warning to be safe echoed in my head, sounding more meaningful than he probably meant, and I pushed that thought away for a later time, too. When next updating my resume, I should put "procrastinator on personal issues" under special skills. I can also drive a five-speed.

The warehouse looked about as inviting as I remembered, "Fuck This $hit" painted on the side in an array of colors and scripts. Perhaps it was the wrong time for nostalgia, but the graffiti evoked my earliest memories, the tagged subway cars pulling into our station at 103rd Street. There were so many names competing for attention that they blurred together into one monster ego. And I thought of the city that way, as well, a sort of dragon that let me pass unharmed past the neighborhood brownstones, skyscrapers in the distance. From our building's roof, we could see all the way to the Twin Towers, and I believed them to be the animal's nest. When I had asked my mom why there were two, she told me the dragon was waiting for a friend. I wasn't sure I wanted to meet another monster, but I grew up. I was ready now.

I tried knocking this time, banging my good hand against the sheet metal. It rattled, but summoned no beast. The pad-lock had been replaced, but I'd come prepared and pulled the bolt cutters from my bag. They were hard to maneuver one-armed, but getting creative with my knees, I managed to snip the small security chain. Inside, the film canisters greeted me, alien in their uniformity, such nondescript vessels for fantasies. Hallooing to make sure that I was as alone as I seemed to be, I crept toward the meeting room. It was deserted, folding chairs strewn and chalkboard wiped. Still bright enough to hurt my eyes. My heart thrilled at the sight of the proper open door in the back, and I scurried toward it.

"Leader Cronos," I called out one last time, smug when no sounds greeted me. I was already well inside the makeshift office that rivaled my own in lack of personality. Aside from a desk and a filing cabinet, there was no other furniture, not even a chair for sheep ready to be let into the flock. I went straight for the laptop, wanting to get a glimpse at the Excel sheet of targets that Agent Thornfield had mentioned.

In my undergraduate course on cybersecurity, I'd learned that most breaches are caused by carelessness. That is, pass-words are less likely to be hacked by geniuses in Prague than they are to be left lying around. The leader had done one better. His computer wasn't locked at all, and the desktop image of himself on a mountaintop could be ignored. The spreadsheet was as horrible as I had anticipated, rows of men and women with mysterious letters next to their names. "E" for eliminated, I speculated, shuddering. But no, there were too many. I took photos of each page with my phone, hoping that the resolution would be good enough to read later.

The smarter half of me knew that I should skedaddle, be satisfied with this information. The other half said "in for a dollar," and that chirpier voice was too hard to resist. The top drawer of the filing cabinet creaked as I pulled it open, and I paused, listening for any visitors. The warehouse was tomb quiet minus the occasional flapping of pigeons that had gotten trapped inside. The Zeus Society member files were thin, filled with basic contact information and hastily marked attendance records. "Kate Manning" didn't even warrant one, yet, nor did John Thornfield. The second drawer was more interesting, its files labeled with city names, a range from Los Angeles to Portland, Maine, with plenty of stops along the way. I yanked New York City from where it was nestled between Philadelphia and Boston, flipping it open to see photos of nearly every LGBT club in all five boroughs. Sure enough, among some other storefronts, there were Tongue and The Pink Parrot. Earl the security guard was standing in front of Big Mamma's famous venue, glaring at whoever was taking the photo. There was no date on the back, but it looked recent. I tucked it into my bag, not really caring if it were missed. Did I mention that I was angry now?

I moved along to the final drawer, which was less organized. An assortment of random papers, binder clips, and rubber bands. None of the contents looked promising, but I swept my hands through it anyway, pausing when I got to a familiar-looking piece of stationary—silver paper, crimson font, and a tiny black noose. My palms started sweating in anticipation, the nauseating thrill of concrete evidence. It was another funeral invitation, this one made out to eight rather than seven Pink Parrot employees. Taylor Soto had gotten a promotion, a bonafide A-lister, at least according to this group. He hadn't lived long enough to enjoy—or regret—his newfound notoriety. They must have known that he'd be marching in the parade, but how?

Before I could speculate on possible informants, a gunshot reverberated throughout the building, letting me know that I definitely wasn't alone anymore.

CHAPTER TWENTY-THREE

A voice repeated "in for a dollar" in my head, but it was less confident this time, more like a question, and I stuffed the invitation into my bag. If anyone saw me sneaking around, they probably wouldn't believe my cover story, but I wasn't about to let someone shoot me without at least trying. The only way out that I knew was back the way I came, and I tiptoed through the meeting room and into the storage space. Another gunshot rang out, and I ducked behind a row of films as the pigeons squawked from the rafters. If I peeked between the shelves, I could make out the silhouette of Leader Holt, his Winchester pointed up and away from his body. I couldn't tell what was happening until another shot was fired, followed by the thud of a bird hitting the concrete floor. Cronos Holt crouched down over it, and for a moment, it looked like he might caress the smashed head. Instead, he lifted the creature by its feet and flung it toward a far wall where it joined two of its brethren.

"'I hate that mann like the very Gates of Deeeath / who says one thing but hides another in his hearttt,'" Leader Holt said, enunciating each word slowly. I didn't remember that passage from my hasty reading of *The Iliad*, but I was willing to bet this was a favorite verse. He aimed his rifle back toward the ceiling, and another pigeon fell down beside him. "Come see, Miss Manning."

I guess it was too much to ask that this sociopath hadn't noticed me. The overhead lights made my body cast a long shadow on the concrete. I stood up and walked around the corner, keeping my eye on the muzzle of the gun. It was pointed at the ground, but I wasn't feeling comforted, especially when he began quoting again. His recitation took him awhile, and I had time to both recall how many pages I'd skimmed in freshman English and gather my wits.

"Much better than the Lord's prayer, don't you thiiink?"

"Beautiful, but nothing beats the Lord's Prayer in my book. Leader Holt, I'm so glad it's you," I said, pulling my bag in front of me and doing my best doe-eyed expression. Under the circumstances, acting like a deer wasn't the safest choice, but I thought vulnerable might get me further than vindictive. "The shots frightened me."

"This one's still breathing," Leader Holt said, ignoring my comment and motioning me to come even closer. I obeyed in time to watch the bird's chest expand once then stop. "They sayyy a pigeon is a type of dove, but a type isn't the same. No one's paying for wedding pigeons, are they?"

I shook my head, taking a step back. The leader swiveled the gun toward me, then rested the base on his upturned palms. "Walnut. Unadulterated walnut. It belonged to my grandfather."

He held it out to me, and I moved to take it, but he pulled it back toward his chest, holding the weapon as if it were a toddler. "I don't imagine you can kill much of anything with that busted arm."

"Probably not," I said, squashing the suicidal impulse to say "try me" instead. My list of people deserving some head smashing was growing. "Listen, I wanted to talk to you, but I understand if now's a bad time. We all need time to, um, decompress."

I pulled my cell phone from my jacket pocket as if to oh-so-casually check the time, but Cronos yanked it out of my hand. I had assumed by his laconic speaking tendencies that he wouldn't be quick, but I was wrong. He moved like a damn pit viper.

"I tell you what, Miss Manning. You do me a personal favor and kill one of these vermin for me—what do the city folks call them? You catch one of these *rats with wings*, and I'll let you make a phone call to whomever you like."

"How generous. A man of his word, I presume."

"Yes, ma'am." He held the rifle toward me again, and I reached to take it. I wasn't shocked when he snatched it back toward his chest, but my mood wasn't improving.

"I see what your word is worth, Mr. Holt."

"You see nothing. That's your problem. That's always the problem. Do you know the story of David and Goliath, Miss Manning? Of course you do. Everyone knows that one, but what about Nestor? Nestorrr." The name took longer when he repeated it, but still didn't sound familiar. Never to fear, Cronos was going to enlighten me. "Young Nestorrr came first, taking down his own giant to be a hero. It's one of my favorite stories. Later he became king."

"How about that?" I said, but was ignored.

"Not for being a hero, mind you. All his siblings were dead. Do you know the story?"

I shook my head, waiting for a moment when the leader might leave himself vulnerable to an attack. His slow enunciation was grating on my nerves as much as his misguided self-righteousness. "Siblings" took him particularly long to spit out.

"This great big warrior underestimated his opponent and was taken down by an upstart."

Leader Holt held his gun with one hand as he reached into his back pocket for a slingshot. When he held this out to me, I knew he wouldn't jerk it back, but part of me wanted him to be joking. I'd never actually used a slingshot before and doubted my beginner's luck would land me a poor man's dove.

"No wonder you were at the Halloween parade, Mr. Holt. You seem to like charades."

The leader shook his head, digging again into his back pocket to pull out three marbles. They were iridescent, pink and gray, as if chosen with their targets in mind. I slipped my arm sling off and pushed it into my bag, my fingers grazing the handle of the bolt cutters. A bad plan was better than no plan. Just call me Miss Glass Half-Full.

My elbow ached as I extended my arm slightly to hold the base of the slingshot. The doctor had said there was no risk of permanent damage if I took it easy for a few days. But that was like those Tylenol warnings, right? No more than six pills a day. More guidelines than rules, I'd always thought. It didn't help that my hands were shaking, but I managed to cradle the marble, then select a target. I picked the fattest bird I could see, hoping that his weight would slow him down. No dice. Even if my aim had been more accurate, the marble would have breezed right past him. We all move fast enough when our lives are in danger.

"I wasn't at the parade, Miss Manning. I don't go out of my way to expose myself to filth."

I'd been so focused on the task at hand that I'd forgotten about my attempt to gather information. Thankfully, Leader Holt had not.

"Just large quantities of porn." I didn't gesture behind me, but he knew what I meant, shaking his head again, bemused.

"For our campers, of course. I onllly watch enough to make sure they could make men or women commme back to their natural states."

I cringed at his enunciation of "come," not sure if the emphasis was intended or not, but uncomfortable either way.

"But you sent the funeral invitations to The Pink Parrot. No sense in denying that," I said, turning to meet his eyes.

The leader held out his hand for me to select a second marble, and I took it from him. This time I aimed quickly and released, trying not to overthink this rigged carnival game. The marble hit a rafter with a loud ping, but didn't do any damage to the animals.

"Yes, but you'll fiiind we rarely get our hands dirty. I'm a wealthy man, chapters in every major market, donations rolling in. Whyyy jeopardize my livelihood for a little bit of trash?"

He gestured toward the three dead birds in the corner, and I managed not to gag as I snatched the last marble and took aim again at the row of live pigeons. Why they returned to the scene of their attack was beyond me. Of course, they didn't have much to fear from me, as my third and final attempt flew wide. I dropped the slingshot and kicked it toward Cronos who *tsk tsked* my poor attitude, then bent down to retrieve his toy. I yanked the bolt cutters from my bag and knocked them against his rifle with as much force as I could muster one-handed. The gun flew out of my opponent's hands, and I kicked him hard in the chest. When he fell over, I crawled on top of him and held the bolt cutters awkwardly against his neck. He could have knocked it away easily it he tried, but perhaps he didn't know that. He made no motion to disentangle himself.

"Let me assure you. My hands have been dirty plenty of times. Cell phone. Please," I added.

I expected resistance, but the leader handed over my disposable phone with no complaints, and I leapt up to sprint toward the door. My dramatic exit was unnecessary since my opponent made no move to follow me or retrieve his weapon. Hunting practice was over.

⊶

Once outside, I cradled my aching arm while running toward the train station and, more importantly, crowds. It didn't take long to be back in civilization, and I ducked into the ninety-nine cent store to make that one phone call I had been so rudely denied. Agent Thornfield arrived faster than I would have believed possible. The DEA must have their own cars on call.

"This is one of the few stores in Texas that sells plastic flowers," he said by way of greeting.

I glanced down at the assortment of fake carnations and lilies, wondering who he needed them for. In my experience, these are only acceptable at memorials and grave sites. I hadn't visited my parents' cemetery since before being hired by the NYPD and thought about buying a bouquet. No, that wasn't a road I was ready to travel, yet.

"Good tip," I said instead, turning away. We walked outside, Agent Thornfield keeping an eye on my arm, then helping me get it back into the sling. I knew the pain wasn't bad enough for my elbow to be dislocated again, and I thanked God for small favors. "I'm not sure if Cronos Holt sees himself as David or Goliath or some guy named Nestor, but he's the hero of his story. Claims to be too wealthy to bother with violence."

"He's wealthy, sure enough. Cleared 2 million last year from speaking engagements alone."

"People hire this fruitcake? I hope they don't pay him by the hour."

Agent Thornfield spat on the ground, lost in thought for a moment.

"There doesn't seem to be a link between Cronos Holt and the Magrellis. I kind of wanted there to be, but there's not. I'm headed back into The Skyview this week."

"You don't think that your cover's been compromised?" I asked.

"You're the only one who's seen me here, and I'm betting— no pun intended—that Kennedy S. Vanders won't be reappearing for a little Texas Hold 'Em."

"No bet. Nor Lars Dekker. You know he's missing, right?"

"Yes, ma'am. And I think of all the little tails I've been chasing, that one might lead to my rat."

"You think he's been taken by the Magrellis?' That scenario had crossed my mind, too, but didn't add up unless Lars was in debt to The Skyview somehow. Had Eva lent him money?

Agent Thornfield touched the side of his nose and gestured toward a black Lincoln Town Car that had slid into view. "I've yet to meet a young investigator who doesn't have a reputation for chomping at the bit, so I won't bore you with old biddy gossip. I'm not much of a mother hen. I would have come on out here myself, too, based on nothing more than a wink and a promise. And most guys my age? We're looking to retire. Don't take a busted arm in stride so much anymore. I guess what I'm saying is—may I at least give you a ride home?"

I awkwardly rummaged in my bag for the invitation and held it out to him. "Not home. Cronos Holt's been sending these invitations, that much he admitted."

Agent Thornfield took the paper from me, but didn't show any emotion beyond a small shake of his head. "Cartels use this tactic, too. But you must know that."

"I know they follow through sometimes, too. Heads on railroad tracks, that sort of thing. I guess what I'm saying is that I've got my own rat to chase."

"I can respect that."

CHAPTER TWENTY-FOUR

Mr. Thornfield allowed my silence during the ride. I was lost in unpleasant memories, part of me hoping that the DEA agent was as capable as he seemed. Maybe he could take down the whole cartel without me having to get closer than a football field to any Magrelli ever again.

On my last night undercover, the Maritime Sapphire had slid into view like a ghost ship. I swear I could hear the bones of former captives rattling as the vessel docked and a dozen or so crew members worked to secure the chains. It was sleeting, but I was chilled for reasons entirely unrelated to the weather. When I had called the lieutenant about my lead on the Magrellis' cocaine shipment, I had expected to be brought in immediately. After all, I knew the ship name and port name. They could take it from there. The S.W.A.T. team would be fully outfitted—helmets, gas masks, bulletproof vests—and prepared for any scenario. But the lieutenant wanted me on site in case I was wrong.

What he really meant was that he wanted me on site in case I wasn't done, yet. In case I had to return to my filthy excuse for an apartment in the Bronx where I hadn't talked to anyone who actually cared about me in nearly two years. Some days, I didn't think that there was a "me" left anyway, so what did it matter? But standing on the cold, dark platform in nothing but some tight jeans and a fake leather jacket, I had been mad enough to care. My status as disposable to the NYPD had been made abundantly clear.

Frank Magrelli and his associate de Luca were nearby, but tucked in their luxury cars, a different one for every occasion. Salvatore was prowling, making sure his crate made it off first and into the waiting van. In the bad weather, the crew seemed to be having some problems stabilizing the ship, and the process was taking longer than usual. At least that's what Zanna told me. I'd never actually been present for an event this big before, and the machine guns were making me nervous. I recognized a few of Salvatore's enforcers, but not all of them. A small mistake, and I could end up an "unavoidable casualty." Not the dream obit I had in mind.

Zanna had managed to shake off her cocaine fit, and Nino and I had unchained her from the radiator. When she had woken up on the couch, she didn't remember telling her brother and me about Port Jefferson. And she didn't ask about the burns on her wrists and hands. By the way she was dragging on her cigarette, she wasn't feeling 100%. Her job was to discourage any prostitutes from making their way down to the docks until we were ready to leave. The ladies arrived early to stake their claims. There were a few favorites, men who were a little bit kinder than the rest or at least more generous. Most of the men were too tired by 5 A.M. to do much damage, but a few liked to hit as much as they liked to fuck. Those were left for the new girls, the ones who didn't know to arrive earlier for a little flirting, a little heckling. Or if they knew, they weren't allowed into the circle, yet.

My nickname might as well have been Tagalong since that's what I'd been doing since the first day I'd met Zanna. Usually she just wanted company, but tonight she'd slipped on her heaviest rings, and I knew she wanted an audience. If she'd directed her talents to Ultimate Fighting, she would have been a star by then. Or dead.

The first two women to arrive had a good hundred pounds on us, but this seemed to make Zanna happy. I did what I could to intervene for them, offering them twenty bucks apiece if they'd come back later.

"Such a pussy," Zanna had said, laughing and snatching the bills from my hand. The women weren't taking my bait anyway, and I didn't have any more.

"Oooh, this one's got a mouth on her, huh?" one of the women said to her friend. "Such a pretty mouth, too. She can suck my dick any time."

I should have been thinking about how to deescalate the situation, but instead I was thinking about buy and busts. Most undercover cops buy some weed, arrest the seller, then go home for beers and baseball. It's not the life of Riley and the suicide rates are high, but it bested being left to hang by your precinct. As far as I could tell, I wasn't going to get out of this night with anything less than a beating. I eyed the girls, picking the one with the blue lipstick as my target. She must have agreed with my choice because before Zanna had finished cursing out her friend, she'd dived into my gut and thrown me onto the ground.

I could feel gravel cutting into my jeans, and I thrust my hips up to get her off of me. She'd latched on like a boa constrictor, and her legs were stronger than seemed possible. I bucked back and forth, trying to throw her off to no avail. When her friend screamed, she was distracted, and I managed to slide out from underneath her. I jumped to my feet, kicking wildly at her legs, trying not to hurt her much while still appearing to fight. I was ready to defend myself as soon as she got up, but the sight of the other woman made me lose my breath. There was a gaping hole in her right cheek, and Zanna was wiping flesh off one of her rings.

"You want more, bitch," Zanna yelled, but her arm was caught mid-swing. Salvatore could have sent one of his minions, but this live wire was about to be his sister-in-law and he was a hands-on kind of guy. He sliced her cheek open before I even saw the knife.

If the Texan objected to dropping me off at a drag club, he didn't make a show of it. Instead he wished me well and told me to stay in touch. Earl stood in front of the door as I approached, and I suddenly became self-conscious of my pilled gray dress. The twenty-something snickering in front of me didn't help, and I was pretty sure I couldn't pay her to wear my white socks and black penny loafers with her 7 For All Mankind jeans.

"I.D.," Earl said without giving away his opinion on my ensemble. I handed him my Kate Manning Connecticut driver's license along with one of my rare, real business cards to which he raised a skeptical eyebrow and stared intently into my face. "For real?"

"For real," I said.

"Ms. Burstyn said you were good, but you're a piece of work." I took that as a compliment. As he opened the door for me, I paused to ask him if he'd seen anybody snooping around, taking photos in the last month or so. I doubted that Earl ever laughed, but his lips quirked a little. In answer, he gestured across the street where I turned in time to see a young man and woman pointing their phones toward me. I covered my face celebrity-style, but recovered quickly. They weren't interested in me, but in the flashing neon signs and flamingo guardians of the place. It was a sight, especially so far-removed from the brashness of Times Square. This was a tree-lined, high-end block. There was no doubt in my mind that Big Mamma had paid off some neighbors—if not some city officials—to keep this place rocking late into the night. Sometimes the party didn't even get started until midnight. Thankfully, it was earlier than that when I moseyed over to the bar, looking for Big Mamma and Dolly.

They were easy to spot near the garnishes, having a heated tête-à-tête. I couldn't hear what they were saying over the Pointer Sisters blasting from the speakers, but I doubted it was whether manzanilla or picholine olives went best with martinis. Big Mamma was poking a pink drink umbrella right into Dolly's chest. I'd never seen her so much as scowl at him, and I was alarmed. When I started toward them, my friend caught my eye and shook his head. I dropped onto the nearest barstool and didn't take my eyes off them, not even when the bartender brought me a daiquiri "courtesy of Earl, sugar." Rum-heavy and blue-tinged, it wasn't my taste, but the gesture was nice. Professional solidarity or something.

Dolly took the paper umbrella from his boss and slipped it behind his ear. He wasn't working tonight, that much was clear from his jeans and T-shirt, but he looked more sure of himself than he had that morning. His crew cut didn't do anything to hide the burn, but it was dark enough at The Pink Parrot for customers not to notice. They eyed him as they took their seats and eyed him as they left later. I eyed him as he walked toward me and claimed the barstool next to mine.

"What'd you do to deserve an Earl special?" he asked.

"I think I surprised him."

Dolly signaled to the bartender, who brought over a concoction that couldn't be called The Grover or The Cookie Monster. "I prefer my drinks without food dye."

"I was kind of betting on blueberries."

"Optimistic, but maybe you should take a break from gambling."

I pushed my drink away from me and pulled out the silver invitation, flattening it onto the granite bar. In other clubs, I would have been concerned about the paper getting sticky, but The Pink Parrot was don't-let-the-name-fool-you classy. Ms. Burstyn wouldn't have it any other way. Speaking of the boss lady, she was heading toward us, and I straightened up, determined not to let her intimidate me anymore. If she was bullying my friend, then she was messing with the wrong queen.

"Down girl," she called when she was near enough for us to hear. "I'll let Darío fill you in on his genius plans."

"She knows, Mamma. I told her this morning. This city's trying to kill me."

"You don't think you're like to be killed elsewhere? Miss Stone, I expect more sense from you."

That was news to me, but I picked up the invitation and handed it to her. "Hard to argue when the savages send calling cards."

There wasn't another empty seat in the vicinity, so Big Mamma squeezed herself between Dolly and me to let some customers get by. She smelled like gardenias despite having been at the club for at least twelve hours. "Never let them see you sweat" was her enviable motto. I thought she might be caving to Dolly's desire to head back to Florida, but when she spoke she started with Taylor Soto, the forgotten float victim. "Now, how in God's green earth did they know Taylor was being considered for a promotion?"

The record stopped, and for a moment, I thought the quiet was in my head, a reaction to the news that the busboy-turned-bartender was about to become a performer, maybe even a star. But no, the music really had stopped to let an emcee take the stage to introduce the evening's first floor show. Three men in matching long wigs waltzed out, trailing sequined boas behind them. Their hips moved from left to right in an exact rhythm. Olympic synchronized swimming teams had nothing on their precision. And they were mesmerizing. When they started their lip-synched routine to "I'm So Excited," the crowd hooted in delight. Big Mamma gestured to the one in the middle. "He got Taylor's spot."

I took a closer look at the performer, identifying him as Herman White despite the makeup. "But he was already a performer."

"Yeah, the other young man in the running got the hell out of Dodge after the explosion. Didn't even show up for his last paycheck. Too scared to even walk through the front door, poor love."

"So you never got an invitation like that one? With Taylor Soto included?"

"No. He wasn't in the lead, but he wanted it so bad. I don't know how anyone outside of this place could have known that I was even considering him."

"He could have been bragging about his promotion."

Big Mamma grunted at my theory, and I took that to mean "Maybe." I was ready to grunt, too, in frustration for leaving this victim out of my calculations. It seemed possible that he wasn't collateral damage after all.

"Everyone here has a pretty large social media following, including the waitstaff. Maybe the Zeus group found out that way? They keep tabs on all the LGBT clubs in the city. And beyond for that matter."

I thought about my photos of the spreadsheets, but decided not to show them. If I had been creeped out by the lists, how would the spreadsheets make them feel?

Big Mamma grunted again, then elaborated. "How 'bout we nail these bastards to the wall, convince Miss Dolly that chicks and dicks alike dig scars, and call it a day." She stepped forward to shout at the trio onstage. "Sing it, honeys!" They turned in perfect unison to beam at their patron saint. They blew kisses in my direction, too, seemingly less impressed by my disguise than Earl. It takes one to know one, I guess.

CHAPTER TWENTY-FIVE

All the other benches on the street were illuminated by streetlights, but I sat in semidarkness, under the one burned-out bulb. It would flicker an orange glow occasionally, and a few persistent bugs would try to kill themselves in the warmth. They didn't succeed. It was late, and I should have gone home. Instead I found myself staring into the windows of the unofficial gym of my former precinct. It was going on midnight, so there weren't that many cops inside. Those not on patrol were home with their families, watching *The Late Show* or snoring their beers off.

I may have passed for homeless. I'd pulled on a clean sweater, but my dress certainly wasn't smelling any better than it did when I put it on that afternoon. And with my sling, I couldn't even pretend that I was spontaneously interested in a month-long trial membership: "Join Now! A New You Awaits!" Sometimes I felt like an anomaly, reinventing myself every morning and sometimes again in the afternoon. Then again, weren't we all looking for that next reincarnation? The one that would once and for all make us glossy magazine happy.

That night I wasn't looking for my next self; I was looking for Marco Medina's. I couldn't be sure from my distance, but I thought that was him, putting all his efforts into clobbering a punching bag. I'd fought that enemy before, but the demon's there in the morning no matter the number of swings. The glow above me popped on for a moment, and I could see the outline of a moth. Its wings beat excitedly until the light went out again.

The facility was keycard entry, so I sat on my bench and watched my former lover fight with his conscience and fear. No one could accuse him of botching his undercover assignment. Two upper echelon gang leaders would never see the outside of Sing Sing again. A dozen more members arrested. If anyone could be called a Gotham City hero, it was him. His name had been left out of the papers to protect him, but he wouldn't have wanted the publicity anyway. I'd never met anyone as intent on self-sacrifice. He would have preferred if his punching bag hit back.

My plan was to vacate my spot long before he exited the building, but the city had a tendency to hypnotize me if I wasn't on guard against its powers. The streets weren't as busy as my morning breakfast with Dolly, but there were still people walking their dogs or scurrying home from late shifts. The corner deli was open, and there was a steady stream of customers ducking in for bottled waters and snacks. I watched a man rip open a packet of white, powdered doughnuts with his teeth and asked myself what I was doing there. I had reached the point of fatigue when my ears start to ring, and my costume needed to be washed or maybe burned.

Still I sat, mulling over what Big Mamma had told me. That Taylor Soto had wanted so badly to be a star. New York City may have been headed for a record-low annual murder rate, but that wouldn't matter to the twenty-one-year-old's parents. And there was no getting around it; I had to talk to them. Maybe that's what I was doing on that bench, holding off the morning.

When he finally exited the building, Marco looked straight at me without recognizing me, and I thought I would let him walk away. He'd lost weight since I'd seen him last, since he'd asked me to go away with him and I'd said no. Some part of me must have known that I wasn't going to chase philanderers my whole life, that running away had lost some of its appeal. But I hadn't said any of that, and I wished I had now that I was watching this hollowed-out version of Marco stare through me. I called his name because I couldn't help myself. He jumped as if he'd heard a gunshot.

"Checking up on me?" he said, and we both pretended not to notice his reaction. He sat down, and I wasn't sure who was more pungent. My eau d'fish was giving his workout some competition.

"Something like that."

He leaned his head on the back of the bench. I worried about when he'd slept last. It hadn't been restful based on the dark circles under his eyes. He'd let his hair grow back out and was clean-shaven. There was none of the bravado that his undercover persona had flaunted. He looked far removed from gang life despite the Los Guardias brand on his forearm. I reached out to trace the keloid that had formed after they'd seared his flesh. Marco tensed, then let me touch the smooth, raised surfaces.

"Coat hanger and a lighter, can you believe that?"

I shook my head. I'd been imagining something more elaborate to make such an ugly mark. The L and G were somewhat legible, but only if you knew what to look for. Would Dolly's face look like this?

"Like cocoons," I said, rubbing the tunnel of the L.

"No butterflies are going to emerge from here, trust me."
He looked at me, and I froze, my finger hovering above his
skin. I suddenly knew why I'd come, to resurrect ghosts,
and I could feel my face flush as Marco laced his fingers in
mine and squeezed. But he was in no position to give me
any comfort.

"Moths, maybe. I've always liked them better anyway, not
flaunting their colors around like big business bugs." I gestured
above us, but the light had gone out entirely. The moth had
probably moved on to a livelier target.

Marco didn't respond, and I squeezed his fingers back. He
was looking at me like his old mentor, not his lover, and I
understood. He wanted me to guide him through acclimating
to the real world again, but who was I to give advice on that?
I'd all but erased myself and was slowly building a person
again, ashes up.

"This case. Both cases," I said, not ready to think about what I
could or couldn't give Marco. "The motivation is stumping me."

"What you got?"

"A bunch of sad parents." The Giabellas at the memorial
service, the Belascos in their plastic-protected living room,
and now the Sotos. I didn't want to face any more grief of that
magnitude. If I didn't go home, I wouldn't have to wake up
and take the train to the Lower East Side where Mr. and Mrs.
Soto would pretend to be okay with answering my painful
questions.

"What else?" Marco prompted.

"We wretched men / live on to bear such torments," I said. I
stared at Marco, wondering not for the first time what eye color
was listed on his driver's license, his real one. In our little pool
of darkness, his irises looked black, and I was sure that mine
did, too. "This hate group and its leader with a god complex.
The guy keeps quoting *The Iliad* to me, and all I can remember

from freshman English is 'We wretched men / live on to bear such torments.'"

"I'm not a poet, and I could have told you that."

"But if the group profits from their sick conversion programs, why would they kill potential clients?"

Marco was silent for awhile, letting me come to my own conclusions. When he spoke, his voice was softer, and I knew the complicated emotions of speaking about time undercover. "On the other side—" he began, then stopped.

I knew that he had been seeing someone, that he had cared about her. I could even imagine what it was like for her, rising one morning to find out that her boyfriend had vanished. When the community put two and two together, they'd realize she'd been dating a snitch. I hated to think about what would happen. The best she could hope for was ostracization. Would Marco try to contact her from out here? That would be suicidal. I'd left my fake friend Zanna in better shape, at least, protected by her family. It was hard for me to rustle up any sympathy for her anyway. I'd seen people twisted by poverty, but Zanna was always vicious if even half the stories were true.

"On the other side," Marco said, pausing again. "There was this guy everyone called Cigarillo because he chain smoked them. Swagger like you wouldn't believe. Girls flocked to him. A new one every month. He'd leave them, then call them 'bitches' or 'crazy' or both. I knew some of them, and they were decent girls. A few with tempers maybe, but when you live in that way—well, there's nowhere for the anger to go."

"Not crazy," I said.

"Not crazy," he repeated.

I knew he was warning me against insanity as a motive. Sure, your serial killers are out there, but Marco might as well have been saying, "Repeat after me: Victims are more likely to know their murderers."

"Let me see you home," he said.

I shook my head and stood up, expecting him to do the same. Instead, he leaned back on the bench again and closed his eyes.

"I don't think you can sleep here," I said, trying to keep my tone light, but my anxiety was apparent.

"I don't think I can sleep anywhere anymore."

When I'd first moved back into my real apartment, every sound in the alley behind my building jerked me awake. Once, I woke to what I swore was a man in the corner of the room. Then my eyes adjusted, and I could tell the shadow was created by construction lights on the George Washington Bridge. Still, I'd opened my nightstand and checked the chambers of my Smith & Wesson. Why hadn't I anticipated that Marco would have the same fears? I guess he'd always seemed invincible to me, an example of dedication to the force.

I watched him rise slowly and look toward the subway station. I made a motion to walk in that direction, but he turned back toward the gym entrance instead. He walked inside without looking at me again. No one had claimed his spot at the punching bag, and he crouched defensively in front. In my mind, I could hear the steady beat of his fists hitting the leather the whole ride home.

CHAPTER TWENTY-SIX

B aby powder didn't completely soothe the rash that had spread across my chest, and I threw my gray hatemonger dress into the garbage, silently praying that I hadn't brought home some new roommates. I didn't often consider leaving the city, but news of bedbug infestations could send me into a panic. I hadn't sat on a subway bench in months following a report that the wood provided safe havens for the little pests. To be safe, I yanked the trash bag out of the can and took it down the hall to the shoot. I wouldn't be needing that disguise anymore.

I'd slept restlessly the night before and not because I woke up multiple times to claw at my skin. Marco's warning that crazy wasn't a viable motive had stuck, so I moved on to ambition. But Taylor Soto's rival for a promotion had been at the movies the night of the parade with multiple witnesses to vouch for his alibi. Moreover, he seemed genuinely scared when I spoke to him on the phone that morning, tearing up at the very mention of Halloween.

"I know this sounds awful," he had said. "But I'm glad I wasn't there. I've never been so glad to be at a Wes Craven film in my life." That's when he started crying for real, and I thanked him for his time before getting off the phone. I knew in-person interviews lead to more accurate readings, but I felt pretty good about my instincts. The NYPD could fly out to Arizona if they wanted, but I wasn't booking a flight. My next task made that call seem like a merry-go-round, and I secured my Katya Lincoln brown bun wig to my head with a sigh. Dolly would say that there were better hairpieces in the Revolutionary War, but he wasn't here, and I wasn't telling him where I was headed.

I shook my black suit out of its dry cleaning bag and awkwardly slipped on the pants. A disguise wasn't necessary, but Katya was my P.I. getup, and I needed the confidence boost. The previous day's exertions had left me sore but not disabled. *Who's winning at life now*, I thought as I tucked in my blouse. I had to leave one jacket sleeve hanging loose, my busted arm resting in a sling underneath. The result was somewhat severe, but I was going to be as upfront as possible with Taylor Soto's parents. I hoped I wasn't too late to sort through the victim's belongings. Both his Twitter and Facebook accounts had been deleted—no "in memoriam" pages created—but I was keeping my fingers crossed that the Sotos hadn't cleaned out his room, yet.

When my personal cell rang, I glanced down at the caller ID, startled to see Lars's name. I almost dropped the phone in my excitement, but managed to gush that I was glad to hear from him before noticing the silence. "Hello?" I tried again. "Are you there?"

"Kathleen. I was going to leave a message," Lars said.

Relief flooded my system, but he sounded awkward. For a second, I wondered if he had disappeared to get away from me. That wouldn't account for the gunshots on Ellis's voicemail, so I squashed my self-doubts and asked if he was okay.

"Yes, fine. Everything's fine. Listen. You need to stop looking for me."

I let that sink in before responding. "Your brother's upset."

"I'm fine. Tell him I'm fine. Busy with work," he said, then hung up before I could ask about the gunshots.

What work, I thought. I would be lying if I didn't admit that I was embarrassed, considering that I had obviously misread Lars's romantic interest. Worried all the same, I dialed the other Dekker heir to relay my concerns.

"I'm not sure we should call in hostage negotiators."

Ellis was joking, so I knew that a weight had been lifted from him. His brother was alive. That didn't mean he wasn't in danger, and I tried to impress upon my audience the seriousness of the situation. "I told Meeza about Lars's car, and twenty-four hours later, I get this cryptic call."

"Detective Cowder will look into it. It's a non-priority now."

I guess hanging up on your audience was a Dekker family tradition. My exclusion had been pointed, but I didn't react. Ellis was probably right. The call was a good sign, and I should focus on the case actually paying me, considering Lars didn't seem too interested in the murder of Ernesto Belasco anymore. *Detective Cowder will look into it.*

The train ride to the Lower East Side gave me too much time to consider the loss of young lives occurring every day in the United States, often fueled by prejudice and its ugly cousin hate. I didn't want to visit another set of forlorn parents, be reminded that Ernesto was twenty-two, Taylor Soto twenty-one, and Bobbie Giabella nineteen. Kids who would never have called themselves kids while they were alive. Bobbie thought he was robbing the cradle by dating a seventeen-year-old. Taylor had hustled his way up the food chain in one short year, from busboy to bartender to almost-performer. Of course, there was only so far hustling could get you.

I introduced myself to Mrs. Soto through the intercom, noting that this family wasn't as freewheeling as the Belascos in terms of visitors. When I reached the second floor, Taylor's parents were waiting for me, eyes dry but sunken—small symbols of defeat.

"We were wondering when you'd come," Mr. Soto said, holding his hand out to shake my good one. I wasn't sure what to make of his remark, but guessed that Big Mamma had notified everyone involved that I would be investigating. "A week and change. Not bad," he added as he turned back into the apartment.

"I'm sorry for your loss," I began, my face warming not at how long it had taken me to visit them, but at the accusations I was there to make. The parents nodded, not as in sync as The Pink Parrot trio from the night before, but simpatico nonetheless. I doubted that I needed to interview them separately to get the same story. I didn't want to hear it twice anyway.

The entryway led directly into the kitchen to reveal a shoebox on the table. It had my name on it, and I backed away as if it could bite.

"We were betting on you rather than the cops. My brother's a cop," Mr. Soto said when he saw my reaction.

"It's true then," I asked, my voice catching on "true." I had known it would be, but was praying for some kind of misunderstanding, some sort of miracle. I was ready for the villains to be villains, for the victims to stay victims.

In answer, the mother lifted the lid on the box for me to look inside. No severed fingers, but something equally chilling—letterpress funeral invitations matching the one still in my bag. They were tied with a red ribbon, two or three death threats presented like a bouquet.

"But he wasn't sending them," I said, glancing first at the mother then the father. They were looking at each other, their eyes no longer dry but shining with something that looked like relief. They didn't have to carry this secret around anymore, let it pull them into an abyss.

"Please sit," the mother suggested, running water into two cups. She took one for herself and held the other out to me. I gripped the glass, but didn't drink, an image of Ernesto choking to death flashing in my mind. I shook my head to make it vanish, forcing myself not to confuse the boys. I'd been doing that for long enough. Still, I didn't touch the water.

"No," the mother continued, sitting down across from me and pulling the box toward her. She held it protectively, as if she knew I would take it with me when I left. And I would. "The first threat scared him, of course. It scared all of us. He talked about quitting, and we—well, we encouraged him to get a real job."

I doubted that they objected to the paychecks, only the lifestyle. Whether they objected to the late nights or the company, I would never know because I didn't ask.

"But then?" I prompted instead.

"I think wanting to quit gave him the idea. He had been talking about this promotion for months, promising us he was going to make big money, get health insurance, the works. But there was this other fellow up for the same position. His boss couldn't make up her mind."

I hoped that she would continue, but she didn't. She stared at her wallpaper, a green paisley that might have once looked inviting—maybe when Taylor was a boy—but was now flecked with grease stains. The Sotos had all but given up their son themselves, but I could travel the last few feet for them. "He set up the float, hoping to scare his rival, get him to leave The Pink Parrot."

"I don't think—he didn't mean to kill anyone," Mr. Soto said, reaching into his wallet to remove a receipt from Al's Hardware and Repairs. Taylor Soto's Mastercard has been charged for ammonium percholate, aluminum foil, and sulfur. $42.95 to kill Bobbie—and himself—by accident.

It should feel better to solve a case. Trumpets should blow, and strangers should cheer. At the very least, I shouldn't have to sit down on the bottom step of a brownstone to put my head between my knees. But there I was, being ignored by college students hustling to catch the bus. I'd never told anyone, not even my department-assignment psychologist, but I regretted joining the police department. I regretted joining the force, regretted going undercover, becoming a detective. Now I wasn't sure how to leave this lifestyle behind. When I quit the NYPD, I thought I might change careers along with identities, but a B.S. in Criminology didn't exactly lead to interviews in advertising or education. I was qualified to follow people around. I suppose I could look into nannying.

The hero complex I'd entertained was tainted, squashed really, by the horrors I'd witnessed, the lack of support I'd experienced. "More evidence" was like some sort of Sisyphean instruction. "Just one more time up the mountain, Kathleen. You can go home tomorrow. With more evidence." It was appropriate that I would be handing over this case to the department with a bow on top.

After the Maritime Sapphire was raided, I'd never seen Zanna again. I couldn't say for sure that she had a scar on her cheek, but I'd been on the receiving end of Salvatore Magrelli's knife a different time and my thigh still boasted the proof. The prostitutes had run off, of course, and Salvatore had suggested that I take my friend to the hospital.

"Fuck you," Zanna had shouted, and it was hard not to be at least a little amazed by her guts. I guess I was cowed enough for the both of us. Salvatore never raised his voice. Instead, he raised a finger to his lips, his whisper plenty terrifying.

"This is the kind of ruckus that must be avoided, you understand?"

He spoke as if he were sending his future sister-in-law to the principal's office, not the emergency room. She slumped down on the ground, and I knelt down beside her, praying that this would all be over soon. I'd said Port Jefferson, 4 A.M., and despite my anger at the NYPD, I knew that they would show. They wanted this drug lord as much as I did, if only for the good publicity. Salvatore loosened his silk tie, and I imagined that he was about to bind Zanna's wrists. Instead, he knelt down beside her with me and pressed the material to her wound. She whimpered, but didn't say anything else, the fight entirely gone out of her. I'd never actually seen Zanna give up on a fight before. The blood soaked through the silk.

Salvatore turned to walk away, then paused to look back at me.

"I need someone quiet," he said thoughtfully. I saw the red, flashing lights before he did.

Part of the reason I was letting myself meander down memory lane was that my next responsibility was calling Big Mamma and telling her that one of her own was a killer. Taylor Soto had planted explosive materials and pushed Indigo Ivan. A sloppy plan at best, but even if the materials hadn't caught fire, they would have been discovered eventually. Panic would have ensued either way. And that's all Taylor wanted. A little mayhem, and his rival hightails it home.

The call had to be placed despite my reservations, and I sat up like a big girl and smoothed the flyways that had slipped out of Vondya Vasiliev's perfect albeit homely creation.

"It was Taylor," I said when Big Mamma picked up, dispensing with niceties because they wouldn't help. I waited for a scream or at least a well-mannered "shit," but instead she waited on the details. I gave her everything I had, gripping the shoebox hard enough to crease the cardboard.

"And we don't have any recourse against the Zeus Clan of Holy Hatred?"

"You can lawyer up, accuse them of aggravated harassment in the second degree. They might claim the invites weren't intended as death threats, just prophesies."

"Right."

There was a pause long enough for me to think that I was about to be hung up on for the third time that day, but Big Mamma spoke again. "Thank you, Miss Stone. Send over a bill. You did good, kid."

I didn't feel good or much like a kid, but I somehow managed to stand up and take the 4 train up to my office. It was about as cheerful as the Sotos' grease-stained kitchen. It had only been a day since Meeza left, but the plants were drooping as if they knew they weren't going to make it under my care alone. I took out the mister and halfheartedly gave the leaves a few squirts. There was a small note scrawled in masking tape on the side: "Try talking to them." Meeza's girlish handwriting flipped a switch inside me, and I threw the plastic bottle against the wall hard enough to make a dent. Since that didn't do anything to alleviate my rage, I pulled out my cell. Lars Dekker might not be a priority for the NYPD, but Meeza Dasgupta was most certainly a priority to me. I found V.P.'s number and typed a message I'd sent countless times before: "Need ride. A.S.A.P."

CHAPTER TWENTY-SEVEN

Always a professional or at least not one to turn down a customer, V.P. responded quickly. A vehicle would be waiting for me on the corner of 77th and Third Avenue in half an hour. I spent a few minutes typing up my case notes and making arrangements to drop off the evidence I'd collected from Taylor Soto's parents. Since the murderer was dead, there was no rush, and I got the feeling that the precinct paperwork would languish for awhile. I wondered if they'd even hold a press conference, let the public know that the explosion wasn't an accident, but that the perpetrator wouldn't strike again. Since they couldn't take credit for solving the case, I doubted it.

There didn't seem to be much point in waiting around the office any longer, so I tossed my Katya Lincoln wig onto a mannequin head and bolted for the elevator. The floor secretary didn't look up as I stormed passed and started jabbing at the down button. If V.P. was responsible for Lars's disappearance, awkward phone call notwithstanding, I was going to find out. Then I was going to convince Meeza that she could do better. Better than V.P. and better than me, too. If I didn't want this job any longer, I couldn't expect her to want it either. Maybe Vondya needed someone to yell at suppliers for her. I'd be happy surrounded by all those possible lives. A bob from Toronto with an amateur interest in ethnology. A mohawk who ran her own dog walking business. The elevator doors dinged open before I could decide which identify I preferred, and I rode down to the street more or less as myself.

Finding your questionably legal rental car was always a bit of a crapshoot. There were usually telltale signs, though, like tinted windows and rusted bumpers. When he remembered, V.P. or one of his cronies would text you a make and model. Of course, when I turned the corner onto 77th, I spotted my ride immediately—an "eff you" in the form of a 2013 Lexus LS. Meeza's favorite. The classiness of the vehicle was diminished when I reached under the passenger side door to peel off the key. This was more of a duct tape rather than an access card kind of company.

I'd only been to the lot once, a trip that I now very much regretted since it threw my assistant into V.P.'s path. Beyond all belief, she'd been as struck with the car thief as he was with her. Even as I started the ignition, I thought I could smell her jasmine perfume mingling with the leather interior. It usually made me calm, but for this mission, I rolled down all the windows, crisp autumn air be damned.

There was plenty of afternoon traffic along the avenues. The stop and start motion allowed me time to gaze upon residences I could never afford, buildings with doormen bedecked like the queen's guard, tipping their hats to passersby. The pristine awnings boasted names like The St. Laurence and The Christopher, evoking bygones days when you could introduce yourself to strangers with a place name, instant pedigree. I'd like to believe that at least separate service entrances were a thing of the past, but I knew they weren't. Not here, and not even in the fancier parts of gentrified Brooklyn where low-income renters were expected to go around back while their high-income neighbors waltzed through the front doors. I grew up somewhere in the middle when there was still a middle to be had in the city. I'd taken out loans to pay for college, but my parents' life insurance policy had allowed me to negate them in one fell, awful swoop.

Eventually, the traffic eased, and I accelerated out of Manhattan and deep into Queens. When I got to the Lucky Day Pawnshop and Diner, I knew that I was getting close and crossed my fingers that my anger would get me through what was sure to be an uncomfortable interview at best. At worst, well, there wasn't much point in thinking about East River graves. At least I'd be laid to rest in home waters. Deciding that it was unwise to show any obvious weakness, I slipped my sling off and stuffed it into the glove compartment while waiting for a red light to change. I felt a twinge as I pulled on my jacket sleeve, but not unbearable pain. I could keep my hand in my jacket pocket to add some support.

The small, dirty Patel Industries sign was hard to spot, but I remembered the gravel driveway and pulled up to the locked gates. My arrival must have been expected because a bulky man sauntered out and waved me through. I pulled directly up to the doublewide trailer serving as the headquarters for this sketchy operation. The front door was rusted, and it looked like a cannon ball had gone through part of the siding. There was no one milling about, but I glanced up to spot the surveillance cameras and waved. Only two, how about that. Maybe V.P. should be more, not less, paranoid. I could give him some pointers.

The door creaked when I opened it, but my host didn't need the added warning. He was smiling at me over the top of his alligator boots, hands folded casually across his stomach.

The grin was the kicker, boyish and shy enough of slick that mothers and judges alike deemed him trustworthy. When I'd had dinner with Meeza's family, they had been delighted with everything from his entrepreneurial spirit to the daisies he'd handed over. He read as not a threat. Now that was a neat superpower.

"Miss Stone, what a pleasure," he began, all but salivating at what he must have deemed a victory. Why would I come to him unless ready to capitulate? Or at least negotiate. I knew I didn't have the upper hand, but I wasn't counting on a stacked deck. "I believe you know my friend Mr. Dekker."

V.P. gestured to an empty doorway, and my stomach dropped, imagining his victim tied up and beaten. Then Lars walked into view unharmed and sipping a glass of wine.

"Hello there. I was hoping to avoid a scene with my call, Kathleen." He ran his fingers through his hair, looking as sure of himself as he had at The Skyview. "Or do you prefer Kennedy? How about Kalida Sanchez?"

My undercover name was top secret, and I'd never told anyone on the outside. In case the neighborhood lines were bugged, I had even used code words when I called in tips via pay phones. My horror was apparent, and V.P. chuckled. I realized he'd laid down four kings to my bluff. *All in*, a voice in my head whispered. I was adult enough to know that wasn't good advice.

"You're working for V.P.," I said, swiveling toward my opponent fast enough to make my arm ache. I thrust my hand into my blazer pocket, and both men started.

"Hang on there. No weapons necessary, love," Lars said, shaking away the wine he'd spilled on his hand. With some effort, I swallowed down the urge to vomit at his term of endearment. I slipped my hand free and held it up, uneasy that the men had both assumed I was packing. I wasn't and hadn't been since Detective Ellis Dekker confiscated my Smith & Wesson. I'd done a halfhearted Google search on permits to carry in New York, but hadn't made it any further than the disclosures page. My delightful hosts didn't need to know about that shortcoming.

"This?" I asked, gesturing around the office with my good arm. "There's a head-sized hole in the side of this building, and the carpet smells like gangrene. V.P.'s running a two-bit operation that caters to thugs."

"No need to call yourself names," V.P. said. I leaned against the wall so that I could see them both. Lars was swirling his wine as if we were at the four- and five-star restaurants he usually frequented, and V.P. was scratching at an invisible spot on his lapel. I'd touched a nerve with one of them at least. He knew that his accommodations weren't winning any awards, and he wasn't happy about it.

"You know what I mean," I said.

"Yes, but do you?" Lars asked.

He took a sip from his glass, but kept his eyes on me. "Pinot Noir, Aubert Reuling Vineyard. 2006, I believe. $150 a bottle at most places, but Eva gives it to me for free."

"What a saint," I said.

"You'll catch on." He swirled the red liquid again and held it up to the light. "Would you like one?" When he laughed, I knew that he was thinking about poor Ernesto Belasco foaming at the mouth, and I crossed my arms in front of me, right cradling left. Would he pour it down my throat if I refused? Instead I didn't reply.

"She's a smart cookie, this one," V.P. added. "But not smart enough."

"Maybe not. We'll see," said Lars, taking a step toward me.

"I'm asking, why link yourself to this bottom feeder?" I said, not flinching at his approach and scrambling for time.

It dawned on me that the sounds on Ellis's voicemail were backfires, not gunshots. Lars had probably meant to leave a message, then hung up when one of V.P.'s cars started acting up.

"You're not thinking big enough, kitten. May I call you 'kitten'? The aliases are so tedious. We have mutual friends after all." I flushed thinking how disappointed his brother would be in both of us. He wasn't talking about his brother, though. "Salvatore—Mr. Magrelli to you, I believe—graciously offered me Ernesto's intended position after his, hmm, after his accident let's call it. The judge surely will. You know about that, don't you, kitten? The guilty traipsing off into the sunset while you go into hiding."

"I never knew you had such a flare for the dramatic," V.P. interrupted, seeming pleased with his companion's dialogue. If I had to describe their attitudes, I'd say smug, ready to put the whole kitty into their satin-lined pockets. Unfortunately, that kitty was me. My panic competed with curiosity, and I was desperate to know how my former assistant's boyfriend was connected to Magrelli.

"How long have you been shilling for a psychopath?"

"Should we compare company watches? Or can I take yours after they find your body?" V.P. asked.

"So this is it, you're saying? I'm about to meet my maker in a rusted-out trailer in the middle of nowhere Queens. My parents would be so proud."

"I wish," V.P. said, his grin dimming slightly. "But Mr. Magrelli thinks you have potential. Has been tracking you since the trial you managed to botch so magnificently."

I took my time in responding, desperately wanting V.P. to be lying, but suspecting that he wasn't. Plenty of times the thought had crossed my mind that I wasn't dead yet because Magrelli didn't want me to be.

"His brother's in prison for life," I finally said.

"And for that, he extends his most sincere gratitude. Not having to bother with that freeloader anymore? You're saving him millions of dollars a year."

It's true that the brothers hadn't been on good terms, Frank preferring the spoils to the wars. I wanted to sit down, sort through all these revelations, instead of focusing on the threats in front of me. If Salvatore Magrelli had been tracking me for years, I had been hiding for nothing. He probably had files on every person I'd ever hugged. I'd been worried that my connections had somehow put Lars in danger. Some joke. My concern reminded me of why I'd barged into this hellhole in the first place, and I thought maybe I could salvage something from this mess.

"What can I do to get Meeza out?" I said. I didn't know what I had to trade, but they could have it.

V.P. swung his boots off the desk and stood up. "Meeza has no part of this, you hear me? Not a damn penny's worth of knowledge."

His protectiveness almost made me feel sorry for him. Almost. Channeling my best Meeza impression, I clucked at him. "Oh *aare bhagvaan*. If you're in, so is she."

V.P. flushed, and he knew that it was true. He'd been saying it all along, just to me rather than himself. His affection for my friend might have been real, but so was her danger.

"I can help her, Vincent," I said, turning my back to Lars and hoping I wouldn't regret that move. I could hear him pouring himself a generous refill. "She can disappear, live her life somewhere friendly. Never see either of us again. You love her, right?"

"I can take care of her," he said.

"All I'm asking is that you consider it. You don't have to answer today." I hated thinking of my friend as an ace in the hole, but it appeared that I had some leverage. V.P. would know that I wasn't bluffing about this. If anyone had given serious thought and research into a fail-proof escape plan, it was me. Trying to disappear in the city had been a mistake, but Argentina? Argentina I could do.

"No deal," Lars said. "Salvatore thinks you can be flipped. He thinks you're halfway there already. Frustrated with the police department, not opposed to violence."

Magrelli's last words to me echoed in the mind, *I need someone quiet.* He'd watched me kick a woman while she was down. It wasn't too far of a stretch that I could be compromised in more ways. But that was Kalida Sanchez. Kathleen Stone was calling the shots now.

"Our dinner was his suggestion?" I asked, swiveling to look at Lars's light blue eyes. His pupils were pinpricks in the lights and reflected nothing.

"His idea of a joke, maybe, although one with a real goal. He wanted to know who killed Ernesto, and you were there, ready and willing. When he figured it out himself, I was off the hook."

Lars held his glass up to me in mock salute, letting the fluorescents shine through the puddle of red, then drained the contents. It seemed to be a sort of confession, a brag really, about taking the life of a potential rival. With Ernesto out of the way, he could step into the vacant role? It didn't add up, and I was amazed by Lars's nonchalance, a gambler through and through.

"Off the hook?" Surely Salvatore wouldn't be complacent about his recruit's murder. Was Lars really that much more of a prize than Ernesto? I suppose his connections were better than those of an immigrant's son, but Salvatore had always valued loyalty above all else.

"If he sees something in you besides this mutt I see in front of me, I could overlook some fleas, too. With his blessing, we could see where things go."

Lars leered at me, but it wasn't his expression as much as the phrase "with his blessing" that made me sick. Why was everyone always capitulating to this man? Even Zanna. Salvatore was scary, sure, but if Lacy "Big Mamma" Burstyn could stand up to the city's mafioso to open her businesses, I could say no to this not-so-tempting offer.

"No deal. Tell Salvatore—" and here I forced myself from saying something I'd pay for later. "Tell Salvatore I send my best wishes on a happy and healthy marriage. I hope no more of his in-laws get killed."

Of course fleeing crossed my mind. I'd never lived anywhere else, but I had a very expensive fake passport, and I'd researched enclaves in Latin American where no one would want to find me. Glacier towns inhabited by guides and adventurous tourists. I could take the cash from my last big-money case and bid adieu to sneaking through life. But it's hard to break those last few ties. And a small part of me still wanted to be that hero I'd set out to become. Maybe I couldn't cut the head off the snake, but I had no reservations about hacking away at the tail.

I stood in front of Ellis's building, weighing the need for an ally against the heartache I would inflict. If our positions were reversed, Ellis would have a speech prepared, know the right words to make this revelation sting less. On the way over, all I'd thought about was if I had enough cash to hide Meeza instead of myself and whether she would agree. How much would I have to explain? And how would she feel about year-round parkas? Sledding dogs? She was probably an animal person, right?

Ellis buzzed me up, and I blurted out his brother's involvement with a drug cartel as soon as I was inside. It wasn't my most eloquent moment. Even still, I hadn't counted on the way family clouds people's judgment. Hadn't Ellis warned me of this moment? Maybe he really was a prophet, but that didn't make his response sting any less.

"You're telling me that you solved two cases for the NYPD in one afternoon. Thank you for your service, Kathleen. The commendation—no *commendations*, pardon me—are in the mail."

Ellis was standing in his bare feet in the kitchen, a picture of relaxed domesticity. I wasn't fooled. The Ellis I knew wasn't sarcastic, so I took his tone as a bad sign.

"I don't know what Lars is doing for Magrelli, but it's lucrative enough to kill for. I think he took out Eva's cousin to have a shot."

"So first my brother's a possible lover and now he's a murderer? You used to take rejection better than this."

I massaged my aching arm, hoping the gesture might help other parts of me that hurt. It didn't. Instead I swallowed and tried to present my case logically. "He had opportunity and motive. He practically bragged about it to me."

"And you have this all on record? I can take some audio to Ellen right now."

"Ellen?"

"Detective Cowder. I can tell her, 'why don't you take it easy this week.' Kathleen Stone's got this one in the bag for us. Excuse me while I call my parents and break their damn hearts."

My old friend had never kicked me out of his apartment before, and I didn't know where to go when I wandered back out onto the streets. Would he convey the information I'd shared? I wasn't sure. Twenty-year-old Ellis would value justice above all else, even the bond of brotherly love. But that earlier version had long since disappeared. I walked north on Sixth Avenue, passing The Fountain, but not seeing Charlotte manning the counter. She'd probably been promoted to CEO, too busy now to get her hands stained by copy machines or customers. It seemed all but certain that the death threats, however upsetting, didn't actually mean their murderous intentions. The Zeus Society was sending them to cause pain, sure, but not physical pain. At least Mr. and Mrs. Belasco were safe. Some comfort.

I walked over to Union Square and sat down on the steps to watch the skateboarders and consider my options. A boy no more than ten tried to ride down a handrail, splaying himself on the sidewalk when he didn't quite make it. A friend chased down the now wayward board before it skidded into traffic. The kid seemed unfazed, hardly checking out his scraped knee before trying again. He landed on his back this time and rolled toward my feet. When I extended my good hand, he hopped up on his own. "Nah, lady, I got this." But he didn't. His third and fourth attempts were near neck breakers, and I started walking again before I was haunted by a child's spinal cord injury. I'd never considered my alter ego Keith to have a death wish, but I was reconsidering, given his penchant for a sport that seemed designed for concussions. Maybe Keith 2.0 could be into spoken word instead of skating.

I never intended to walk three miles to get to my office futon, but by the time I reached Central Park, I figured, what's the point in taking the train now. The sun had set, and the restaurants were full. Of my many sins, envy's not usually on the list, but with the people I cared about most in the world drifting (or already drifted) away, I couldn't help but stare at the happier-looking parties. A group of middle-aged women smiled at me through the glass at Rosie's Bar & Grille, and I turned away.

Somewhere during my undercover crash course, I'd read statistics about failed relationships for those attempting to blend into gangs or terrorist cells. I thought it wouldn't matter because I didn't have any relationships to speak of. Only a friendship with Ellis Decker that I assumed would last, however neglected. A couple of acquaintances that wouldn't look at me twice if I passed them on the streets. As far as I was concerned, I could stay embedded forever, provide endless information to the NYPD or maybe the FBI someday. Then reality set in, and I couldn't believe what I'd signed up for. Would Magrelli kill me now after all this time? Or would his so-called plans for me make him hold out a few more months? It was something of a relief to know that there was no point in hiding in the city anymore. The relief of a blister being sliced open, leaving raw, new skin exposed to the elements. It was what the Sotos were feeling tonight, too, staring at their son's empty bedroom, blaming themselves for his bad decision.

I looked up to see my office building in the distance. It was a mid-sized, glass-windowed monstrosity providing business spaces at discounted rates until the owners decided to remodel into condos. Grateful for small favors, the floor secretary had gone home for the night, and I unlocked my office door, trying not to think about never seeing Meeza there again.

I typed a few notes onto my computer then fell into a restless sleep. When I woke, the sky was turning from black to blue, and a large man was leaning over me, whistling a tune I didn't know.

CHAPTER TWENTY-EIGHT

DEA agents don't have to call up, apparently. They also move like ninjas even if 6'1" and a solid 250 pounds. I bolted upright, blinking when Thornfield flipped on the too bright overheads. They hummed faintly, bees waiting to attack.

"Good morning, sunshine."

"I wouldn't have pegged you for a morning person, Mr. Thornfield."

"Us Texas boys know how to get our work done before the armadillo crosses the highway."

"Excuse me?"

"Before it gets too hot. How are you doing with that? Burned, yet? John's fine, by the way. I ain't dead, yet."

I swung my legs to the front of the couch and stood up, flexing my elbow and noting that it moved more easily than yesterday. All in all, I didn't feel terrible for having lost all my friends and slept on a futon for fear of going home. I switched on a lamp and switched off the overheads. See? Kat Stone, Problem Solver.

"Water's boiling, if that's what you're asking."

John grunted, approving of my attempt to speak his language. I filled him in on Vincent Patel and Lars Dekker, the newest lackeys of kingpin pain-in-my-ass Salvatore Magrelli. When I explained that V.P. had been spying on me since he lent me my first car almost three years ago, John didn't seem stunned. How could I have missed this connection? It would make sense for the car dealer to work with the Magrelli crew. There wasn't anyone else in town running his brand of operation. And why keep your own stack of license plates if the service could be provided for you? I'd even asked myself repeatedly why V.P. had never been shut down, assuming he was crafty not well-connected. Maybe he was both, but I still wanted him as far away from Meeza as possible.

I'd unofficially registered with V.P. under a pseudonym, of course, but he'd figured out my real identity faster than anyone had before or after. Fingerprints, I had assumed at the time. He hadn't been interested in my fake license, but in the evidence left behind on the plastic. Even then, I didn't stress. What did it matter if he knew that I was a former cop? I clearly wasn't signing back up for the force anytime soon. The leap from Kathleen Stone to Kalida Sanchez was more difficult. I had testified anonymously at the trial, and the newspapers withheld my name. But if there were informants inside most criminal operations in the city, there were informants inside every precinct, as well. My name may have been V.P.'s entry fee into the bewitching world of freighter ships, AK-47s, and late night rendezvous with the nastiest ear-slicing, head-chopping so-called "businessmen" that Mexico, Colombia, and Venezuela have to recommend.

"But the Magrellis run mostly with the Mexican cartels, right?"

I was pretty sure John interrupted me to get the conversation back on track, since his intel was as good as mine if not better, more up-to-date. I was only partly aware that my rant had been verbalized. "Yes, as far as I was able to tell."

"The Skyview place seems clean. I would have bet my shirt that it was laundering money, but it's Eva's pet project. A try at goin' legit, maybe. Hottest game in town not withstanding."

"But her cousin was recruited."

"Sharp kid."

His voice softened almost imperceptibly, and I guessed that he liked Ernesto. That seemed to be the majority opinion about the victim except for his boss in Brooklyn, covering shifts after Ernesto was recruited by the Magrellis. No wonder Eva felt guilty about her cousin's death. She was the one always pushing her husband to include her family. Bomber wasn't to blame for Ernesto's sick days, after all. Why take twenty dollars an hour plus tips when promised more money than you can spend? His cheating at The Skyview indicated that he wasn't opposed to risks, especially since it didn't seem like he had any idea who I was. It was a test for new players, half-practical, half-practical joke. *He was always talented*, his mother had said.

"And you're saying Lars killed him," John said.

"I'm saying he had motive and opportunity," I replied, considering Ellis's reaction to the same information.

John grunted again, slapping his cowboy hat over his bald spot and turning toward the door. He would investigate, I was sure. When I'd called him, he didn't seem surprised to hear from me. DEA agents have a reputation for being kamikazes— guns and attitudes blazing at all times. But I had a feeling that John had caught his fair share of bad guys by being patient. Sometimes you have to turn over every rock, and there are always plenty of rocks. In Texas and New York alike.

I heard John address the floor secretary as "ma'am" and imagined her disdain as he tipped his hat. I needed to pick up my check from Big Mamma, but I wasn't looking forward to that errand. One of her own was a killer, accidentally or not. No, surely there was a better use of my time. I considered whether I could do anything right now for Meeza and tried to call her cell. When she didn't pick up, I left a vague message, counting on V.P. to have her phone bugged. Should I tell the Belascos that they didn't need to worry about the death threats? I figured the less they knew the better, but I couldn't stop myself from at least checking on them. They'd lost their son to greed.

The wind was whipping along Atlantic Avenue when Dolly and I got off the train in Bed-Stuy. He'd insisted on joining me when I called to delay my meeting with Big Mamma. I suppose I should have been grateful for the time together, but if he was going to leave, I wanted him to do it sooner rather than later. I'd never liked those sayings that begin "There are two types of people in the world," but I was definitely a ripping the Band-Aid off type of woman. I pulled my scarf over my Kathy Seasons wig, the one I'd been wearing when I first met Ernesto's parents. Vondya had taught me a sure-fire way to get hairpieces to stay in place, but I didn't want to deal with the fallout if this one got tangled beyond my combing abilities.

Dolly was wearing a jacket too light for the brisk November morning, and he shoved his hands into the pockets. On the ride over, he'd been unresponsive, and I hadn't pressed him. When we'd walked a block, he began sharing memories of Taylor Soto, warring with whether to consider him villainous or misguided.

"He made a drink for me. Called it the Jolene Ain't Got Nothing on Me. You know that Dolly Parton song? 'Jolene'? It's about a no-good, scheming husband stealer."

I nodded, though I wasn't sure I'd heard that tune before. Dolly fell silent again, and we approached the Belascos' block. The squad car was still parked outside, offering protection rather than surveillance now. I wasn't going to tell the department that an escort was unnecessary, but I was glad that it was. While I was focusing on that one bright spot, Dolly grabbed my arm and turned me toward him. "I want to apologize. I knew Taylor was ambitious. I should have known."

Dolly's skin was more scabbed than infected now, and I looked into his eyes, wondering how many men had lost their hearts in the view. My own less distinguished eyes narrowed, and I gripped him by the shoulders, ignoring the twinge in my elbow. "Everyone I've ever met is ambitious. They don't try to blow up their friends."

"Whatever you say, kitten." He tucked a loose strand of my hair back under the scarf.

When Dolly called me "kitten," it sounded like a purr, the way you'd call a beloved pet. How had Lars managed to make it sound like a slur? I hoped that I would never see him again, but that didn't seem likely. My best bet was that Magrelli didn't have a need for me at the moment, but he would. There had to be another way to get to him if not through Eva.

Our attention was pulled back to the squad car when it flashed its lights. My old classmate Sammy Carter stuck his head out the window. "If you two lovebirds are done, maybe come say hello, why dontcha. It's boring as shit out here."

I winced as I watched a mother pull her child to the other side of the street, dismayed by the NYPD's ability to make civilians distrust them in every zip code of every borough.

"Hey Sammy," I said. "Keep your pants on."

"Or don't, sugar," Dolly called, and Sammy cursed some more before opening the car door and waving us over.

"*Beats desk duty,* the sergeant said. Really? At least I can take a piss at the station. Shoot the shit. I took over at 6 A.M. and seen nothing. Not even lights. Why are you here anyway?"

I glanced at the Belascos' window and, sure enough, it was dark. My watch said 9, and it was possible that the couple was still sleeping. If anyone deserved a rest, it was them. My gut didn't agree with that assessment, and I forgot what Sammy had asked me as I jogged across the street and rang the buzzer.

"What the hell? You can't do that," Sammy yelled, then followed me, flipping off a car that screeched to a halt to avoid slamming into him.

"Just paying my respects."

No one answered the Belascos' apartment 15, so I tried the neighbor at 16. When a voice crackled "hello," I identified myself as the police, raising an eyebrow at my old colleague who said "Shit" again, then trailed me inside. Sammy wasn't the only one bored that morning, because Mrs. 16 wasn't hiding behind her security chain on this visit. She was standing in the hallway, ready to share her theories on where the Belascos might have gone, but I cut her off.

"Gone?" I asked.

"Yeah, they cleared out. The walls are thin, so I know they're not home. Haven't been since last night. Not a single toilet flush. The front door never opened, so I figure the aliens came for them. They feed on grief, you know. But they won't mind me—"

"Thank you so much for your time," I said, digging my lock picking kit out of my bag. I hoped my dismissal would send the housecoat-clad woman back into her own apartment, but instead she closed the door behind her and waited for a chance to snoop inside the Belascos' place. For all I knew, she had been waiting years for this moment. Who was I to disappoint her?

"I can't let you do that," Sammy said as I tried to jimmy the first pick into the opening, then replaced the tool with something smaller.

"Face the other way. We won't tell anyone. Will we?" Dolly winked at the neighbor who blushed.

"Not us," she said in response, trying to smooth the gray strands that had run away from her long French braid.

Despite having a top-of-the-line picking kit, deadbolt aficionado certainly isn't listed on my resume, and the audience wasn't helping. Sammy had given up on looking the other way, and I doubted this was the first time he'd skirted the law. No one gets assigned desk duty for months without some sort of screwup. The neighbor was practically humming with excitement, and only Dolly was giving me enough space to work. I was sweating by the time I heard the encouraging slide of cylinders, and I said a silent prayer that I wasn't leading my makeshift crew onto the scene of a double suicide.

The living room looked much as I remembered it, furniture still wrapped in plastic, family photos still smiling at me. There was more clutter this time, and as I walked into the kitchen, I was immediately greeted by the smell of ripe garbage. The trashcan was overflowing with a few papers and cans scattered onto the floor. Slow flies hovered around the lids sticky with food residue. Ernesto's bedroom hadn't been touched, but his parents' room was a wreck. Drawers were thrown open, hangers littered the floor, and pillows had been tossed haphazardly onto the bed.

"Shit," Sammy said for the tenth or so time. Then he added, "This wasn't on my watch. I got here at six. Nothing happened to the Belascos while I was outside, got it?"

"Nothing happened to the Belascos period," I said. It did look like the place had been ransacked, but unless kidnappers were in the habit of packing pajamas for their victims, the

Belascos had fled on their own. Down the fire escape by the looks of the open window, avoiding the patrol parked in front. Had their fear of the Zeus group gotten to them? It was possible, but they'd be safer under police protection. I glanced at Sammy, who had his hand on the holster of his gun, his own fear making him look for comfort somewhere. Maybe not. I gestured toward the open window, letting Sammy work out the details himself, and headed back toward the kitchen.

The neighbor was rifling through the trash, throwing packaging on the floor to get to the papers. "This is what they do on the cop shows," she said, holding up a Bank of America bill. She looked over the contents, but apparently didn't see anything interesting because she tossed it aside. I probably should have asked her to stop, but what could it hurt now. I picked up the bill myself, wondering if the Belascos skipped a funeral because of the cost rather than my original homophobia theory. The $135.67 balance was too low to cost them any sleep. A charge to The Fountain print shop, though? Now that was the kind of information to turn a lady's head.

⟶

While Sammy was busy trying to simultaneously distance himself from the missing parents ("Not my shift, not my shift") and me, I was beating myself up over missing the possibility of a copy cat funeral invitation. The death threats had been reported by all of the local papers, but they hadn't mentioned the specific business that would handle such vitriol. How had the Belascos found out? A better question might be, why had they sent themselves hate mail? They must have known that they would need an excuse to run away.

I could hear Sammy using my name while he filled in his superiors on the situation, but I wasn't about to wait around for paperwork. Dolly and I walked out of the Belascos' front door, leaving their neighbor happily helping herself to the dirty secrets she could find amidst the tossed-out leftovers. Detective Cowder was sure to arrive soon, and the possibility that Ellis might be with her caused me to walk a little faster than usual. I had accused his brother of murder with the ill-advised confidence of a rookie, and now the parents might be more involved than they had seemed.

"A bunch of sad parents," I had told Marco. While I hadn't found a newly minted Zeus Society membership card in their sock drawer, the Belascos must have talked to Leader Holt. He could have given them the death threat details, down to the black noose insignia. And that particular bird-killer, I knew where to find.

Sammy wasn't happy when I told him where we were headed, but he'd been instructed to stay put. When I suggested he send someone out to the warehouse, he mumbled something about never being taken at his word anymore. I hoped that whatever mess he had on his record didn't put us in danger, but I couldn't lose any time. The Belascos had already proven themselves to be a flight risk. I knew that Sammy would relay our destination to the detectives who arrived, but I called John Thornfield to update him as well. The drug connection seemed fainter and fainter, but I felt better knowing the veteran agent was aware of our intentions.

"So this is where the monsters dwell," Dolly said as we approached the warehouse. It had started to flurry, and my friend's teeth were chattering. He refused to turn back, even when I warned him that Leader Holt might try his voodoo brain power to turn him straight. Or shoot him for kicks. Dolly had insisted on taking his chances. And the Belascos? I wasn't sure if their hate extended beyond their immediate family, but I wasn't keen to find out. "I'm more concerned about what

Vondya is going to do when you get that pretty red hair wet," Dolly said.

I pulled my scarf more tightly around my head, not exactly nonchalant about Vondya myself. She had some Russian phrases that sounded a lot like curses and, come to think of it, my life hadn't been going as planned lately. For starters, I never wanted to see this entrance to hell again, but there we were—Orpheus and Eurydice or something. I wasn't sure who was who, but neither of us was stellar at following directions. Gods help us.

The padlock hadn't been replaced since yesterday, so I pulled open the door, wincing at the noise. Once inside, Dolly surveyed the canisters, but my eyes went to the pigeon corner. I was relieved to see that Leader Holt was tidy at least. There wasn't a single bloodstain in sight, and I hoped that we didn't find out where he kept the bodies. The warehouse was large, and Dolly suggested that we split up to cover the rooms more quickly. I'd seen that movie and didn't like the ending. Instead, I directed us toward the meeting room, which was more than empty. It was scrubbed clean. Not a single folding chair was left, and I could see my reflection in the linoleum. We hurried on to Holt's office, but it was empty, too. Even the desktop computer was gone. I yanked open the file cabinets to find a few paperclips and rubber bands left behind. Nothing useful.

"We're too late. It looks like everyone's jumped shipped, Belascos in tow," I said, picking up the empty trashcan to make sure I hadn't missed something. A written confession would be nice.

"Come on, there must be some untried nooks and crannies in this creepy ass place."

The only other room that I'd seen had been my own interrogation room when John Thornfield had grilled me on what little I knew. My information was better now, but I could almost feel the bad guys slipping away. Finding out that Taylor Soto had killed himself and Bobbie Giabella by accident had left me feeling lost. There was no justice to be found there. But maybe there was still some left for Ernesto. The last hand he'd dealt had been to me. *What a waste of talent*, I thought, using his mother's adjective. I could admit that I was slightly in awe of his ability to trick a room full of big spenders. No wonder Salvatore wanted him. I doubted Lars Dekker had half the skill.

Nobody was waiting inside the interrogation room, and I began to lose hope. Then the sound of muffled voices in the next room made my body freeze. I recovered in time to beat Dolly to the door. A Winchester rifle was aimed at my chest.

CHAPTER TWENTY-NINE

Shall I lead this time, Cronos?" I said. The Belascos cowered behind their leader, too frightened to appreciate my bravado. By Dolly's whispered "holy hell" behind me, I suspected that he wasn't impressed either.

"Who are you?" His slow speech made him sound like the caterpillar from *Alice in Wonderland*, and maybe we'd all fallen down the rabbit hole. Magic couldn't have made the situation worse.

"You told me that you don't like to get your hands dirty, so unless you want me to compliment your barrel, let's aim it elsewhere."

Leader Holt's confused expression smoothed. Apparently he hadn't menaced too many people lately—in person at least—because he introduced me to his company as Kate Manning, trespasser and sympathizer. I've never been prouder.

"Kate Manning?" Mrs. Belasco said. Her voice was raw as if she'd been shouting, and she took a step away from the leader. "No, these are Ernesto's friends. They came to visit us."

"Your neighbor in 16 says hello," I said. "She was worried when you disappeared last night."

Cronos made a frustrated sound and turned his head toward the Belascos without putting the gun down. "You swore no one would know you'd gone."

The rifle was about a foot away from my chest, but I was scared to grab it. The room was small for five people. Even if the bullet missed on its first pass, it might ricochet.

"Sally Ann is a busybody, but not too bright. I didn't think she'd notice."

"If Leader Holt convinced you to kill your son, Mrs. Belasco, your sentence might be more lenient," I said, too afraid to spare any pity for the underestimated neighbor.

"You're not a friend of Ernie's," she asked, her voice cracking at her son's nickname. Ernie and Bobbie, the saddest pair I could imagine. I hoped they found each other in the afterlife.

"No, I met him once. Right before he started choking. Don't believe the celebrity hype. Poison's not pretty."

At this Mrs. Belasco started to cry, and her husband pulled her toward him protectively. It was clear that however they felt about homosexuality in general, they hadn't hated their son. What could have pushed them to such extreme measures? *Who* was a better question.

"Be strong, Maria," Cronos said. "Don't say anything."

"Mrs. Belasco?" Dolly took a step toward the grieving mother, and Cronos swiveled the gun toward him. I didn't consciously decide to attack and was almost stunned when the bullet blasted through the ceiling, sheetrock raining down on all of us. The leader held onto his weapon, but it was still pointed at the ceiling. I was close enough to knee him in the groin. When his grip loosened, I yanked the Winchester toward me, and the momentum made me fall hard, smacking into the concrete floor. The gun may have been in my possession, but there wasn't much I could do with it. My elbow had snapped back out of place, and all I wanted to do was pass out. Luck was not on my side because Cronos recovered quickly and headed for me. I held the handle tight to my chest with my good arm, hoping I could survive a beating. Leader Holt only got in one weak punch before Mr. Belasco grabbed him and pulled him away.

"Enough," he said. "We appreciate your help, Cronos, but not like this."

Dolly had taken two more steps toward Mrs. Belasco and was now holding her while she sobbed. She didn't seem to mind his touch, and covered in dust, they looked like statues. Cronos couldn't have looked further from divine as he snarled at Mr. Belasco to let him go, ranting about gays being to blame for the downfall of the Greek empire. That explained the mystery of the group's name, at least.

"If you turn yourself in, you'll be safe," I said to the Belascos instead. From my position on the ground, I probably didn't seem very authoritative. The pain had brought along some clarity, and I thought I knew why the Belascos had killed their son. "At least for awhile. The Magrellis can't get to you inside."

The mother stopped crying, and I could almost see the resignation in her face. She thought she'd done right in keeping her son from a drug cartel. She thought a life under Salvatore Magrelli's thumb was a fate worse than death. Maybe she was right, though I doubted a jury would agree. I wanted to know what she had said to him before he left for The Skyview. Did she say she loved him after poisoning his dinner, knowing it would react if he had even a sip of alcohol? The righteousness was rolling off of her, and as angry as I'd like to be, part of me felt it was justified, too. What would Ernesto have become? One life sacrificed to save many? A devil's bargain maybe, but it seemed like the devil was the only one making deals these days.

Agent Thornfield arrived first, and Cronos Holt didn't have any difficulty recognizing him. The words "son of a bitch" might have come out of his mouth, but John didn't seem to notice. He whistled in appreciation as I handed over the Winchester.

"Unadulterated walnut," I said through clenched teeth.

"An antique, sure enough," he replied. Dolly got cups of water for Mr. and Mrs. Belasco, who sat quietly, waiting for the NYPD to arrive. They didn't seem like flight risks anymore and confessed to sending the invitation to themselves. Representatives from the Zeus Society had been at Ernesto's burial not to protest but to present their twisted brand of comfort, the "now he can't sin anymore" tagline that the Belascos admitted they hated. It had given them an idea, and they knew that if anyone would help them get out of the country, it would be this group.

We'd moved back into the main storage space, and I leaned against a rack of porn, hoping that the EMTs would get there soon. A tougher broad might have popped her own partially dislocated elbow back in place, but even the thought of that made black spots swim in my line of sight. A lone pigeon flapped against a high window, desperate to get out. I could sympathize.

"Still got that slingshot?" I said to Cronos. He would probably be charged with obstructing justice—something minor, but it would stir up a little bad publicity at least, maybe cut into his speaking fees. I hoped that Big Mamma would press charges for the death threats, too, though I wouldn't meddle with her business. Despite his vulnerabilities, Cronos was acting surprisingly calm. The certainty of the rich never ceased to amaze me. He believed that he would make bail in an hour tops. I could hear his spin already, helping people in their greatest time of need. The weapon of David and Goliath fame—or Nestor and whoever—was still in his back pocket. He handed it to me and I passed it along to Dolly, who looked at me quizzically.

"Hit a bird, get a priiize!" the leader said gleefully. He held out a marble, but Dolly passed. Whether he disapproved of the ammo or touching the man's fingers, I couldn't tell. Instead my friend moved around a few bits of debris until he found a healthy piece of concrete. He cradled it in the pocket, then pulled back the elastic much farther than I had managed. When he let it fly at the window as I knew he would, the glass shattered, raining down on the concrete floor. The pigeon didn't fly away immediately, scared by the noise and blast of cold. Eventually he made a break for it, and within seconds had disappeared from view.

"You'll pay for that," Cronos said, no longer amused.

"We'll see. I think you'll be paying for awhile."

I hoped Dolly was right. So did Detective Cowder, who arrived shortly after to handcuff him and the Belascos. I wasn't in so much pain that I didn't notice Ellis's deliberate avoidance of me. He kicked at the dirty glass pieces on the ground and looked everywhere but in my direction. Detective Cowder asked all the questions, and I filled her in on what I knew. The Belascos had known that their son was being recruited by Magrelli; they'd solved the problem themselves. They probably would have killed Eva, too, if they could have gotten their hands on her. Somehow Magrelli had found out, and they really were fleeing because they were afraid.

I was glad when the paramedics arrived, so that I could be excused. Solving this case didn't feel much better than solving the float explosion, and I wondered if I should enroll in night school for nutritional sciences. A young paramedic extended my arm. "Sedatives or pain killers?" he asked.

"Both?"

He rolled his eyes at this comment and dug two pills out of his bag. After I assured him that I wouldn't operate any heavy machinery, he gave me a small cup of water, too. Five minutes didn't seem long enough for either medication to kick in, but the man was ready to wrap up this non-life-threatening scene and popped my arm back in place with enviable precision and not a little sangfroid. I staggered out of the ambulance seconds before he slammed the doors shut behind me.

Ellis had my bag slung over his shoulder, as if we were at the movies and I'd merely stepped into the ladies' room. "You've been playing the wrong game all along," he said.

"What's that?"

"Driver's licenses for three different states, currencies for multiple countries, two cell phones, tape recorder, gum, a brochure for trapeze school, something called 'No Slip Tape,' bolt cutters, a lock picking kit, and an arm brace. I'm telling you, Kathleen, you would clean up at Let's Make A Deal."

He wasn't smiling, but he wasn't hostile. He held out the brace and helped me slip it over my head, pulling me close to his chest in the process. I didn't pull away, and he didn't make me. Was it a truce? It might have been the meds starting to work, but the possibility made my face warm. It was more concern than embarrassment that made me ask about his brother.

"Lars gets bored easily," Ellis said.

"A family trait?"

"I'm not in law enforcement for the health insurance, if that's what you mean."

The thought of company-provided health insurance made my heart flutter, but I suppose not everyone's as easily swayed. Plus, the NYPD made sure you used your coverage, detracting from the appeal.

"He didn't kill Ernesto. I'm sorry I accused him."

"Lars is nothing if not opportunistic."

I didn't know what to say to someone whose brother had thrown away his life of luxury for crime sprees. If Ellis was the Bruce Wayne of the family, who was Lars? I didn't want to find out, but I had a sinking feeling that I would. In a way, it was why I had wanted my two cases to be linked. Cartoon villains are easy to spot. These others with good intentions? Mothers protecting their sons? Young men wanting to succeed? They could be any of us with the right push, the wrong voice whispered in our ears. And I had a lot of voices. Little scared me as much.

The police cruiser with Cronos Holt inside flashed its lights and pulled away. I didn't want to, but I forced myself to take a step away from Ellis. He was watching the leader squint at us through the window.

"All their weapons land, no matter who flings them."

"Please don't start," I said, still chagrined that I couldn't remember more than the "wretched men" lines from *The Iliad*. What had I been doing in English class besides studying?

Dolly was wearing John Thornfield's coat when he exited the warehouse. Bundled up, he looked even more vulnerable than usual, but I knew better. He waved at me with one of the too-long sleeves, and I waved back.

"Friend of yours?" Ellis asked.

"Easy bet."

Meeza was gripping my hand in the dark as we waited for the lights to come back on.

"I'm nervous," she said. "Should I be nervous?"

I smiled at her even though I knew she couldn't see me. There was a tea candle on our table, but it barely illuminated the penis-shaped confetti that Big Mamma thought set the right tone for fundraising. "Of course we're still mourning," she'd said when I held up a shiny blue one for her inspection.

"But you don't get far by looking over your shoulder. You feel me?" I'd "yes ma'am"ed her, and she'd walked me to the front of the crowded room. Our front-row table was reserved and labeled "VIP." That was definitely a first. I was feeling fortunate that night, though. Meeza had agreed to be my date even if she hadn't agreed to leave the country or stop seeing V.P. My concerns were touching, she had decided. It was a start. And that nagging concern that her boyfriend had asked her to keep tabs on me? I shoved it to the back of my mind.

The disco ball was illuminated first, but because of our location, we could see Dolly walk out from the wings. He was wearing a gray, silk gown with pink feathers skimming the ground. On anyone else, the dress would have looked like a maid's duster, but Dolly looked glamorous. He started singing "Rocket Man" before the other lights were turned up, and a collective sigh eased through the crowd. His scheme had been for the evening to be his farewell performance, but Big Mamma and I persuaded him that a welcome-back would be more appropriate. I'd like to think that I had some influence over his decision, but we all knew he never wanted to leave in the first place. Nobody wants to be run out of town.

The lights turned up a notch, and I could now admire the blonde bob that Vondya had made special for the evening, staying up until the wee hours of the morning to get the bangs right. They grazed the star's eyebrows in a nearly perfect horizontal line. Paired with black silk gloves, it was if the accident had never happened. At least not for an hour or two.

When joined on stage by Cassandra and Juniper, the tempo changed, and soon Kylie Minogue was blasting over the speakers. Everyone was on their feet, Meeza shaking more provocatively than I would have believed possible. I excused myself and headed toward the bar to avoid the crowd. I was being extra careful with my banged-up arm, heeding the warnings this time. I had a better view from the back anyway.

Dolly had descended into the crowd and was swinging Meeza around. The dancers near her did little to hide their jealousy, but the overall vibe was hopeful. Big Mamma would have been proud of these patrons, not a single one staring over their shoulders. We all had a good chance of making it out of there alive. If that wasn't cause to celebrate, what was? I felt more like myself than I had in years since there was no point in hiding anymore. I may have been wearing Dolly's Kiki wig because he insisted it was festive, and my I.D. may have said Kate Manning or Katya Lincoln or Kathy Seasons—take your pick—but I was humming along to "Can't Get You Out of My Head." The view in front of me wasn't all sunshine and sequins, but at least I was facing the right direction.

ACKNOWLEDGMENTS

It's hard to tell whether luck is on Kat's side, but she's definitely on mine. I was fortunate to work with agent Penn Whaling and wish her the best in her new career. The entire Ann Rittenberg team is superb, including Ann herself and Camille Goldin. Over at Pegasus, superstar editor Maia Larson continues to impress me with her insight and patience. I'm also grateful to Claiborne Hancock and Iris Blasi. Charles Brock designed the gorgeous cover, and I hope Nashville suits him. Elizabeth Cramer introduced me to the granite moth, more evidence that teachers can learn from their students. Without the support of my friends and family, I can't imagine writing a single chapter. Special thanks to Ricardo Maldonado, Matthew Pennock, Kristen Linton, Katie Meadows, Tayt Harlin, Toral Doshi, and Chris Shiflett though there are many others whose encouragement is invaluable. Adam Province makes this strange journey worthwhile. And of course I thank my parents, Kevin and Paula Wright, to whom this book is dedicated.